"What's wrong

"We have a bit of a situation..." CJ started. "There's no key."

"No key?" Erica asked.

"Yeah...I guess someone forgot to leave it in the ignition and then left without checking that our ride was...uh, rideable."

"What are you saying? Are you saying we're...freaking stranded?"

"Yeah, we're stranded."

"Nooo," Erica groaned. "What are we going to do?"

"Well, we can't spend the night in this golf cart. Come on, let's find a place to hang out until someone comes looking for me."

"Are you sure someone will come?"

"I mean, I'm the star."

"Stranded on a movie set in the middle of nowhere. Great. And likely to catch pneumonia by morning."

"Actually, I think I have an idea. Follow me."

"Is this a...brothel?" Erica asked as he led her into the made-up bedroom above the saloon on the set.

"That's a bed with real blankets, so we actually have bedding. But we might need to cuddle to conserve body warmth."

"If I didn't know better, I'd say you did this on purpose."

"I didn't, I swear it. It beats the old 'stuck in an elevator' scenario, right?"

Dear Reader,

I am truly honored to have been invited to contribute to this series. Successful series writing demands a commitment to teamwork and a shared vision, ensuring each book seamlessly connects to form a compelling narrative that captivates readers across multiple volumes.

I am delighted to join this creative team. The aspect I enjoy the most about our project is how it harmonizes diverse writing styles and strengths. Although the story I've written is designed to be exciting on its own, I highly recommend exploring the entire series for a more complete reading adventure.

Your feedback is a joy to me. You're welcome to connect with me on social media or email me at authorkvanmeter@gmail.com.

Kimberly Van Meter

COLTON'S
REEL DANGER

KIMBERLY VAN METER

Harlequin

ROMANTIC SUSPENSE

Special thanks and acknowledgment are given to Kimberly Van Meter for her contribution to The Coltons of Arizona miniseries.

Harlequin®
ROMANTIC
SUSPENSE™

Recycling programs for this product may not exist in your area.

ISBN-13: 978-1-335-50277-3

Colton's Reel Danger

 Harlequin Enterprises ULC
22 Adelaide St. West, 41st Floor
Toronto, Ontario M5H 4E3, Canada
www.Harlequin.com

Printed in Lithuania

MIX
Paper | Supporting responsible forestry
FSC® C021394

Kimberly Van Meter wrote her first book at sixteen and finally achieved publication in December 2006. She has written for the Harlequin Superromance, Blaze and Romantic Suspense lines. She and her husband of thirty years have three children, two cats, and always a houseful of friends, family and fun.

Books by Kimberly Van Meter

Harlequin Romantic Suspense

The Coltons of Arizona

Colton's Reel Danger

Big Sky Justice

Danger in Big Sky Country
Her K-9 Protector
Cold Case Secrets
Cold Case Kidnapping

The Coltons of Owl Creek

Colton's Secret Stalker

The Coltons of Kansas

Colton's Amnesia Target

Military Precision Heroes

Soldier for Hire
Soldier Protector

Visit the Author Profile page
at Harlequin.com for more titles.

Chapter 1

CJ Knight's arrival in Arizona felt like walking into a mirage, the lines between reality and nightmare blurring under the relentless sun. The last place he wanted to be was in the heart of memories he didn't trust anymore.

Yet here he was, dragging his feet across the tarmac, a sense of duty overriding his dread.

What he wouldn't give to be back in LA poolside, drowning the shock beneath a waterfall of rum and Coke, but Hollywood didn't care about your personal trauma unless they could sell it for a buck.

God only knew how long it would take for someone to try and sell his situation to a streaming service. People loved sordid stories attached to celebrities, ate 'em up like candy from a bowl.

Three months ago, the news had hit him like a desert storm: his manager, Doug DeGraw, a murderer. The man he had trusted implicitly, confided in and called a friend, now a headline in every tabloid.

CJ's world had spun off its axis, leaving him grappling with a betrayal that cut deep. He and Doug had been close—or so he'd thought. Now, in the aftermath, he was forced to question if he'd ever known the man at all because he never would've thought Doug capable of murdering anyone, much less a woman in a fit of rage.

But the facts were hard to ignore. Doug was a cruel, worthless piece of trash who'd tried to cover up a horrific crime without so much as a blink of conscience until he'd gotten caught.

And CJ was left to find a new manager.

Not to make it all about him, but the search had been less than productive, something he'd complained about with his buddy Landon Rollins, another actor still waiting for his big shot.

"Man, what the hell? You didn't have a clue about De-Graw?" he asked, flabbergasted, lathering sunscreen on while soaking up some rays poolside at CJ's place a few days before CJ left.

Landon often house-sat for CJ when he was on location, which worked out for him because he was perennially broke and usually couch-surfed.

CJ shot Landon an aggrieved look. "It's not like he acted like a stone-cold killer around me. He was, like, normal. *Trust me, I've been questioning everything I thought I knew about the guy, but the bigger issue right now is I'm without a manager."*

"Yeah, that's rough," Landon quipped derisively. "You still scheduled for that Arizona shoot? Did you know I tested for that part, too?"

Yeah, sure you did, buddy. *CJ suppressed a groan and the urge to roll his eyes, but it was too late to get out of that commitment. "Shooting starts in a week. I'm leaving for the airport in a few days. Are you still good to watch the house?"*

"I'm here for you. You know that."

"Thanks," CJ said, although he wasn't stupid. The minute he was gone, Landon would act like he owned the place, throw parties and probably break something in the process that CJ would have to fix when he returned.

But even with that said, CJ trusted Landon to keep things mostly under control until he returned. Landon might've liked playing "Lord of the Manor," but he was a pit bull about keeping out thieves and troublemakers, and that was worth the cost of a party cleanup.

"You shouldn't have a problem finding a new manager," Landon said confidently, settling against the chaise lounge as he adjusted his sunglasses with a sigh. "You're, like, box-office gold. Everyone wants a piece of CJ Knight."

Box-office gold. Ka-ching was all they heard when CJ was part of the conversation. And the minute news had hit that Doug had been busted and was out of the game, the sharks had scented blood and started to circle.

The whole thing made him sick and made him feel covered in grime, even though he hadn't done anything wrong.

"In the meantime, chill, man. Enjoy the rays, get some vitamin D and rest up before you have to get back to work."

CJ chuckled wryly at Landon giving him advice about anything remotely adult-ish. Landon was a giant kid who refused to grow up, but he sure knew how to capitalize on his strengths. Too bad he was a terrible actor and didn't take anything seriously enough to improve his craft.

"Where in Arizona?" Landon asked.

"Back to Sedona."

"Mmm...hot chicks in Sedona."

There was only one hot chick in Sedona who remained stubbornly set in his memory, and it was the one woman

*who would probably set him on fire if he so much as looked
her way.*

*Probably not unwarranted, either. He'd really screwed
up any chance of making anything of that connection.*

*So, no big surprise that hiding out in his Hollywood
Hills home was more palatable than leaving his sanctuary to return to Sedona, Arizona, to film another project.*

*But when the job rang, you answered—because an actor
without a ringing phone was an actor without a future.*

Still didn't make the doing any easier.

Amazing how something so beautiful could suddenly
change in the blink of an eye. Whereas the last time he'd
been here he'd been in awe of the towering red rocks, now
he just felt the oppressive heat trying to squeeze the air
from his lungs.

The vast open skies, once a canvas of freedom, now felt
like an unending void.

Dramatic much? Yeah, but he wouldn't be an actor if he
couldn't feel all the feelings, right?

He walked, his steps echoing the turmoil within, a discordant rhythm to the usual airport hustle.

It was easy to let his mind run away with him because
he was already uncomfortable in his surroundings.

Times like these, his mind was merciless.

With every step, his mind replayed the revelations, the
lies unraveling like a film strip gone haywire. How had
he not seen it? The signs, the oddities? Doug's charming
facade had masked a darkness that CJ could barely com-
prehend.

He had been so blind, so naive. It gnawed at him, this

gnarled knot of guilt and anger, coiling tighter with each thought.

He had almost made it through the terminal, his thoughts a whirlwind, when he saw her. *Ahhh, crap. I don't need this right now.* And suddenly, the urge to spin on his heel and run in the opposite direction was hard to fight.

Erica Pike.

The universe had a sick sense of humor.

Good God, the woman was hot. The sight of her was like a jolt, snapping him back to a reality he wasn't prepared to face.

It'd only been three months, but it felt like a lifetime ago that he'd been the recipient of her dazzling smile, and the taste of her kiss lingered in his mind.

Except what could've been fantastic between them— well, he screwed that up in royal fashion.

And now, judging by the chill emanating from her moss-green eyes, a happy reunion was not in their future.

However, if *awkward* reunions were an Olympic sport, this moment would win gold.

Why was she here? The last time he'd seen her at the airport, she'd been picking someone up, a lawyer or something? But she locked eyes with him, and it felt purposeful, as if she'd been waiting for him, and if that didn't make his insides get all wobbly, nothing else would.

Ahh, crap, he realized. She was his ride.

But he was an actor, right? If he couldn't fake a pleasant, civil exchange and act like all was well, he needed to hand in his SAG card.

"Uhh, hey, Erica. We gotta stop meeting like this." He tried making light of the fact that he'd essentially ghosted her after they'd had sex. It hadn't been intentional, but his life had imploded, so Erica's feelings hadn't exactly been the top priority. When she failed to oblige him with an obligatory chuckle, he went for the compliment. "Man, you look great. Your hair… I love it like that." He gestured to the loose bun of dark hair spun on top of her head, loose tendrils teasing her soft jaw.

She wore a gauzy white linen pantsuit that looked effortlessly classy and yet sensual. With those long legs, Erica had a model-like gait that lent an air of sophistication everywhere she went—and people always turned to stare, wondering if she was famous.

But she might as well have been a robot for all the emotion she was showing. In fact, the subtle twist of her lips at his compliment barely qualified as a smile as her gaze raked him up and down, responding coolly, "You look… comfortable."

Yeah, he probably deserved that. He looked like he had rolled out of bed, finger-combed his wavy hair, pulled on a pair of jeans and grabbed the first thing his fingers could find that was relatively clean, which, in this case, had turned out to be a classic-rock tee.

Because that was exactly what'd happened.

Was he wearing deodorant? He resisted the urge to take a discreet sniff, wishing he'd taken the time to shower before catching his flight from LA.

And why hadn't he paid better attention to his travel itinerary?

He hadn't even noticed where the production company had booked his lodgings; otherwise he would've balked at staying at the resort where Erica was the executive assistant.

Erica delivered a frosty but professional smile, her hands clasped in front of her. "Hello, Mr. Knight. I'm here to pick you up and take you to the resort. We have a car waiting to take you to the heliport. Did you check luggage?"

There was nothing rude about her delivery, but the chill coming from her eyes could've rivaled the Antarctic.

Mr. Knight. Ouch. CJ hefted the small carry-on bag. "Just this. I like to pack light."

"Very good. This way, please."

Say something. Anything, a voice urged, but his lips remained sealed shut as he followed her through the busy terminal to the awaiting town car.

"So…how'd you pick the short straw to come get me?" he asked, trying for humor. When all else failed, shoot for the joke.

"I always handle our VIP guests," she answered without missing a beat or humoring him with an obligatory chuckle. They exited the terminal, going straight to the sleek black car idling at the pickup curb.

Erica opened his door for him, which felt weird, and after he'd slid in, he started to offer a seat beside him, but she closed the door and went to the passenger-side front seat to ride with the driver—leaving him alone.

Most people climbed all over themselves to spend a little one-on-one time with CJ.

Not her, though.

Do you blame her? That judgy voice was getting on his nerves, but the censure was warranted. He owed Erica an apology for how he'd handled their…thing. It wasn't like they'd been dating, but…there'd been a spark. Definitely something between them that'd felt different.

Until he'd bailed.

But to be fair, all hell had been breaking loose and his life had imploded. That had to warrant some leeway, right?

CJ released a long sigh, leaning back against the plush leather, rubbing his palms along his jeans as sweat prickled his temple. It was only May, but the temperature was already kissing the backside of the nineties and the car air felt stale.

He tapped the darkened window separating the front from the back, and the divider went down, revealing Erica with a blandly expectant expression. "Yes?"

"Uh, it's kinda hot back here. Can you adjust the air?"

"Of course, Mr. Knight," she said with a short smile, hitting the button and disappearing again.

The air changed minutely, and CJ realized with a chuckle that Erica was purposefully keeping the air less than crisp.

He supposed he deserved that.

Hopefully it wasn't a long ride to the helipad.

Erica had indeed drawn the short straw when she'd realized it would fall to her to squire CJ Knight from the airport to the resort.

As the executive assistant at Mariposa Resort and Spa, her duties included managing all VIP guest relations.

There was a reason Mariposa had gained a reputation for catering to exclusive clientele. She wasn't about to let their reputation slide just to save herself from seeing the man who'd left her feeling like a wadded-up piece of scratch paper.

But it wasn't the professional obligation that gnawed at her; it was the personal sting. That night with CJ had felt like something more than just a fleeting connection. How wrong she'd been. He'd vanished, leaving her with a mix of embarrassment and bitterness. Not even a text or phone call—just silence—as if she'd meant nothing and didn't warrant his attention after he'd gotten what he'd wanted.

Argh! The red-hot button of rage in her heart was something she wasn't accustomed to dealing with because she never allowed herself to be in these kinds of situations.

She wasn't the one to get awestruck by celebrities—if anything, she found Hollywood types too cliché in their perceived self-importance, but CJ had seemed different, and that was where she'd screwed up.

It wasn't just that he was good-looking. Sure, he wasn't hard on the eyes, but it was something else, something in him she'd thought was sweet and kind. But then it had all turned out to be bullshit, and the mortification of being played was something that ate at her on the daily.

He was just another Hollywood player, and she'd been foolish enough to think otherwise.

She'd spent a week prior to this moment preparing herself for the inevitable rush of feelings upon seeing CJ again, but it was one thing to write a plan on paper, entirely another when it was time to put the plan in action.

The car rolled to a stop at the private helipad owned by the resort and put her mask of professional distance back in play. *You can do this*, she told herself. *He's just another entitled rich guy who thinks he can do whatever he wants.* She had plenty of experience dealing with that type.

Erica opened the door and gestured for him to follow—her fake smile felt painted on, but at least she wasn't snarling.

The helicopter's blades whirred into life, filling the cabin with a relentless buzz that drowned out most sounds. Erica sat opposite CJ, her expression a mask of professionalism. She noticed CJ's lips moving, obviously trying to strike up a conversation. This was her moment to play ignorant.

"Yeah, so, Arizona, huh? Quite the place," CJ shouted over the noise, attempting to bridge the awkward silence. His words were mostly swallowed by the rotor's din, but his expression was unmistakably one of forced casualness.

Erica glanced at him, her face blank. She tapped her earphones and shook her head, mouthing, *Can't hear you!*

CJ leaned forward, raising his voice. "I said, Arizona's quite something!"

Again, Erica shrugged, pointing to her earphones and feigning a frustrated frown. She couldn't suppress a smirk as she turned her gaze out the window, secretly relishing in thwarting his attempt at small talk.

He leaned back, defeated, and they spent the rest of the flight in silence. CJ would occasionally try to say something, gesturing wildly to be heard, only to be met with Erica's exaggerated shrugs and pointed taps at her earphones.

There was nothing wrong with her earphones—Mariposa always made sure anything attached to the resort was state of the art, but CJ didn't know that, and she didn't want to waste the energy listening to the sound of his voice.

By the time they landed, Erica was almost impressed with CJ's persistence. The humor of the situation didn't escape her, but she kept her amusement firmly locked away. This was business, after all, and CJ Knight was just another guest. It was her job to see that they were delivered safely—not engage in chitchat.

As they disembarked, Erica kept her demeanor cool and

detached. She showed CJ to his room with practiced efficiency, her tone polite but distant. "If you need anything, Mr. Knight, don't hesitate to ask," she said crisply and turned to leave, but CJ tried again to talk.

"Erica, wait…"

She turned, mildly irritated. "Yes?"

"Are we going to talk about—"

She cut him off with a quick "If you have a preference for breakfast, please let our staff know, and we'll make sure to accommodate your needs" and then left him and his question behind.

Her heart was thundering in her chest, a reminder that she wasn't as emotionally removed as she'd like to pretend.

Did she want to talk about why he'd ghosted her after their night together? No, not really. She wasn't going to trot after the man, begging for a reason. Her mother always used to say, *When people show you their true colors, it's wise to believe them*, and CJ had shown who he truly was when the cameras weren't making him into a screen hero.

No, CJ would find that she wasn't like the women he was used to having around, and she had zero interest in being part of his adoring fan club of empty-headed fame chasers.

Drawing a deep breath, she smoothed nonexistent wrinkles from her linen suit and kept walking, punting thoughts of CJ into a mental waste basket, where he would stay.

Chapter 2

CJ knew what he ought to do—study his lines, immerse himself in his character and adhere to his meticulous pre-shoot routine before being summoned to the set in a few days.

That was the professional thing, the expected thing.

But it wasn't what he *wanted* to do. His mind was stuck on thoughts of Erica, a conundrum that felt more complex than any role he had ever played.

He couldn't fathom why her opinion suddenly held such sway over him, especially after he'd left without a whisper the last time they'd met.

It was an enigma that kept him restless, pacing the confines of his luxurious room at Mariposa.

This resort, an oasis of opulence in the scorching expanse of Arizona, endeavored to be paradise on Earth. Yet amid its grandeur, CJ felt displaced, his thoughts orbiting around Erica.

He tossed his script onto the bed, its pages landing in a disheveled heap, and left his room.

As he navigated the lushly landscaped grounds, his eyes scoured every corner, every hidden nook where Erica might've been hiding.

The resort was vast, a labyrinth of exclusivity and secrets, but suddenly he had tunnel vision. He had to talk to her and smooth things over. Why? He wasn't exactly sure, but the urge compelled him like no other.

But as he continued to wander without seeing her, his frustration grew. Had she vanished into thin air?

If he could just explain how the chaos of DeGraw's crime had upended his life, she'd understand.

And then what? What was he hoping for? He hadn't thought that far, but he wasn't used to working so hard for someone's forgiveness, and the effort felt clumsy and foreign.

Maybe it was the challenge that drew him. Erica was certainly that.

His fame had been of no consequence to her, and while she hadn't been overtly rude, she hadn't been easily charmed, either. Yeah, the chase had intrigued him, but it was more than that. Erica had been different, and he'd liked that about her.

He rounded the corner and nearly ran smack into her as she talked with maintenance personnel.

"Erica," he called out, hoping he sounded chill and not needy.

Her expression, ever the mask of professionalism, betrayed none of her inner thoughts as she excused herself from the conversation and approached him. "Mr. Knight. How can I assist you?" Her tone was cordial yet distant.

But now that he had her attention, that driving need deserted him, leaving him tongue-tied. Worse, the audience of her staff made things ten times worse.

CJ hesitated, his gaze flitting around the area. "Can we go somewhere private to talk?" he asked.

Erica glanced at her watch, her brow furrowing slightly. "I'm sorry—I'm on a tight schedule. Is there something wrong with the room?"

"The room is fine. I want to talk to you about the last time we saw each other."

Erica's expression remained impassive, though her lips tightened subtly. "That's not necessary, Mr. Knight."

Enough with the *Mr. Knight* bullshit. He'd seen her naked, twisted into positions that would make a notable entry in the Kama Sutra, and she was treating him like they were strangers. Of course, she was doing it on purpose. He hadn't taken her for the passive-aggressive type.

He gestured for her to follow him for more privacy. She relented with a barely suppressed look of annoyance.

"C'mon, Erica, I know what you're doing," CJ said once they were out of earshot. "Is it really necessary? We're both adults, right?"

"And what am I doing?" Erica's question was calm, her hands clasped in front, a posture reminiscent of a concierge dealing with a difficult guest.

CJ gave her a look, not buying her fake robotic act. "I get it, you're a great executive assistant. Top marks. If I needed help with the accommodations, you'd no doubt fix things without blinking an eye and I'd appreciate your efficiency, but…we've got history, and your *Mr. Knight* bull is obviously a passive-aggressive dig at me. Maybe I deserve it, but can't we talk things out?"

"As I see it, there's nothing to talk about."

"Let me, at least, apologize," he said.

"An apology isn't necessary," Erica interjected, her professional mask slipping for a fleeting second to reveal a glimpse of underlying hurt.

"I disagree. I know I hurt your feelings—"

Her breath hitched, but she shook her head. "Your apology is noted, Mr. Knight. Is there anything else?"

No, he wasn't going to let her ignore his attempt at apologizing. She wanted him to play the villain, but he wasn't going to make it easy for her.

"There's this tension between us. I want to clear the air."

Erica's demeanor shifted, a hint of steel entering her voice. "Mr. Knight, I assure you any personal issues will not affect my professional duties."

"I know that," CJ insisted, his patience wearing thin. "I'm trying to make amends, Erica. I genuinely regret how I left things. I should've been more considerate."

"Considerate?" Erica's composure cracked, a flash of anger crossing her face in a rare appearance as if that single word had punctured the professional reserve she clung to. "You *disappeared* without a word, CJ. You made me feel like garbage after getting what you wanted. You pretended to be a different person so I would sleep with you. That's more than being inconsiderate—that's slimy and gross. And now you expect forgiveness? A clean slate? Sorry— I don't hand out clean slates to people with dirty fingers."

Her words were a knife to his ego, but he couldn't deny their truth. Damn, she really wasn't pulling any punches. "So that's it? You're not even willing to hear my side?"

"Why should I? It's not necessary, CJ," she cut him off, her tone rising. "You have your work, I have mine. Let's keep it professional."

Flabbergasted by her rigid stance, he admitted, "I didn't think you'd react like this."

"Like what? A woman who demands more respect from the people she sleeps with?"

CJ's cheeks burned. Maybe he'd become too immersed in LA culture. One-night stands were common, and no one blinked an eye or called anyone out for not sending a text afterward. But standing there before Erica, her censure made him feel small, even though he was a few inches taller than she was.

Erica forced a hollow and fleeting smile. "All right, well, if you're finished with what you needed to say… I have work to do."

"How about we start over?"

"No."

The finality in her answer left CJ with nothing more to say. He wasn't about to chase after her, to grovel for her attention. He was used to adulation, not rejection.

As Erica walked away, CJ stood rooted, the weight of their exchange pressing down on him.

He had hoped to bridge the gap between them, but he had only widened it. Watching her retreat, he grappled with the unfamiliar sting of rejection. He had always prided himself on being grounded, unaffected by the trappings of Hollywood fame, but now he was forced to confront a harsh truth—Erica saw him as just another self-absorbed celebrity.

Was she right? No, not even close. She had no clue who he truly was, and it was rude of her to assume she knew the measure of his character based on one situation.

If she'd just listen to him…

The notion spurred a fleeting desire to chase after her, to prove he was different. But Erica was unlike the women he usually encountered, unsettling his confidence and sense of self.

She believed he had disrespected her, a perspective he struggled to understand, but something bothered him.

Yes, a crisis had upended his life, but would he have reached out to her otherwise? The thought was unsettling. He enjoyed his freedom and his lack of commitment, but Erica… Erica was different. There had been a spark, something genuine and unfamiliar.

C'mon, man, this is a waste of time. Let her go.

He had lines to memorize, a character to embody. He couldn't afford to be sidetracked by a brief connection, by a possibility that had no place in his current trajectory.

With a final, resigned glance at Erica's disappearing figure, CJ turned and returned to his room. The door closed behind him with a sense of finality. His focus needed to be on his career, not on a spa resort manager who couldn't accept an apology, no matter how heartfelt.

Erica watched CJ walk away, his retreating figure a silhouette of unfulfilled intentions and lingering regret. The corridor, usually bustling with the quiet efficiency of the resort staff, now seemed oppressively silent, echoing the chaos inside her head.

Despite her poised exterior, Erica's thoughts churned with conflicting feelings, and that wasn't like her.

His unexpectedly sincere apology bothered her more than she wanted to admit.

So, he'd apologized. What did that mean? Did he expect they could just be buddies after he'd humiliated her?

Start anew on a different, more honest footing? *Oh, hell no.* The idea scraped against her dignity, reminding her of the vulnerability she had exposed that night they'd spent together.

Under normal circumstances, she wasn't the type to slide into bed with just anyone. But CJ had seemed different—their connection had been mesmerizing.

Nope, correction—none of it had been real, remember?

Embarrassment surged at the memory, a reminder of how she had allowed herself to be swept away under what now felt like false pretenses.

She had believed in the connection, the spark between them, only to wake up to an empty bed and, later, zero communication.

Her pride, wounded by that abandonment, refused to bend, to give him the benefit of the doubt that part of her yearned to offer.

Screw him and his attempt at smoothing things over.

Recalibrating her thoughts, she forced CJ from her head and busied herself with the usual duties required of her position.

It was all good until she had a breather, a quiet moment between crises, and Erica found her mind replaying their brief encounter.

The warmth of his touch, the intensity in his eyes, the way he had made her feel both desired and understood—these memories burned with a vividness that she couldn't seem to purge. It was irritating how such a brief moment could leave such indelible marks on her psyche.

Objectively, the sex had been good. Probably better than just good—but it hadn't been mind-shattering, she thought, purposefully dredging up a college memory with her ex-boyfriend, Denzel, that still had the power to leave her blushing.

Except, in all fairness, Denzel had never made her feel seen or heard like CJ had. The emotional connection between them had left her spinning into the ether, amazed at how they'd seemed connected in ways that went beyond physical.

And that was why she was still mad—it'd all been fake. *Argh! Stop thinking about CJ, and move on.*

She'd be so happy when CJ Knight was no longer her problem. *It's only for a few days*, she consoled herself as she dove into her work responsibilities.

Laura Colton, one of the owners and assistant manager of Mariposa, hustled over to Erica, motioning for her to wait up.

She smiled, genuinely happy to see Laura, practically glowing with the love of a smitten woman—Noah Steele was a lucky man—and waited for her to catch up.

Cheeks pinked, Laura laughed breathlessly at how winded she was from the quick jog. "I knew I shouldn't have canceled my gym membership. If I keep declining at this pace, I won't be able to stay on top of all the activity around here."

"Hush—you're in no danger of that," Erica disagreed, shaking her head. The woman was drop-dead gorgeous and always looked like a movie star, but she was a consummate professional and always knew what was happening around the resort. "What's up?"

Back to business, Laura said, "I saw the actor CJ Knight was on the VIP guest list. Are you okay with that? I can take over for you if you want."

Erica hated being considered weak, and Laura's offer to step in only made her feel like some fragile bird needing shelter—and that wasn't Erica. She forced a bright smile. "Goodness, no, you have enough on your plate without adding my responsibilities to the pile. I'm fine. Honestly, I don't even care." At Laura's dubious expression, Erica doubled down, saying, "Seriously, totally fine. Please— stop looking at me like that. I'm perfectly capable of sepa- rating personal from professional."

"Oh! I know you are," Laura exclaimed, as if worried she'd inadvertently insulted Erica. "I was just… I don't know…actors are such…well, they can be a lot and…"

Erica saved her boss from continuing to stumble on her words, gently letting her off the hook. "You have a wed- ding to plan and a resort to run—please, let me handle CJ Knight. Besides, it's just for a few days here, and then he'll be someone else's problem. I heard they're shooting on lo- cation somewhere in Sedona."

"That's true," Laura said, biting her lip. "I'm sorry— I'm scatterbrained right now. Of course you can handle whatever comes your way. I'm just overthinking things."

"Understandable."

"Well, please let me know if you need any help," Laura said before heading to the next item on her to-do list.

Even though Laura was a sweetheart, Erica wished she hadn't shared what'd happened between her and CJ during a pity party moment. Erica liked to keep her personal life private—messy personal details had no place in her professional life—but she was human, too. And CJ had really hurt her feelings.

The hardest part was acknowledging that a part of her, a part she fiercely repressed, wanted to forgive him, to explore the what-ifs that haunted her quiet moments.

But she couldn't. She wouldn't.

Her pride, her sense of self-worth wouldn't allow it. She had built her life on being strong and independent, not the kind of woman who succumbed to charming actors with mouths full of pretty lies.

As the day wore on, Erica became increasingly distracted, her thoughts returning to CJ and the unresolved tension between them. It was more than just wounded pride. It was a battle between her rational mind, which admonished her for even considering forgiveness and the part of her that longed to rewrite their story, to give it a different ending.

She ended the day feeling drained, and the emotional turmoil left her mentally exhausted.

By the time she put Mariposa out of her mind to go home, she was worn out and irritated that CJ's presence was dominating so many of her thoughts.

Mostly because it was unlikely that CJ was thinking of her at all.

Chapter 3

True to her word, Erica was completely professional whenever they had to suffer each other's presence, but by the time CJ was called to set, he was grateful to leave the uncomfortable situation with Erica behind.

It shouldn't have been this hard to put someone in his rearview mirror, but something about Erica nagged at him, refusing to let him move on.

During an unhinged moment, he'd considered having flowers delivered to her desk—something big and ostentatious and something she couldn't ignore—but then he'd come to his senses and realized he'd have better luck getting her attention if he flushed money down the toilet and clogged the septic.

It was a relief to return to something he understood—the chaos of a film set.

"Caroline Briggs, first assistant director. Welcome to base camp," said the harried woman with a wild spray of graying hair springing from her hastily pulled-back bun. She unabashedly gushed, "Mr. Knight, I love your work. Forgive me for fangirling for a minute, but I absolutely jumped at the chance to work on this film because I'd heard you were signed on. Seriously, you're, like, a legend."

It was unusual for an AD to be awestruck by a celebrity. They were usually too overworked and crushed by the weight of their enormous responsibilities to bother with celebrity stuff, but after Erica's cold shoulder, it felt good to be liked again.

"The pleasure's all mine," he said, smiling.

"Your trailer is stocked per your rider, and if there's anything you need, please don't hesitate to grab me. Here's my personal cell. A driver will come to transport you to set, which is a few miles down the road." She handed him a business card, gesturing to the luxury set trailer reserved for him. "If you could report to makeup in an hour, that would be great."

He smiled, familiar with the drill. "Got it." He pocketed the card and headed for his trailer. Stepping inside, he nodded with approval. The small table was filled with fresh fruit, containers of assorted nuts and his one indulgence— sour gummy bears—which were hard to come by when he was on a strict meal plan during shooting. He liked to keep his body and mind sharp when filming, which meant cutting out many processed foods, but a man couldn't live on chicken and broccoli alone. Even though his nutritionist balked, he insisted on the gummy bears—they were sometimes integral to his sanity.

This film—a Western period piece—was bound to be grueling due to the location, the heat and the fact that period pieces always had so many more moving parts to consider when filming.

Base camp, a cluster of trailers that formed a makeshift community, was a hodgepodge of craft services, equipment rigs and the star trailers a few miles from the set so as not to disrupt any of the filming. Still, sound carried in a place like Arizona, so signs were everywhere to remind people to keep the noise to a minimum.

He watched as a special dirt hauler trundled down the road toward the location.

Special dirt for the main set was hauled in and meticulously combed to look organic to the area. However, it was specially made to create little to no dust, which could create continuity problems later.

But then, someone had to manage all that "movie dirt" so it was ready for the next shot.

The business of make-believe was a robust business, and everyone wanted a piece of the pie.

He remembered the first time he'd stepped on location for his first real gig. He'd been overwhelmed by the sheer scope of the operation. It was a mini mobile town with its own heartbeat and community. It was easy to understand how people fell in love with their coworkers or costars during shooting when they lived in a manufactured bubble of altered reality.

Hell, he'd even made that mistake—falling for his co-star—and he'd stubbornly believed she was The One. But while Mimi Watson was ethereal on-screen, she was a headache in real life. He'd learned real quick that he'd fallen for the illusion of Mimi, not the petulant, spoiled brat that she was when the cameras were off.

The first time she'd snapped at a waitress for a small mistake had been the moment he'd realized they weren't compatible.

After that, he'd made it a point to keep a professional distance from his costars or anyone he worked with.

Maybe that was why Erica's judgment felt so wrong. He wasn't the guy she believed him to be, and it stuck in his craw that she wouldn't budge in her opinion.

Let it go, Knight. He sighed and exited the trailer to report to makeup.

He grinned with true pleasure when he saw his favorite makeup artist waiting for him.

"There he is," said Julian Reed, the best in the business and the world's biggest gossip. "Come here and give me some sugar."

CJ bent forward for the expected air kiss that Julian demanded and dropped into the makeup chair while Julian fussed around him. "Feels like a hundred degrees already, and it's not even eight a.m. yet," he groused. "Thank God you have your trailer set to frigid."

"Honey, I can't have my babies sweating off all my hard work," Julian said, adjusting the many bangles on his wrist. "Now, tell me what's new? I mean, aside from the whole murder thing with your manager, Dougie DeGraw. That's something you don't hear every day."

CJ didn't want to talk about Doug, but he liked Julian and supposed he could indulge his curiosity. He shrugged, admitting, "Your guess is as good as mine. I've been hiding in my house since the news broke. I wouldn't know if the second coming of Jesus was happening and tickets for the event were being sold for the Hollywood Bowl."

"Oh, honey, that would be something, wouldn't it?" Julian clucked his tongue and finger-combed CJ's hair, pursing his lips. "Who has been cutting this mop? This is a disgrace. You should pop into the stylist's trailer before going on camera."

"Jules, it's a Western period piece, I doubt anyone's going to notice if my ends are a little off-point."

"Fair," Julian admitted. "But just so you know, this kind of thing gives me hives. Anyway—" He pulled two wet wipes and thrust them at CJ. "Wipe your face so I can start the magic. Your pores look big enough to require their own zip code. Good lord, have mercy!"

CJ laughed, shaking his head. "You're the expert."

"Indeed. Now, give me the good stuff. What the actual hell… Did you know that Dougie was a murdering psycho?"

And here it goes.

He supposed he ought to get used to that question but didn't know how he ever would.

Erica sighed in relief, knowing CJ was finally out of the resort. For days, she'd worked overtime to avoid interacting with the man, but she'd invariably catch a glimpse of him in the hallway or, worse, coming from the pool.

That memory, in particular, seemed stuck in her brain.

She'd sucked in a wild breath at the shocking sight of CJ, a thick towel wrapped around his torso, his abs glistening, his wild mop of hair adorably mussed—and that brief flicker in his eyes when he'd seen her had nearly caused her to miss a step.

She'd quickly ducked into a storage room, acting as if she'd purposefully been heading that way, when in fact she'd simply been waiting for the coast to clear.

So much for acting like a responsible adult, her inner voice had quipped as she'd leaned morosely against the stacked linen tower. *You're literally hiding in a closet.*

Not hiding, she'd corrected, her gaze roaming the small room, *doing inventory.*

Aha! Her sharp gaze had caught a small gap in supplies. *See?* Erica would need to ask Martha to order more shampoo bottles from that cute boutique shop in town. Feeling slightly less stupid, she'd straightened her blouse and stepped boldly from the storage room with a purposeful stride but had been secretly disappointed that CJ hadn't been standing outside the door waiting for her.

Argh. That's some twisted logic.

So, yes, CJ checking out was a blessing. Now life could return to normal.

Bella, one of the younger maids, found her. "I saw that Mr. Knight checked out. So he's not returning to the resort?" she asked.

"No, he's not. Is there a problem?" Erica asked, perplexed. Had CJ trashed the room or something?

"Oh, no—no problem. I was doing my end-stay cleanup routine and found something he must've left behind by accident," she clarified. "I didn't know if he might want it back. I mean, I figure he probably will, though. It's kind of expensive."

Bella produced an electronic tablet, and Erica wanted to groan. "Yes, thank you, Bella," she said, accepting the device with a quick smile. "I'll see to it that his property is returned."

Bella's smile warmed Erica's heart—the girl had been horrifically assaulted but had emerged the other side stronger and braver than anyone she'd ever known. "Awesome. He's so nice. I'd hate to see him stressed out over losing it," Bella said, leaving Erica to finish her shift.

Erica stared at the tablet and fought the urge to swear beneath her breath. She could send it by courier but ran the risk of it getting damaged, which would make the resort liable for its replacement.

Or she could just run it over to the production and drop it off, ensuring that it was intact when it left her possession.

What were the chances she'd run into CJ? Pretty slim. She could take those odds.

Holding the electronic to her chest, she resigned herself to hand-delivering CJ's property.

After detouring to her office to get the secret production location and the contact information, she popped into Laura's office to let her know where she was going and why.

With an apologetic grimace, Laura looked conflicted, saying, "I wish I could take it for you, but I'm supposed to meet with the florist in about forty-five minutes and I'll never make it back in time."

"Oh, don't worry about it." Erica waved away her concern, hating that her boss thought she was incapable of making a delivery. "I'll drop it off with the production office and head back. It should be a quick trip."

"You're a rock star," Laura said with relief before glancing at her watch. "Oh! Damn it, I forgot I have to go over those carpet swatches before the carpet rep returns later this afternoon."

Erica chuckled, leaving her boss to her chaos, and headed for her car.

The resort flew in the guests, but there was a small road the staff used to take them in and out.

Wiping away a bead of sweat, she climbed into her car

and immediately turned on the AC. Arizona heat was relentless, even in late spring.

It was no wonder CJ had been in the pool so much while he'd stayed at the resort. She shook her head, immediately irritated at herself for dredging up that memory again.

Deliver the item. Leave. Forget CJ Knight.

Stick to the plan.

The production was filming on a private ranch in Sedona. When she rolled up to the gate, she found two production assistants monitoring the flow of traffic into the location.

She rolled her window down with a smile, showing her ID badge from the resort. "Hi, I'm Erica Pike, executive assistant at Mariposa Resort. CJ Knight just checked out, but he left behind his tablet," she explained, gesturing to the tablet on the passenger-side seat. "Thought he might like it back."

The assistant nodded. "The trailer camp is just up the road. You can't miss it. The AD's mobile office is the first one on the left."

Erica thanked the assistant with a smile and rolled on.

This would be quick and easy—no different than any delivery.

So why was her heart rate fluttering?

Chapter 4

Erica scanned the bustling base camp, her eyes drawn
to a large trailer with the words Assistant Director written in bold black letters. She approached and knocked on
the door, but there was no answer. As she waited, her gaze
wandered the organized chaos of equipment, props and
people rushing about.

As a seasoned executive assistant at Mariposa Resort,
Erica was used to seeing high levels of organization and
efficiency. But this world was on a whole other level. It reminded her of the behind-the-scenes operations at Mariposa, where everything ran like a well-oiled machine to
provide guests with seamless luxury and the guests never
caught sight of the chaos behind the curtain.

Lost in thought, Erica didn't notice when a production
assistant stopped beside her. "Can I help you?" he asked.

Smiling, Erica stepped down the metal steps and introduced herself. "I'm Erica Pike from Mariposa. I called ahead
to let the assistant director know that we found some property belonging to CJ Knight in his room after he checked
out this morning."

"The AD is on set—something about the horse wrangler not showing up this morning. I can take you there if you want."

"Oh, that's not necessary. I can leave it with you if that works," Erica said, starting to hand the tablet over, but the man vehemently shook his head.

"Sorry—I can't accept personal property. It has to go through the AD, or it'll be my head. Jump into the Jeep, and I'll drive you over. It's a few miles away, so you definitely don't want to try and walk there in this heat."

She resisted the urge to groan when she realized she'd likely see CJ—a prospect that made her palms sweat.

"I don't want to interfere with your work," she hedged, wondering if anyone else could accept the property.

"Don't worry about it," he assured her as he reached out to shake her hand. "Caroline can be pretty strict about protocol on this high-value production. Rocko Bellini—it's a pleasure to meet you."

"Only if it's no trouble," Erica replied with a smile. She could tell from his demeanor that Rocko probably had his own Hollywood dreams. Without hearing his whole story, Erica guessed he was working his way up while hoping for his big break.

"Rocko Bellini…that's a great name," she commented, trying to make conversation as they drove.

Rocko laughed, navigating the newly paved road stretching into the horizon. "Actually, my name's Eric Jones, but that's not exactly a name that rolls off the tongue. Besides, there was already an Eric Jones listed with SAG, so I figured, why not pick a name that really says something? Something with old-school class and charm? And then one day, I woke up and the name *Rocko Bellini* just jumped into my head like it was divine intervention or something. I figured that's a sign from the universe, so I went down to the SAG office that day and officially became a new man."

Erica hid her amusement, nodding. "Sounds like it was a sign, definitely. Have you been on any productions I might know?"

"Well, just some small parts, but I did have a speaking part on *Grimm*—do you remember that show? Great show. I was hoping for a recurring gig, but the series ended, and it was back to California. It was filmed in Portland, Oregon—did you know that?"

"I didn't. I actually didn't watch the show. Not much of a supernatural fan. I prefer crime dramas, stuff like that."

"Yeah, that's cool. Well, since then, it's been small parts here and there—enough to keep my SAG card active, but not enough to pay the bills. My cousin got me this gig as a production assistant and it's been pretty dope, but I'm ready to get my shot. Someday it'll be me above the line."

Erica chuckled, enjoying his enthusiasm. "I hope you get there."

"Oh, I will. Mark my words. Hey, if you get the chance, watch episode four, season six of *Grimm*. I'm in the coffee shop scene. I had some funny lines—not laugh-out-loud kind of lines but kinda dark humor, you know? I think I delivered."

Erica nodded, offering a half-hearted promise to check out Rocko's suggestion. In reality, she knew she wouldn't. But for now, Rocko's charismatic energy was enough to distract her from the looming prospect of running into CJ.

They pulled off a safe distance from the filming area, and Rocko apologized with a charming smile. "We'll have to walk from here. The sound guys get grumpy if there's any unwanted noise in their ears."

"I understand," Erica replied, stepping out of the vehicle. The warm Arizona sun kissed her skin as she took in the scenery around her.

The desert landscape was surprisingly beautiful, with its rolling hills and vibrant wildflowers scattered throughout. Despite being so close to her own resort, Erica had forgotten how stunning Arizona could be.

"Watch for snakes," Rocko warned, gesturing for her to follow.

Erica nodded, her eyes scanning the ground. She wasn't particularly fond of snakes, but she was determined not to let her fear get the best of her. Rocko led the way, navigating the rugged terrain like he'd been born to the area and not an LA-Hollywood type.

Erica couldn't suppress the nervous energy tickling her insides as they walked. The distant sound of voices directing actors became louder as they approached the filming area.

Finally they reached the edge of the set, concealed behind a curtain of tall saguaro cacti. Erica's heart raced as she caught her first glimpse of the action. A group of actors dressed in old Western attire stood in a dusty street lined with weathered wooden buildings. A saloon sign swung lazily in the desert breeze.

"This entire set was built for this production," Rocko whispered, motioning toward the "Main Street," which looked plucked straight out of the movie *Tombstone*.

"Impressive," she murmured as her gaze searched for CJ among the cast.

Her heart skipped a beat. There, near the makeshift hitching post, his dark hair hidden beneath a worn cowboy hat, CJ leaned casually against the wooden post, laughing and joking with his costars, looking like a Western snack.

Even dressed like a dusty old cowboy, he was nice to look at. He exuded an air of confidence and charm as if he'd been born to be a star. Okay, so objectively he was hot, she allowed, folding her arms across her chest, but his character was as ugly as they came.

Still, Erica's breath caught in her throat as she watched him. Memories of their one-night stand came flooding back. Stolen glances from across the crowded building, playful banter at the bar and then one unforgettable night when they had shared a dance under a star-filled sky before heading back to his hotel room.

Heat flooded her cheeks as she pushed the memories away. Rocko nudged Erica gently, pointing toward a small tent adjacent to the set. "That's where you'll find Caroline," he whispered. "She should be able to assist you from this point forward. Nice to meet you." He tipped an imaginary hat and headed off toward his next assignment.

Erica tore her gaze away from CJ, forcing herself to focus. She approached the small tent where Caroline, the assistant director, was frantically pacing back and forth while talking on the phone.

"What do you mean you don't know where he's at? We need that wrangler here now!" Caroline's voice crackled with frustration as she continued her conversation. She glanced up briefly and offered Erica an apologetic smile before returning her attention to the call.

Stepping inside the tent, Erica waited patiently, understanding the stress that the assistant director must've been under. Stacks of production paperwork cluttered the table, scripts lay open on every available surface and a large cork-board was covered in colored sticky notes that seemed to represent the intricate web of scenes and shots for the film.

This was where the magic happened, where dreams were brought to life on the silver screen. She sighed, wondering what it must've been like to live this kind of life. She'd never been the creative type—more of a linear thinker—but she admired anyone who could make something out of nothing. Give Erica a spreadsheet over a right-brained task any day.

Caroline finally hung up the phone and let out a weary sigh. "Sorry about that," she said with a harried smile. "Welcome to the madness."

Erica returned the smile. "Thank you. I totally understand." She produced a business card from her linen pocket. "Erica Pike, executive assistant at Mariposa Resort. We spoke on the phone."

"Yes, something about a tablet CJ left behind at your resort?"

Erica quickly produced the tablet. "Yes, here it is. The resort takes a hands-on approach to personal items of value left behind by VIP guests. I didn't feel comfortable sending it by courier given that it's an electronic device. You never know how it might be handled."

Caroline agreed. "Lord knows that's true. I ordered a replacement phone, and it was delivered looking like it'd traveled through a tsunami. Ended up being broken and had to exchange it at the local store. Totally frustrating."

"Well, I see that you're dealing with your own crises, so

I'll let you get back to it. Do you know where Rocko went? I'll just catch a ride back to base camp where I'm parked."

Caroline grimaced. "I'm sorry, I know it's asking a lot, but would you mind hanging out for a bit? I can't really spare Rocko right now. We've been struggling with some setbacks lately, and it's an all-hands-on-deck situation."

Erica hid her alarm—not only because she had things to do back at the resort but also because hanging around could mean more unfortunate time spent with CJ. But what could she do but agree? "I don't want to create any problems," Erica said. "I'm happy to wait."

"Thank you." Caroline breathed a sigh of relief. "You don't by any chance know any horse wranglers in the area that might be willing to work for scale on short notice?"

"Off the top of my head, no, but I could probably find someone for you back at the resort. One of my bosses, Joshua Colton, might know someone."

"Good to know," Caroline said. "I'll keep that in my back pocket as a viable Plan B. Go ahead and grab something from craft services. Help yourself. We're dead in the water until we find that damn wrangler—or someone to replace him. God, what I wouldn't do for a margarita right now. Or maybe we'll move the shooting schedule around," Caroline left, muttering to herself as she grabbed her cell phone. "Damn that wrangler."

Erica hesitated, unsure if she should leave or wait as Caroline suggested. However, she sensed that Caroline needed some privacy for her next round of phone calls, and out of professional courtesy, Erica decided to leave.

She found her way to craft services, ordered an iced

coffee with a protein bar and found a quiet place in the shade to wait.

With some luck, CJ wouldn't even notice she was there.

However, as CJ somehow swiveled his stare her way at precisely the right moment, their stares locked, and Erica knew luck wasn't on her side today.

CJ couldn't believe his eyes—was that Erica over there at craft services? An unbidden thrill nearly coaxed a surprised smile from his lips, but he managed to stop it from forming. Should he go over there and say hello? She was on his turf now. Wouldn't it be rude to ignore her?

But Erica had made it clear she didn't want anything to do with him. So, did he stay put and pretend he hadn't seen her?

They'd locked stares—pretending that he hadn't seen her seemed out of the question.

She already thought he was a toad; he didn't want to do anything to cement that belief.

Excusing himself, he took a chance and walked over to craft services, acknowledging Erica as he grabbed a blueberry muffin. "Fancy meeting you here, miss," he drawled, going for humor in the face of a potentially awkward encounter. "Begs the question…did you miss me or…do you harbor a secret desire to find yourself on the silver screen?"

"Neither," she answered, sipping her iced coffee. "You forgot your tablet at the resort. I'm simply returning it."

CJ realized with a start he hadn't even realized his tablet was gone, but he was grateful it had been returned. Quickly sobering, he said, "Thanks. I appreciate that. I have pictures on my tablet that I would've been really upset to lose."

"Careful—pictures of Hollywood parties can get you into trouble," she quipped, clearly assuming he had pics of a dirty nature.

He chuckled, correcting her quietly: "No, actually, I have pictures of my grandfather before he died last year of pancreatic cancer. I used to visit him in hospice, and we'd use the tablet to play games. When I was there, I showed him how the camera worked, and he thought it was the coolest thing. He'd always been fascinated by gadgets. So, I'd wheel him around the garden area, and he'd use my tablet to snap pics. Used to make him happy, and seeing him happy...well, it made me happy."

Erica's expression faltered, and she looked embarrassed that she'd taken such a left turn in her assumption. "I'm sorry. I... That was crappy of me." Humbled, she said, "I'm glad I was able to return your tablet safely."

"Me, too."

"I'm just waiting for my ride," she blurted when a beat of silence hung on for too long, explaining, "Your AD is working on finding someone to take me back to base camp. She said I could get something from craft services." She lifted her coffee. "This is really good. The crew is well taken care of in the food department."

CJ nodded, a flicker of relief passing through him at the change in subject. He hadn't meant to make her feel like an ingrown toenail. "Yeah, they do a decent job here. Keeps us going during the long hours." He glanced around, adding, "Also helps keep tempers in check if you keep people fed well. Today's shooting schedule is a mess. Everyone's starting to get antsy."

"Yes, I heard something about that. Your wrangler didn't show up to set?"

"Yeah, we can't do any work with the horses without the wrangler present. Union rules. And because today's shooting schedule was slated with the horses, we're stuck twiddling our thumbs in this heat while we wait for direction."

"Your AD is working hard to get someone here," Erica shared. "But she looks pretty stressed out."

"Yeah, I don't blame her. When things go wrong, the AD takes the heat from all the upper-level people."

"Meanwhile, the stars get to enjoy pastries and iced lattes," Erica said in a faintly teasing tone.

Was that the tiniest sign Erica was thawing in her attitude toward him? He hoped so.

"Would you like a tour?"

A glimmer of interest flashed in her eyes, but she seemed reluctant to accept his offer. "I don't want to distract you," she said.

"You're not distracting me—you're keeping me from losing my mind from boredom," he said. "C'mon, I'll show you the cool stuff. Maybe it'll take your mind off the fact that you hate me."

"I don't hate you, CJ," she said, exasperated. "I... Never mind. If you'd like to give me a tour, that would be a nice treat."

"Great." He grinned, tossing his half-eaten muffin. "Follow me for the grand tour of Main Street in Dry Gulch—a town where the West wasn't exactly won, but it was a place to wet your whistle and stock up supplies before moving onto bigger and better."

The fact that Erica laughed with genuine amusement

gave him more than a spurt of hope. Let's face it: he was charming, and if given half the chance, he'd show Erica he wasn't the bad guy she thought he was.

Or at least, she might leave the set willing to hear his side of the story.

Maybe even let him take her to dinner to make amends.

Okay, maybe that was a tall order, but a man could dream, right?

Chapter 5

Erica probably should've declined CJ's offer, but she couldn't resist the opportunity to experience the behind-the-scenes of an actual Hollywood film.

It wasn't that she was awestruck by the celebrities—it was the sheer amount of work and expertise she saw at work to make movie magic happen.

And CJ seemed to understand that.

"Are you sure you're not needed?" Erica asked, following a quick tour through the wardrobe tent, which the costume director had temporarily set up for wardrobes changes or emergency costume fixes.

"It's fine," he assured her. "From what I heard, our entire shooting schedule has to be reworked, and we're already losing daylight. Likely the whole day of shooting will be lost because of the missing wrangler."

"I don't quite understand why a wrangler needs to be on set for the horses," Erica said.

"Union rules. It's a safety issue for both the actors and the horses. Just to make sure everyone is doing things by the book and cautiously. Horses can be dangerous to work with if you're not careful."

"Can you ride?" Erica asked.

"Enough to look convincing on camera," he answered with a wink. "But I wouldn't call myself an actual rider."

She appreciated his honesty. He could've just as easily lied to try and seem impressive. The simplicity in his admission, the absence of pretense struck a chord within her. "I can't ride, either," she admitted. "I'm a little afraid of horses, actually. I had a bad experience when I was a kid that stuck with me."

"What happened?"

Erica hesitated, not sure she ought to share anything so personal. The vulnerability of the moment was palpable, a rare opportunity to share a piece of her past that she usually kept hidden. "Well, I was at a friend's birthday party, and the parents had paid for a company to bring horses to offer free pony rides. Except they weren't ponies—they were actual horses that the company had purchased at an auction. I suppose the upside was that they were saved from the glue factory, but the downside was that they were surly and totally ill-suited to working at a children's party. Several of us were bitten—some badly enough to break skin." She reluctantly slipped her linen blouse down to reveal her shoulder, unveiling the thin white line on her shoulder. "I was one of the kids who needed stitches."

CJ's brow furrowed as he peered at the faint scar. His expression softened, a mix of empathy and concern washing over his features. "I'm sorry," he said. The sincerity in his voice was unexpected, almost disarming. "That must've been terrifying."

Erica forced a short laugh, admitting, "It was. I haven't gone near a horse since. I mean, I think they're beautiful, majestic creatures, but I have zero interest in being next to one ever again." The laugh didn't quite mask the lingering shadow of that childhood fear.

"I wasn't bitten by a horse, but one time I was scratched by my grandmother's cat and got cat scratch fever. I ended up in the hospital overnight for high-power antibiotics."

"I've never heard of anyone getting sick from a cat scratch."

"Yeah, it can happen. Now I'm religious about washing my hands anytime I handle an animal, just in case."

"Did the experience make you scared of cats?" Erica asked, thinking of her own cat, Mitzy, at home.

"No, but it did give me a healthy appreciation of good old-fashioned soap and water. The doc told me if I'd washed out the scratch right when it happened, I probably wouldn't have gotten sick."

A reluctant smile found her lips even as she tried to stop it. This easy energy between them...it was unnerving, given their history, yet impossible to ignore when he was this genuine, this disarmingly real.

As they continued their stroll through the bustling set, Erica couldn't help but notice a commotion near the stables. Crew members were frantically whispering to each other and casting worried glances in that direction.

Curiosity piqued, she tugged at CJ's sleeve. "What's going on over there? Is everything all right?" she asked, concerned.

CJ turned toward the stables with an unsure frown. "I don't know, but it doesn't sound good."

"Do you think it has something to do with your missing wrangler?"

"There's one way to find out," CJ said, gesturing for her

to follow, but she held back until CJ slipped his hand into hers, assuring her everything would be fine.

She should've pulled her hand free, but there was something about the warmth of CJ's hand in hers that calmed her apprehension.

CJ hailed one of the production assistants assigned to the area where the horses were corralled, and the assistant, immediately recognizing the movie's star, hustled over.

"Is everything okay?" CJ asked.

"Sorry, Mr. Knight—one of the horses got loose, and we don't have anyone qualified to go after it. I mean, I used to ride horses at my grandparents' ranch, but I haven't sat a horse in almost twenty years."

"You haven't worked with horses in twenty years, but you're working with the horses?" Erica asked, confused.

"Ma'am, no disrespect, but when someone in production asks if you can ride a horse, you say yes and figure it out later. A job's a job in this business."

Didn't seem very safe, but Erica kept her feelings to herself. Her professional instincts bristled at the cavalier attitude, a stark contrast to the meticulous standards she upheld at the resort. She would never run Mariposa like this, but it wasn't her operation, so it was best to keep quiet.

For his part, CJ seemed to understand, commiserating, "I once said I was bilingual just to get a part."

"Are you bilingual?" Erica asked, curious.

"Hell, no. I can barely manage decent English most days," CJ replied without any shame. "But this business is hard. Nothing more terrifying than a closed door to opportunity."

The sound of hooves on the ground, thundering against

the hard earth, echoed through the set as a massive quarter horse, bucking and rearing in excitement or fear—it was impossible to tell which, crashed through the flimsy wall divider aimed at keeping the animals shielded from production.

Erica shrieked in fear, her childhood memory rearing its ugly head. Her heart raced, the old terror surging back as the horse's muscled body shone with sweat in the midmorning sunlight and its eyes were wild with unbridled energy.

CJ jumped into action, putting himself between Erica and the horse, using a soft and calming voice to soothe the animal.

"He's scared and in an unfamiliar place," CJ explained smoothly, his hands up to keep the horse at bay. "Horses respond to energy. Everyone needs to stay calm. Whoa there, buddy, you're okay, but you're scaring everyone. C'mon now, it's okay," he said, in a gentle tone while slowly gesturing for the production assistant to hand him a carrot.

The production assistant grabbed a carrot from a bucket and inched his way over to CJ to hand him the vegetable and then quickly backed away.

"There, there, buddy, see? It's not all bad," he said, allowing the animal to sniff at the offered vegetable, assessing the situation. The horse whickered and snuffed but accepted the carrot, crunching loudly. "Pretty good, huh?" CJ said, gently running his hands along the strong neck while surreptitiously securing the lead on the halter. "There you go. All better, right?" He motioned toward the production assistants watching in awe as the calmed horse walked easily behind CJ, possibly hoping for more treats, while CJ secured the horse inside the makeshift corral, locking it securely. He fished another carrot from the bucket and gave it to the horse with one final rub on his forelock.

Erica stared, her breath still caught in her chest, but not out of fear. The sight of CJ, so unexpectedly capable and gentle, stirred something in her, a flutter of admiration she hadn't anticipated. Maybe it was a little dramatic, but had CJ just saved her?

It felt that way.

And she didn't know how she felt about that.

After the commotion settled and the quarter horse calmed, CJ's first thought was of Erica. The incident had unfolded so quickly, yet her shriek of fear, raw and piercing, still echoed in his ears.

He turned to her, searching her face for signs of distress. "Are you okay?" he asked, his voice laced with concern. The fear he'd seen flash in her eyes was something he hadn't anticipated facing today, yet here they were, her vulnerability laid bare by the runaway horse.

Erica nodded, her breath still uneven. "Yes, I think so," she managed, attempting a brave smile that didn't quite reach her eyes. The encounter had clearly shaken her, bringing forth memories she'd rather have kept buried.

CJ felt a twinge of guilt for having exposed her to this, even though the circumstances had been beyond his control.

The fear slowly leached from her gaze as she recovered, commenting, "You were amazing with that horse. I thought you said you weren't a good rider."

"I'm not, but I never said I wasn't good with animals," CJ teased, clarifying. "Every summer I used to work for an old neighbor who had a couple of horses. For a few bucks an hour I'd muck the stalls and throw out the hay. The old man was too frail to do the job himself, but he wasn't willing to rehome the horses. I helped him out so he could keep them. He couldn't teach me to ride, but he taught me a few things about how to calm an agitated animal."

Erica's expression softened with reluctant marvel. "Every time I think I have you figured out, you go and do something that makes me question everything I thought I knew."

"I'll take that as a good sign, given our history," he said.

She blushed and grudgingly nodded. "Maybe so."

His concern for Erica momentarily pushed aside the myriad of questions swirling in his mind about the loose horse.

However, as the immediate worry for her well-being subsided, his thoughts returned to the situation at hand. It was highly unusual for a horse, especially one as well-trained as those on set, to break loose in such a dramatic fashion.

Someone had to have unlocked the gate, an act that seemed too intentional to be a mere oversight.

"What's wrong?" Erica asked, catching his expression.

"Something's not right. Someone would've had to unlock that gate and spook the horse to send it running like that."

"I'm sure it was an accident," Erica said, but she seemed to share his concern. "Should you tell the assistant director?"

"Yeah, probably."

But the production assistant, a young man named Alex, overheard them and hustled over, anxiety etched on his face. "Please don't tell Caroline. It was my job to watch the gate, and I left for a few minutes to grab a bite to eat at craft services. I swear I was only gone for ten minutes tops, and when I came back the horse was out, but it's all good now, right? No harm, no foul."

CJ nodded, appreciating the young man's candor and understanding his anxiety. "I get it, Alex. It's important to acknowledge when we've slipped up. But tell me, what exactly happened?"

Alex took a deep breath, too nervous to lie effectively. "I left to grab a quick snack—I hadn't eaten all day and thought it would be a quick trip. But that's no excuse. I was responsible for monitoring the gate, and someone must have unlocked it."

Erica, observing Alex's earnest demeanor, softened slightly. "It's good of you to come forward, but why didn't you report this immediately? The situation could have been much worse. Someone could've been really hurt."

Alex's shoulders slumped, the weight of the potential consequences hitting him. "I was scared," he admitted. "Scared of the repercussions, of being blamed for putting the production and everyone here at risk. I mean, this is my first gig, and I didn't want to jeopardize the chance of getting hired on another production."

But CJ understood the guy's anxiety. No one wanted to take the blame for anything going wrong on a multimillion-dollar production. "Look, I've got some pull. I'll make sure you're good. Just make sure it doesn't happen again, okay?"

Alex bobbed a nod, and CJ motioned for Erica to follow him toward Caroline's tent.

The missing wrangler's absence now seemed more suspicious than unfortunate. "Do you think the horse being let loose has anything to do with the missing wrangler?"

CJ mused aloud, more to himself than Erica. The idea that someone might've been trying to sabotage the movie set seemed far-fetched, but in an industry rife with competition and envy, it wasn't entirely out of the question.

Erica followed his line of thought. "It does seem oddly coincidental, doesn't it? Both the missing wrangler and now this." She hesitated but asked with a subtle cringe, "Do you think someone on the crew could be responsible?"

CJ frowned, considering the possibility. "I don't want to jump to conclusions, but something doesn't feel right. I've been on plenty of productions, and this is the first time I've felt this black cloud at my back."

Maybe it was because of what'd happened with Doug, but CJ's sense of security was tilted on its axis—a feeling he wasn't accustomed to.

"You were pretty incredible," Erica admitted, glancing his way, catching his gaze. "I mean, I can't believe how scared I was. I felt like a little kid all over again and about to pee my pants with fear."

The idea of Erica—Miss Professional—wetting her drawers in fear because he'd encouraged her to come and see the horses made him feel ten times worse. "I'm so sorry for putting you in a position where you felt unsafe."

"It's not your fault. You couldn't have known that was going to happen," she said, letting him off the hook. "I'm just glad you were there to handle the situation the way you did. The upside of all this might be if your movie career doesn't pan out, you've always got an in as a horse wrangler."

He chuckled, but he couldn't shake the feeling that this was no accident. They arrived at Caroline's tent only to find it empty. "Damn," CJ muttered, but then caught sight of the production manager walking past.

"Hey, man, can I talk to you for a minute?" he called out.

The man, immediately recognizing CJ, stopped and waited. "Everything okay?"

CJ made quick work of sharing what'd happened, making sure not to point fingers at anyone, least of all the poor production assistant who was probably crapping himself with fear over potentially losing his job.

"The guy stepped away to grab a bite to eat, and then the horse was let out. It's probably a poorly thought-out prank, but I thought someone ought to know, given the fact that the wrangler didn't show up to set today."

He didn't want to say the word *sabotage*, but it clung to his thoughts.

"We'll look into it," the production manager assured CJ, his expression perplexed. "Looks like we might need to install security cameras to make sure this kind of thing doesn't happen again." He rubbed his forehead as if the very thought of adding one more item to his to-do list gave him an instant migraine. His cell phone chirped, and he whipped it out to read the message. "Hey, looks like they're looking for you on set. Caroline got the shot list changed."

"Thanks, man," CJ said, watching as the man jogged away to handle another crisis. Turning to Erica, he said, "Want to watch me in action?"

She blushed, and he realized too late the sexual innuendo was too big to swerve. He chuckled, clearing his throat and clarifying, "I mean, watch me in the next scene. Could be entertaining."

Erica smiled, shrugging. "Seeing as I'm stuck here until

I can catch a ride back to base camp, sure—as long as it's not a scene with horses."

He chuckled. "You're safe with me," he said, adding with a wink, "I promise."

But even as he smiled and seemed chill about the situation, deep down, he was still troubled. Someone had compromised the set. He could feel it in his bones. He wasn't a detective by any means, but his gut instinct told him that horse getting loose had been no accident.

The question was, why?

The incident had not only threatened the film's production but had also endangered Erica, something he found he could not forgive or forget. She hadn't asked for his protection, but she was going to get it anyway.

Maybe if someone had looked out for Allison Brewer, the yoga instructor Doug had killed at Mariposa, she'd still be here.

Maybe if he'd seen some kind of sign that his manager was a murderer...

Shake it off, man. Time to work.

Chapter 6

After her unexpected adventure by the horses, Erica found herself being gently ushered toward the heart of the film set. The director, a woman known for her sharp eye and even sharper wit named Anna Wilson, greeted Erica with a warm, if somewhat distracted, welcome. "Any friend of CJ's is welcome to hang out with us," she said. "I'm just annoyed that of all days to visit the set, it would have to be one where all hell is breaking loose. Sorry, but we're not usually this chaotic."

"Sometimes things are out of our control," Erica commiserated. "I'm the executive assistant at Mariposa Resort. Usually we say that if it can, it will go wrong, and we just have to pivot to accommodate."

Anna barked a short laugh and popped an antacid. "Amen to that. Okay, places, people. We're behind, and we're losing daylight."

Caroline, the assistant director, echoed Anna's direction, and the whir of activity started as people took their appropriate places in the production.

"This next scene is crucial," Anna shared. "We weren't scheduled to shoot this scene until a few days from now, but we adapt when we can—all because of one damn horse wrangler. I knew we should've planned for two instead of relying on one person."

Sitting beside the director, Erica felt a flutter of excitement mixed with nerves. She was about to watch a movie being made from the inside, an experience far removed from her day-to-day life at the resort.

As the preparations for the next take were finalized, Erica's gaze found CJ. He stood apart, his focus inward as he morphed before her eyes into someone entirely different.

The transformation was startling, a testament to his skill as an actor. But this shift, this ability to become someone else so convincingly, stirred a discomfort within her.

This was how it felt when he'd ghosted her after spending the night curled in each other's arms. *Jarring* wasn't the word for how it had felt in the aftermath.

The scene began, and Erica watched, captivated, as CJ and the actor playing the antagonist squared off. The tension between them was palpable, even from a distance, their exchange laden with threats and underlying danger.

CJ's character was a far cry from the man she knew—or thought she knew. He was intense, his presence dominating the scene, his voice carrying a weight that seemed to pull the very air tight around them.

Erica found herself enthralled by the performance, by the sheer talent it took to bring such a character to life. Yet this admiration was tempered by a nagging reminder of the role CJ had played off-screen.

The man who had charmed and lied, who had used his skills as an actor not for art but to manipulate her. The contrast between CJ's heroism with the horse and his deceit in their personal encounter left Erica wrestling with conflicting emotions. His actions earlier had shown a care and concern that had felt genuine, a stark contrast to the manipulation she'd experienced at his hands. But which version of CJ was real?

As the director called "Cut" and the tension on set dissolved into a bustle of movement and conversation, Erica remained seated, lost in thought. She was amazed by CJ's talent yet troubled by the duality of his character. How much of what she'd seen in those moments of crisis had been the real CJ and how much was just another role he played effortlessly?

The director turned to her, a knowing look in her eye. "Impressive, isn't he?" she asked, clearly proud of her leading man.

"Yes, very," Erica managed, her voice neutral. "He's very talented."

But her compliment felt hollow, overshadowed by the complexity of her feelings. The director, oblivious to anything but her film, returned her attention to the monitors.

Erica's thoughts drifted back to the scene she'd just witnessed, to the palpable tension and the undeniable charisma CJ brought to his character. It was a performance, yes, but one that highlighted the fine line between reality and pretense.

So, swallow your damn pride and just have a conversation with the man, a voice in her head counseled with enough hint of exasperation to make her wonder whose side the voice was on.

The conflict within her remained unresolved as the director called for a break, and Erica found herself standing, almost mechanically, her applause for the scene automatic.

She was caught in the dichotomy of CJ's world, where fiction and reality blurred, leaving her unsure of her footing—and that was an unfamiliar feeling for Erica.

She preferred much more straightforward situations where there was clearly a right or wrong answer. Checking her watch, she tried not to fidget as time continued to slip through the hourglass. Let this serve as a lesson to never leave her cell phone behind under any circumstances. She supposed she could ask to borrow someone's phone, but she already felt like a burden when there was so much chaos all around her.

Anna motioned for CJ to come to her, and he obliged, moving swiftly, his expression still locked in his character. Erica swallowed a shiver of awareness as her heart rate fluttered at the intensity in his energy. How did someone change their vibe so effortlessly?

"CJ, doing a good job, but I have some quick notes."

"I'm all ears."

"Okay, so you know when you deliver the line 'I know you were at the Buford Homestead the night Clarissa was killed'…?" At CJ's quick nod, she instructed, "I really need you to deliver that line as if it's taking every ounce of strength in you not to shoot him in the head. Like, you want to so bad, but you can't because you're the sheriff in a lawless town, trying to make a difference. Got it?"

"Yeah, got it." He wiped at the sweat beneath his worn cowboy hat, returning to his mark but not before cutting her a short glance with a subtle hint of a smile that sent butterflies rioting through her stomach.

Unfortunately, the director caught that look too and

chuckled, warning, "Careful—that man's been known to break a few hearts on set."

Erica's cheeks flushed as she fought the fluster from her voice. "Oh, no worries of that. We're not even... I mean, we barely know each other. Actually, I should probably go find a phone. I need to call my office. Thanks for letting me watch you work. Fascinating stuff!"

And then she popped from her chair and practically ran from the set to find someone—anyone—who might have a phone she could borrow.

CJ's heart was still racing from the intensity of the scene as the director called "Cut," signaling the end of the take. The rush of adrenaline was familiar, a testament to his immersion in the role, but as he stepped out of character, a different concern began to take shape. His eyes scanned the bustling set, searching for Erica. He hadn't noticed her departure during the filming; his focus had been total, consumed by the demands of the scene.

"CJ, you ready for another take?" Anna called out, waiting for his thumbs-up. He couldn't hold up production to go look for Erica, but it bothered him that she'd bailed. Had she found a ride back to base camp, eager to be rid of him?

Tension prickled at the back of his neck, a mix of disappointment and worry settling in his stomach. He'd wanted her to see him work, to perhaps understand a part of his life that was so crucial to him, but also to share more of himself, the thing about him that he cared most about.

And maybe his ego was in there, too. He wanted her to see him in his element. She might even be impressed enough to give him a second chance.

CJ reluctantly gave a thumbs-up and returned to his mark, settling back into character. He had no choice but to finish what he was doing and then try to find where Erica had gone.

Finally, after what felt like hours, the scene wrapped, and he was cleared to take a break. He immediately made his way through the throng of people, his stardom and purposeful stride parting the sea of crew members with ease.

He approached one of the production assistants. "Hey, have you seen Erica Pike, the woman from the resort who was with me earlier? The woman who was sitting with the director during the last scene?"

The assistant shook his head, apologetic. "Sorry, CJ, I haven't seen her. But I've been all over the place. Maybe she's around craft services. That's where I always find people."

CJ thanked him and continued his search. The set was a labyrinth of equipment, trailers and temporary structures, a daunting place for someone unfamiliar with its chaotic order.

In a stroke of luck, he found Erica near the AD's tent. She looked up when she saw CJ approaching.

"There you are. I thought maybe you bailed."

"I would have," she answered honestly. "But everyone's still too busy to take me back to base camp. How long are these shoots?"

CJ admitted, "Pretty long. I think we had a twelve-hour day scheduled, and that was before the wrangler didn't show up, so having to pivot has made the day even longer."

Erica groaned. "I'm tired, my feet hurt and I'm hungry."

"I can help with the hungry part. Let's swing by craft

services and see what's cooking. I overheard someone say burgers were going on the grill tonight."

"I need to find a phone," she said, stressed. "I'm surprised Laura hasn't called Search and Rescue out on me yet."

"Why didn't you say something? You can borrow mine." He produced his cell from his back pocket. "It's almost dead, but it should have enough juice to make a call so no one worries."

"Are you sure?" Erica asked, unsure. "I don't want to use up all your power."

"I'll find a charger somewhere. Go ahead," he said, handing her his cell.

Erica accepted the phone with a grateful smile. "I really appreciate this. Thankfully I have the resort's number in my head, but heaven help me if I can remember anyone else's number without my phone."

He chuckled, stepping away to give her some privacy.

"Hi, this is Erica Pike. Can you transfer me to Laura, please?"

CJ could only faintly hear Erica's end of the conversation but caught the gist.

"I'm basically stranded until someone can take me back to base camp. I'm so sorry… Are you sure? I feel terrible… No, you have enough on your plate already. I'm fine. It's more of an inconvenience. I wish I could tell you what time I'll be back, but CJ says we're going to be here for a few more hours at least. Long night of shooting scheduled." Erica murmured something he didn't quite catch and then clicked off, handing him the phone with a chagrined expression. "I used up the last of your juice. I'm sorry."

He shook his head, feeling bad that she was trapped with

him. "I'm sorry this day turned out so differently from what you might have expected. Is there anything I can do? Anything you need?"

The offer hung between them, an olive branch extending into the space of their complicated history.

"I...actually, I think I'll take you up on that offer to get something to eat. All I've eaten is a protein bar, and it didn't go quite that far."

CJ grinned, relieved that he could be useful. "Absolutely. Let's see what's available."

Erica's suddenly shy smile was like sunshine on his soul, even if it was gone in a flash. One thing he was learning about Erica: she held her feelings close to the chest and didn't trust easily, which explained why his actions had hurt her so much.

He couldn't understand why her opinion of him meant so much to him, but it did. Maybe she'd give him a chance to prove that he wasn't a jerk. Nothing like a full belly to extend some much-needed goodwill.

Chapter 7

As the production broke for dinner, Erica sat at a make-shift table with CJ and the director, their plates piled with grilled southwestern burgers. If there was one thing Erica couldn't pass up, it was an expertly grilled burger oozing with cheese and spicy jalapeños.

"Damn, girl, just one of those suckers would take me out," CJ joked as Erica ate her second pepper. "How do you have any taste buds left?"

Erica chuckled. "You can't grow up in Arizona without acquiring a taste for the good spicy stuff. Besides, as my dad used to say, 'Puts hair on your chest.'"

Anna laughed. "Ha! I haven't heard that saying in ages. My dad used to say it, too. But it was usually when he was eating ptcha, calf's foot jelly. I wouldn't touch the stuff, but my dad thought it was good eating."

Erica tried not to grimace. "I, uh, can't say that I've ever tried that dish."

"And if you're lucky, you never will. Like I said, I don't even like it, and it's part of my culture. I'll give anyone a pass to decline a dish of that stuff."

Having Anna as a buffer between her and CJ made dinner entertaining. CJ, for his part, seemed content to listen and enjoy his burger while Anna and Erica chattered about life in the movie business as opposed to running an upscale resort.

"Look, I know this is probably counterintuitive because of the business I'm in, but I can only imagine how exhausting it must be dealing with a bunch of over-privileged jerks," Anna said, biting into a fry. "I mean, the egos on set can be a real pain in the ass, but at the end of the day, I'm not seeing to their comfort, I'm doing a job, same as them. Catering to their bullshit? No, thanks. I'd rather eat a plate of ptcha."

Erica laughed. "It's actually not that bad," she said. "We've been really lucky in that most of our guests are well-mannered and just happy to have a relaxing time at a nice place."

"There has to be some nightmare stories you can share," CJ teased. "C'mon, we're all ears."

Erica blushed beneath the force of CJ's playful smile but shook her head. "Sorry. All of our guests have been wonderful."

Anna grinned at CJ. "This woman's a professional. Page Six couldn't pull the tea out of this woman. Good for you. I respect that. If you ever decide to get out of the hospitality business, I could use someone like you on my staff."

"Flattered, but I don't think I'm cut out for the movie business."

"Fair enough." Anna shrugged, accepting Erica's answer, and the conversation circled around to the film and the day's events. Anna praised CJ's performance in the day's tense scenes. They teased each other in good fun about one another's talents, and from Erica's point of view, it was fun to catch the behind-the-scenes.

However, it wasn't long before the topic shifted to the day's earlier disruption—the missing wrangler—and the vibe shifted.

"The wrangler, he's a local guy," Anna mentioned, picking at her burger. "Came with good references. It's strange he'd just bail without any warning." Her gaze swiveled to Erica. "Any chance you know the guy? His name is Kyle Jefferson."

Erica shook her head. "Sorry—he doesn't ring a bell."

"So there's no word on him yet?" CJ asked. "He hasn't called in or anything?"

"Radio silence on his end, but when Caroline was trying to find him, she dug up something interesting."

Both Erica and CJ were all ears.

Anna hesitated, her fork pausing midair, as if unsure if she should share. "Well, I'm not one for gossip, but given the recent circumstances, I'd hate for there to be some kind of connection," she admitted, her tone lowering.

"Connection to what?" CJ asked.

"Allison Brewer—the girl Doug DeGraw is accused of murdering."

CJ stared, unsettled by the news. "How so?"

"It could be a rumor, but sounds like they were dating," Anna said, wiping her mouth. "The thing is the minute Allison died, a spotlight shone on everyone in her sphere. A murder is one of those situations that contaminate everything. Nothing is ever just a simple thing anymore. The notoriety of a murder follows everyone attached to the victim."

"That's terrible," Erica murmured. "I hope he's okay. Maybe he took a mental health day or something."

"Maybe, but a phone call would've been nice," Anna said, wadding up her napkin and tossing it to the paper plate. Before Anna could continue on that topic, a production assistant approached, whispering something into Anna's ear. She cursed beneath her breath, standing abruptly. "Sorry—have to handle another crisis. You two enjoy your dinner." With that, Anna was gone, leaving Erica and CJ alone.

After a moment of silence, Erica decided to broach the sensitive subject. "I can't even imagine how it must feel for you with the whole murder situation. How are you coping?"

CJ sighed, setting down his burger. "I don't really want to talk about Doug," he admitted. "But yeah, it's been tough. His actions...they've made me question everything I thought I knew about him. I don't like to make it about me, but Doug was more than my manager, he was my friend... but it feels wrong to grieve over losing a friend when that friend turns out to be a murderer."

Erica got that. It was complicated, for sure, but the honesty in his voice revealed a vulnerability that resonated with her. She reached across the table, covering his hand with her own in support. "I can't imagine how that feels, but you're not responsible for his actions."

CJ looked at her, his eyes a mix of gratitude and sadness. "Thanks, Erica. It's just...it's a lot to process, you know?"

She nodded. Although she couldn't quite imagine the weight of that burden, she knew how it felt to feel alone in something. "Yeah, I do. But you'll get through this."

CJ smiled at her, his eyes shining. "I hope so," he said, then cleared his throat. "So, you up for dessert? I think I saw chocolate chip cookies."

Erica hesitated, then smiled. "Sure, why not? I never turn down an opportunity for something sweet."

"Good to know." CJ flashed a smile that made her stomach flip, and she wondered if she owed CJ a second chance or if she was just falling into the same routine as before.

The night scenes stretched on, each take blending into the next until CJ could barely remember his lines without a prompt. He was used to this, but he felt bad for Erica. She tried to put on a brave face, but he caught the surreptitious yawns as she sat beside Anna take after take.

It seemed forever before they were able to finally wrap, Anna's voice cutting through the desert night air like a beacon of relief. The set erupted into a flurry of activity and structured chaos only film crews could master. Everyone was beat, their movements sluggish yet efficient as they began the nightly ritual of wrapping up.

CJ, usually whisked away by a diligent production assistant, tonight felt a pull to do things differently. He managed to sweet-talk the assistant assigned to their ride, a wide-eyed kid who looked like he'd do anything CJ suggested, into letting him take the wheel of the golf cart meant to shuttle him and Erica back to base camp.

"Trust me—I've driven in worse conditions," CJ assured him with a grin, glossing over the fact that navigating a golf cart through a deserted movie set hardly qualified as challenging.

But fate, it seemed, had a sense of humor. As the set emptied and silence took over, CJ and Erica were the last to leave.

Erica shivered at the quiet set. "It's a lot different when it's not crawling with people," she said.

"Kinda spooky, huh?" CJ winked. "Don't worry—I'll protect you."

Erica rolled her eyes. "Just get me to base camp in one piece so I can get home. I feel like I've lived an entire life on this set in one day, and I need to sleep for a good twelve hours."

CJ chuckled. "Welcome to my life, baby," he said, climbing into the golf cart as she joined him. "Life moves at a different pace on set. It's always a little jarring to find your feet again in real life. Sleep helps."

CJ reached for the key that should've been in the ignition, but his fingers grasped nothing. He peered at the ignition and realized with a sinking feeling—the key hadn't been left behind.

"What's wrong?"

Damn, this was embarrassing. "Um, so, we have a bit of a situation…"

"A situation? What does that mean?"

"There's no key."

Erica's eyes bugged. "No key? What?"

He chuckled with chagrin. "Yeah… I guess someone forgot to leave the key in the ignition and then left without checking that our ride was…uh, rideable."

"What are you saying? Are you saying we're…freaking stranded?"

Did he want to say that? No. But was it true? Yeah.

He fished his phone from his back pocket and realized too late that he had forgotten to put it on the charger. "Okay, so…yeah, we're stranded."

"Nooo," Erica groaned, looking ready to cry. "What are we going to do?"

"A solution will come to me," he said, though his mind was terrifyingly blank. He'd never been in this position before. He was a freaking movie star. He hadn't had to troubleshoot a problem in ages—and he was out of practice. But he couldn't have Erica terrified, not on his watch.

He flashed her an apologetic smile that he hoped conveyed both *I'm sorry* and *We'll laugh about this later* and said decisively, "Well, we can't spend the night in this golf cart. Come on, let's find a place to hang out until someone realizes I'm not back at base camp and comes looking for me."

"Are you sure someone will come?" she asked, following him out of the golf cart and rubbing her shoulders at the chill in the air.

"I mean, I'm the star," he said, but when he said it out loud, he was suddenly less sure that anyone would notice. It wasn't like he had a bodyguard who was in charge of his safety, and filming had gone on so much longer than anticipated. Everyone was probably exhausted and ready to go to bed. CJ Knight's whereabouts were the last thing anyone wanted to worry about.

"Stranded on a movie set in the middle of nowhere. Great." She shivered. "And likely to catch pneumonia by morning."

An idea came to CJ. "Actually, I think I have an idea. Follow me." He slipped his hand into hers and led her to another section of the set that hadn't been used that day because of the rearranging of the shooting schedule.

"Is this a…brothel?" Erica asked as he led her into the

makeshift bedroom that was supposed to be above the saloon.

"Oldest job in the world and probably what made the Wild West…well, wild." He grinned, gesturing to the bed. "But that's a bed with real blankets, so not only are we sheltered from the elements, we actually have bedding. But we might need to, uh, cuddle to conserve body warmth."

Erica laughed despite the situation. "If I didn't know better, I'd say you did this on purpose."

"I didn't—I swear it," he said in earnest, but a part of him wasn't sorry it'd happened. "Hey, at least it beats the usual 'stuck in an elevator' scenario, right?"

Erica shook her head with silent mirth and climbed into the bed, snuggling into the blankets with a sigh. "This is the weirdest day of my life, but you're right—it's warm and surprisingly comfortable."

"All right, scoot over, bed hog," he teased, kicking his boots off and climbing into the bed beside her. Immediately, the warmth of her body brought up memories he had no trouble recalling.

Judging by the sudden silence between them, Erica remembered, too.

"We're just sharing the bed for warmth," she said in a trembling voice. "Nothing more than that."

"Of course not," he said. "One question, though…"

"Yeah?"

"Is cuddling out of the question?"

A beat passed between them before Erica grudgingly allowed, "I guess in the interest of keeping warm, some cuddling is fine."

CJ tried to keep the grin from his mouth as he gruffly agreed, "Yep. Just for warmth."

It was either going to be a long night or the best night of sleep he'd had in years.

Chapter 8

As the Arizona night stretched on, cold and unyielding, Erica found herself nestled against CJ in a prop bed set up for a scene that never got shot that day.

The absurdity of their situation wasn't lost on her—a pair of adults, wrapped up in blankets on a movie set, pretending the chill didn't seep into their bones. Yet beneath the surface absurdity, a current of something more profound pulled at her, tugging at the threads of her resolve and her feelings for CJ.

Despite it being May, the wind outside whistled across the desert like a pack of hungry wolves, the echoes carried by the desolate landscape surrounding them.

"I never would've imagined a film set being creepy when everyone's gone," she said. "Feels like a completely different place when it's bustling with people."

"Do you believe in ghosts?" CJ asked playfully.

"No." Erica's quick answer was followed by another shiver, prompting her to add, "Well, I mean, I believe in *science* more than the supernatural, but I'm also not interested in challenging my belief structure. If ghosts exist, I'd rather not know. Besides, in my experience, the evil that exists in the world is most definitely human."

"No argument there," CJ murmured.

Shivering, Erica pulled the blankets tighter around her body as she rested her head on CJ's broad chest. She could feel his heartbeat beneath her ear, steady and strong. She breathed in deeply, taking in his woodsy scent that mingled with the dusty smell of the desert air. A sense of calm washed over her as she listened to the rustling of leaves in the nearby bushes and the distant creaking of metal contraptions used for filming.

"I remember this feeling," she whispered softly, her voice barely above a whisper. "Being next to you felt so natural, which is the exact opposite of how I usually feel."

"What do you mean?" CJ asked.

In the darkness, she felt safe to be more exposed and vulnerable than she ever had before.

"I'm not really the kind of person who lets people in. My circle of trust is very small, and it usually takes years to gain access, but somehow you managed to slip in beneath my radar, and I still haven't quite figured that out."

"And then I hurt you when I disappeared," he finished quietly.

She nodded, her throat closing. "Yeah."

He stroked her hair gently, a familiar gesture that sent warmth coursing through her veins despite the cold. They lay there in silence for a while, lost in their own thoughts and memories until Erica mustered up the courage to ask what had been on her mind all evening.

"Why did you ghost me?"

Her question hung in the air like a weighted balloon waiting to be popped, suspended between them like an elephant on a trapeze.

"I don't like to use it as an excuse, but it's true—it was the perfect storm of circumstances. The night we hooked up, I was scheduled to leave anyway, but I'd fully planned to invite you to come see me in LA. Except the news broke about Doug, and it blew my world apart. I know it sounds superficial, but my world isn't like yours. Losing a manager in this business is like losing a vital part of yourself. They hold your career in their hands, which is why it's so important to find the right one. I hate to say it, but Doug was magic for my career—which makes it doubly hard to stomach that he might've been magic for me but he was lethal to someone else. I mean, I can't even wrap my head around it. To be honest, when it all went down, you were the last thing I was thinking about, but when the haze cleared and I wanted to call you, it was too late. I knew that window had shut, and I moved on."

It made perfect sense. Her logical brain understood, but it stung to know that she'd been so easily forgotten, even in the face of a tragedy. But maybe that was unfair of her to think that.

"I would've understood if you'd given me the chance," she said, although a part of her questioned if that were true. She didn't usually grant second chances to people who'd hurt her.

"I should've called. I'm sorry."

Did he mean that? Was it possible she was holding too tightly to her hurt feelings and not listening to the truth he was offering?

"I'll just say it now—I've missed you. I know we haven't had much of a chance to really get to know each other, but… I'd love the chance to start over and do it right."

"Do you mean that?"

"I do," he answered solemnly.

"Never thought I'd end up spending the night on a movie set," Erica mused, her voice a whisper against the silence that enveloped them. The set, a ghost town under the moon's watchful eye, held them in a bubble of suspended reality.

"Stick with me, baby. I bring the excitement," CJ quipped.

A soft laugh bubbled up in her chest. "That you do," she agreed, meeting his gaze.

In the starlight everything seemed dreamy, more surreal. Was she lying in a prop bed with Hollywood's most eligible bachelor, or was she hallucinating some secret fantasy she hadn't even known existed in her heart of hearts?

Heat grew inside her, stoked by CJ's presence and the memories of their shared past. She closed her eyes, savoring the rhythm of his heartbeat underneath her ear, taking deep breaths to calm her nerves. *Just go to sleep—figure everything out in the morning.*

Great rational advice, but logic and reason had vacated the building, leaving behind growing need and a red haze of desire that was hard to ignore.

Her body trembled slightly as she tried to ignore the goose bumps rising on her arms and legs—a mix of cold and anticipation.

"You're shivering," CJ said, pulling the blankets closer around them. "Get closer—our combined body heat will warm you up."

But it wasn't the cold that was making her shake.

"CJ… I know what I said, and I meant it at the time. But…if we're going to start over…shouldn't we start with what got us all twisted up in the first place?"

Yeah, that was some shaky reasoning, but her brain wasn't in control anymore.

CJ stilled, catching her drift. "Are you sure?" he asked, his voice strained, as if he were fighting the need to be a gentleman and the desire to pin her to the bed.

And right now, she wanted to be pinned, devoured and reminded how toe-curling his moves were.

"I'm sure," she whispered before rising to press her lips against his.

As if in response to her request, the wind died down outside and even the distant creaking sounds faded away into oblivion. They were alone in their own little world, two souls intertwined amid the desolate landscape of illusions and movie magic.

CJ kissed her deeply, their tongues tangling as his hands traveled up and down her spine before cupping her backside possessively with a groan. "Only if you're sure, baby," he said as he helped her pull her clothes off in a feverish motion. Within moments, they were both naked and the chill of the night was forgotten.

"Girl, you've lived in my dreams since the last time we were together," he admitted, filling his palms with her breasts before rising up to suck each tightened nipple into his mouth in turn.

She gasped at the rough lave of his tongue across her sensitive tips, thrilling at the insistent press of his erection against her hot core.

This felt taboo—and yet so intensely hot.

She wouldn't dare admit that her erotic dreams and fantasies had featured CJ front and center, but it was her shameful secret that she'd take to the grave. She couldn't forget how he'd turned her inside and out both physically and emotionally, and now it was happening again.

The exquisite torture was a sensual explosion of the senses, heightened by their extreme circumstances.

Girl, you're playing with fire, the voice in her head cautioned, but Erica was beyond hearing anything resembling reason.

Right about now, going down in flames sounded like the most sublime way to go.

Erica's head fell back against the pillow as she moaned softly, her long brown hair spilling over the rough cotton sheets of the prop bed. The metal frame squeaked rhythmically in time with his thrusts.

Her body trembled under CJ's touch, her hips shifting against his hand in rhythm with his explorations. Her breathing grew deeper, and her eyes drifted shut, lost in the moment.

CJ couldn't believe how good it felt to be inside her—how right it felt. He slid his hand up her side and cupped her breast, his thumb brushing against the hardening nipple. She gasped, arching into his touch as he teased and twirled the tightened bud between his fingers. Her skin was warm and soft against his palm, her breasts full and heavy in his hand.

"You're so damn perfect," he murmured, trailing kisses down her neck, nipping lightly as he went. His lips found her collarbone and then lower still, until he reached the valley between her breasts where he paused for a moment to savor the taste of her skin.

The air was thick with the scent of their arousal, making CJ yearn for more. The sound of their skin slapping together filled the small room, growing louder as their pace quickened.

A bead of sweat trickled down his forehead, adding to the sheen on his skin that glistened in the dim light cast by the full moon and vast expanse of starlight outside the fake glass windowpane. The rustle of the sheets drowned out all other sounds as they moved together like two well-oiled machines. He smiled against her soft skin as her nails dug into his shoulders, no doubt leaving faint red marks that would soon turn to bruises. She gripped him tighter, pulling him closer to her core, urging him to go deeper.

Her legs wrapped around his waist, lifting her off the mattress slightly to meet each savage thrust, their hips meeting in perfect harmony with a desperate rhythm that left them both panting for breath.

His free hand trailed down her side, exploring every contour of her body before bracing himself against the metal frame, holding on for dear life.

He took advantage of this position to thrust even deeper against that velvet heat, groaning at the feel of their bodies joined so tightly together.

CJ's heart raced faster than he thought possible; his chest tightened with anticipation and desire as he buried himself so deep, they were nearly one.

When he climaxed, unleashing a torrent within her, he lost all sense of time and space.

He gasped her name, shuddering as he spent himself, rolling beside her, sucking air as his heart thundered in his chest.

It was several moments before he could collect himself enough to check on Erica—who was in a similar state.

A drowsy but satisfied smile found his lips, but as Erica cuddled up to him, a different feeling started to creep up on him, one that was unwelcome.

The feeling of being watched.

It was improbable that anyone was there with them.

But being alone with nothing to defend themselves with—not even the ability to call for help—made him feel vulnerable in a way he'd never truly experienced.

You're imagining things. Whatever this is, knock it off. Don't screw things up again.

He settled and tried to relax, but Erica caught the tensing of his body. "What's wrong?" she asked.

"Nothing…just a weird place to be stuck in," he said. "I—"

The sound of something banging outside interrupted him, and he bolted upright. CJ's heart thrummed against his chest as the noise outside jolted him back to reality. It was a sharp, sudden sound that sliced through the stillness of the night—a crack, perhaps, or a clatter that didn't belong amid the silence.

"What was that?" Erica asked, grabbing her shirt and pulling it on.

"Probably just a curious animal, but I think I should check it out."

"And do what if it is more than a raccoon? Hurl insults in the hope of hurting their feelings? I think we should just stay put and be quiet," Erica said, her voice a hushed whisper.

Wise, but not very gallant. "You want me to hide in the dark? Should I hand over my man card now or later?"

Erica persuaded him to return to her side. "I promise your man card is well and truly represented."

As much as he was tempted to return to cuddling, he couldn't rest until he knew they were safe. "Stay here. I'll be right back."

"CJ…" Erica called after him, frustrated. "Just—"

"Shhh. I just need to know no one's out there messing with shit."

Erica grabbed her pants and pulled them on. "Then I'm going with you. I'm not going to stay behind like a good little lady clutching her nightie. Besides, haven't you watched any horror films? You never separate."

"Fair point," he said, grinning. "Okay, Annie Oakley, let's do a perimeter search, then."

He slipped his hand into hers, and they went off to make sure no one was prowling the set. But he hoped to God it was just his imagination and not an actual threat because like, Erica had said…he had nothing but his sharp tongue to defend them.

Chapter 9

CJ would've preferred Erica stay behind for safety reasons, but once he stepped outside, he was thankful for her hand in his. They moved together, a pair of shadows adrift in the enveloping darkness of the abandoned film set.

Despite the full moon, the pale light did little more than tease the edges of their path and create more menacing shadows. Every prop loomed like a specter, every flutter of wind felt like breath on the nape of his neck. But there was nothing—no sign of intrusion, no evidence of danger. Nothing but the rustle of leaves and the far-off hoot of an owl keeping vigil over the night.

"Probably just a raccoon," CJ concluded, though his voice lacked conviction and he felt a little foolish for being so jumpy. "I mean, what are the odds someone else is tromping around the set, too?"

"I'd hope the odds are small," she joked. "Otherwise that's creepy in a different way."

He agreed with a chuckle as they returned to their makeshift bedroom.

Back within the confines of the four walls they had claimed as their own, CJ caught Erica's gaze. There was a silent question there surrounding what'd unfolded between them once again. He didn't want to be just another scene in her life, a fleeting moment soon cut and edited out. Yet what was he hoping for? He didn't have an answer for himself, so he sure as hell hoped Erica didn't ask the question.

"People are always so surprised by how cold it gets in the desert," Erica shared as they climbed back into the creaky bed. "Laura said that we ought to consider having a boutique at the resort just for those times when guests come unprepared for the weather."

"Are you and your boss close?" he asked, curious about her personal life.

"Yeah, I guess so. I'm in charge of her bachelorette party, so I think she trusts me enough for that important job. She's a great boss, though. She doesn't micromanage, which is crucial for me. When people try to micromanage me, I get twitchy."

"You seem highly capable on your own. I can't see why anyone would feel the need."

"Thank you," she said, snuggling against him. "Right now this whole night feels unreal, like I'm going to wake up in my own bed and realize this was some fever dream."

"What? You mean you've never spent the night in a closed film set overnight? Girl, this is a typical Friday night."

She laughed at his joke, allowing the easy silence between them to settle. Why did it feel so natural to hold her in his arms? They barely knew each other. "Tell me something about yourself," he said, needing to know more than just the surface Erica that everyone else knew.

Erica yawned, her voice sleepy. "Hmm…what do you want to know?"

"Anything."

"I don't like artichokes."

The simple statement made him smile. "No artichokes. Is there a reason, or just in general?"

"If you must know, I choked on one when I was a kid. I accidentally got one of the thistles in my throat, and my throat seized up. Traumatized me. Haven't touched one since."

"Horses and artichokes—trauma central. Got it. Any other traumas lurking in your childhood I should know about?"

She chuckled. "None that I can think of offhand. How about you?"

"Nothing so dramatic or interesting. I'm allergic to pine nuts, though."

"Pine nuts? Not peanuts?"

"Nope—all good with peanuts, but give me a pine nut and I'll end up in the hospital."

"Good to know. No pesto sauce for you, then."

"Yeah, my love for Italian pasta has been forever shelved."

"There's always Alfredo," Erica murmured, nearly asleep.

He grinned when he heard her breathing change to slow and steady. He held her close, allowing himself to simply enjoy the moment—strange as it was—because he knew when the morning came, everything would change.

The gentle invasion of dawn's light heralded the return of reality. Erica's eyes fluttered open at the distant sounds of voices, the metallic clink of equipment being unloaded... the film crew had arrived, oblivious to the mini drama that had unfolded in their absence.

CJ awoke at the same moment, muttering, "Shit," and they scrambled, a flurry of limbs and fabrics as they wriggled into their clothes to slip from their temporary sanctuary before anyone caught them and started asking questions. "We need to find Caroline," he said, leading the way toward the AD's tent.

Erica appreciated CJ taking the lead, though she was embarrassed to be seen so disheveled. Even though she knew it was unlikely, she cringed at the thought that everyone who saw her would be able to see that they'd hooked up.

Talk about a walk of shame.

"Stranded? You two?" Caroline's voice climbed an octave, her professionalism dueling with concern as CJ shared their unfortunate unscheduled sleepover. "I'll find out who's responsible—"

"Hey, it's okay," CJ interjected quickly, shaking his head. "Everyone was running on fumes last night. Let's not make a mountain out of a molehill. Plus, if I'm being honest, it's more my fault than anyone's. If I hadn't persuaded the PA to let me drive back to base camp, this never would've happened."

Caroline hesitated, then nodded, her expression softening. "You're too kind, CJ."

Erica met his gaze, silently appreciating how he was willing to take the blame and save someone's job.

However, Erica felt compelled to add, "We did have to take shelter in the set with the bed because it was the only one with blankets. You might want to have your set team change out the bedding for sanitary purposes."

"Oh, yes, of course," Caroline agreed. "I'll have someone

take care of that right now, but in the meantime, you both probably want to shower and get back to your routines."

"Much appreciated. Yes, a shower would be amazing right now…and a quick nap in my own bed. I'm thankful for the set bed, but the Old West wasn't big on comfort. I think I have a bruise from the metal springs," Erica joked, but then her cheeks flared at the unintended slip. She was bruised, all right…but not likely from the bed.

She glanced at CJ long enough to catch a smoking-hot look, and her breath caught in her chest. "Yes, anyway, I'd really love to get home," she said hurriedly.

A different production assistant approached, clipboard in hand, ready to shuttle them back to base camp. The return ride was quiet, professional, devoid of the closeness they'd found in the dark. Erica had felt the eyes of the crew on them, curious, speculative, which was an uncomfortable feeling for her.

CJ kept his distance from Erica, a bittersweet tug in her chest. She wanted to reach out, to steal one more moment, but the world was watching now, and she was no more interested in being the subject of everyone's gossip than he was.

Back at base camp, Erica and CJ exited the golf cart, and the production assistant confirmed he'd return in an hour to return him to set before he drove off.

"Wow, you really know how to show a girl a night worth remembering," she teased, pushing an errant lock away from her face as the slight breeze played havoc with her mussed hair.

He chuckled, cracking a short yawn. "You okay to drive back to your place?"

"Yes, I'm fine. I feel bad for you having to return to set for a full day of shooting after the night we had."

"No rest for the wicked."

"So they say," she mused, risking a look his way. Should they make plans to see each other again? What happened next? "Thanks for looking out for me last night…and sharing your body heat."

"My pleasure," he said in a silky tone that sent shivers down her spine. "I'd say let's do it again sometime, but I think we broke about ten different SAG and OSHA rules in one setting."

She laughed ruefully. "I think you might be right." Was it possible to hope that they truly could start fresh? Under ordinary circumstances she didn't believe in second chances, but CJ Knight was no ordinary guy. Maybe the situation warranted a little leeway.

She started to walk away, calling over her shoulder. "You have my number," she said, and let the innuendo fall where it might.

If CJ meant what he said, he'd call.

If not, she'd stick to her original plan and forget he'd ever existed.

Chapter 10

"Okay, break for lunch. One hour," the AD called out on her bullhorn, and bells and whistles sounded throughout the set as everyone prepared to take a break from the grueling sun and grab a bite.

For CJ, he needed a minute to himself. There was too much on his mind—mostly Erica—but also there was something about last night that felt odd.

He used the time to call Landon and make sure his house was still standing.

"Hey, man, how's filming?" Landon asked. "I heard Arizona is heading for a heat wave. Not that it's not already the devil's armpit."

"Yeah, they're planning to erect some cooling stations here on location so people don't drop like flies. But other than that, it's business as usual. How's the house?"

"Everything's still standing," Landon quipped with a grin in his voice. "You know I treat it like my own. Ain't nothing gonna happen on my watch. Although you're going to need to throw some money on the house account because there's nothing to eat in this place."

"Buy your own damn groceries, you moocher," CJ shot back, but he was only kidding, and Landon knew it. "Fine,

I'll put some more money on the house account, but try not to spend it all on beer."

"Beer? Hard liquor, my friend—we're watching our waistlines." But Landon waited a beat before asking, "So, what's going on? What's the real reason you called?"

Landon knew him too well. "You're not going to believe what happened last night. Me and a friend had to spend the night on set. Had to spend the night curled up in a prop bed."

"You're kidding me. How'd that happen?"

"That's the thing—I'm sure it was an accident. The shooting schedule got all screwed up when the horse wrangler was a no-show, and everyone was running on fumes by the time we wrapped. But when I went to hop into the golf cart, there were no keys."

"Seriously? I've never heard of that happening. I mean, every production manager I've ever met is a bulldog and makes sure everyone's doing their job, or it's their ass."

"Same." He couldn't explain how he felt about what had happened last night both with Erica and being stranded, but it all felt unreal, and while being with Erica had been amazing, being stranded had not. "But a lot of weird things have been happening on this shoot. I could've sworn I heard someone walking around in the middle of the night even though I know we were the only ones there."

"Hey, hey, don't go there," Landon said with a chuckle, clearly trying to sound lighthearted. "It was probably just your imagination working overtime. The desert gets to everybody. Or maybe it was a ghost of productions past," he teased, before switching gears. "Now, why don't you tell me more about this friend of yours who stayed over? Are we talking sweaty production assistant or hot Sedona chick?"

CJ didn't like to kiss and tell, but he knew Landon would figure it out somehow. "Yeah, it was Erica. Remember that girl I told you about before leaving?"

Landon whistled low. "Damn. How'd that go?"

"Good. I mean, I think we were able to hash out some things, clear the air, so to speak."

"You like her?"

"Yeah, but she's here, I'm in LA. Not really sure how much of a real future is there."

"I hear you—best not to get too attached. That's my motto every day."

"You're a commitment-phobe," CJ said derisively. "We're not the same."

"Of course we aren't," Landon replied breezily, his words belying the ease with which he drew the parallel. CJ buttoned his lip; arguing about it only made him seem more suspect.

CJ switched gears, chatting about the minutiae of the film set and starting to relax. The real charm behind Landon was his ability to project some kind of inner calm even when his own life seemed steeped in chaos. The man didn't have a stable address, couch surfed at various friends' places and never worried a day in his life about where his next meal was coming from—yet rarely worked.

He could picture Landon sitting cross-legged on his couch with his phone pressed against his ear while he watched one of those reality home-makeover shows that always seemed to be on the television. Ironic, seeing as Landon would likely never own a home of his own.

CJ shook off his thoughts, realizing the time. "Break's

almost over, and I still need a ten-minute nap," he said. "Thanks for holding down the fort."

"No problem, man. You know I got you. Don't get left behind. Get yourself a dedicated driver who doesn't move a muscle unless he's with you. That'll solve that problem."

CJ chuckled. "Thanks. I'll do that."

Landon clicked off, and CJ tossed his phone to the small table in his tent. On location, his private area wasn't much to look at, but at least it had a makeshift cot and a cooling fan. Good enough for a quick snooze before hitting the set again.

When he closed his eyes, all he saw was Erica, which made him wonder…should he pursue her? Or should he let that connection go?

He opened his eyes and stared up at the ceiling of his tent. The fan beside him whirred loudly as the air blew over him, providing some relief from the hot Arizona sun.

Maybe it was better if they didn't keep in touch. It would only complicate things and create unnecessary drama. Plus, what kind of future did they really have? She lived in Arizona and he lived in LA. They were in two completely different worlds.

But then again, CJ couldn't shake off the feeling that there was something special between them. Something worth holding on to. He couldn't remember the last time another person had dominated his thoughts like this. Most days his career took center stage—and he'd liked the simplicity of that single drive.

Maybe it was the whole situation with Doug that had him thinking of things in a different way. Or maybe he was just getting older and realizing there was supposed to be more to life than what he was doing.

His phone vibrated next to him and interrupted his thoughts. He grabbed it eagerly, hoping it was a message from Erica. But instead it was a quick text from the AD that shooting would resume in a half hour.

He sighed and tossed his phone back onto the table. This film project was consuming all of his time and energy, leaving him with little room for anything else.

Maybe that was a good thing.

He couldn't tell anymore.

Erica's steps carried a lightness that only a combination of steaming water and a good hard nap could bestow. She breezed through the lobby of the resort, the clacking of her heels on the marble floor punctuating each determined stride toward Laura's sanctuary-like office.

"Hey," she said, pushing open the door without knocking. The familiarity between them rendered formalities unnecessary—besides, Erica knew Laura was anxious to hear all about her little adventure last night.

Laura looked up from a mountain of paperwork, her eyes widening in anticipation. "You're back! Tell me everything."

"Where do I even start?" Erica chuckled, sinking into the chair opposite Laura's desk. She recounted the surreal experience, omitting the scorching hookup with CJ, and instead painted vivid images of the deserted film set—props casting eerie shadows, the moonlight filtering through the skeletal structures of incomplete scenes.

"Wow, it's like you lived in a movie for a night," Laura

said as she digested the cinematic adventure. "I have to admit it sounds pretty exciting, almost like an urban explorer or something. I'm a little jealous."

"Jealous?" I laughed. "Did you miss the part where I said we had to bunk down on a prop bed? Let me tell you— it wasn't a luxury bed, and it squeaked every time you breathed."

And when you did other things, she left out.

"And everything was chill between you and CJ?" Laura asked, curious. "Last I heard, you two were not exactly friends."

"Oh, it was totally fine," Erica assured Laura quickly. "Nothing like a random stranding to put things into perspective. I was probably too hard on him. I mean, his manager was arrested for Allison's murder—that had to be hard to deal with."

Laura winced, murmuring, "It hurts my heart to even think of what happened to poor Allison. She was such a sweet girl. I still have nightmares about it."

Erica understood. It might've seemed like it was business as usual at Mariposa, but there was definitely a pall of sadness that clung to the darkened corners knowing that a young girl had died there. Laura had even considered having the place "cleansed," but Josh had thought that was a little extreme and shot down the idea.

Laura sighed, returning to Erica's story. "Maybe I'm not cut out for that level of adventure, but it might be nice to be without a phone for a night. I swear mine doesn't stop binging or chiming or yanking on my electronic tether for ten minutes."

"You could always silence your phone, Laura, if you

need a minute to breathe," Erica suggested with a wry chuckle. "No need for anything as dramatic as being stranded in the desert."

"On the surface that sounds like a workable plan, but then I remember my family is so protective that if I was incommunicado for more than a few hours, they'd send a search and rescue team after me."

"Josh would definitely do that," Erica agreed, standing as she checked her watch. "On that note, I have to get moving."

Laura nodded, but her sudden "Oh!" as she reached into her desk told Erica that was more. "I almost forgot. I don't know where my brain is at, but I swear as soon as all this wedding prep is over, I'll be so relieved. There's one more person I absolutely need to have at my bachelorette party. Her name is Willow Sanderson, and she was my absolute bestie in college. If I didn't invite her, she'd fly out from California just to put hair remover in my shampoo bottle and then leave again."

Erica frowned with alarm. "You *want* to invite her?"

But Laura laughed. "I'm kidding about the hair remover, but I'd definitely get an earful, and rightfully so—that woman got me through college. I can't count how many times she saved my ass from horrible dates. We had a system…" Laura remembered Erica was pressed for time, "Sorry— a story for another time. Here's her contact information."

Erica glanced over the paper. "She's in California? Isn't this a bit short notice for her to come to Arizona by next week?"

Laura waved off Erica's concern. "Her parents are loaded. She'll love the excuse to jump in a plane and stop whatever she's doing. Trust me. You'll love her. She's a hoot."

A "hoot" sounded like a headache, but it was Laura's party, so Erica wouldn't say no. "I'm on it," she said with a smile.

Laura winked. "You're the best."

Erica left Laura's office and headed to housekeeping to check in with staff, ensure that all was moving as it should, then met with the carpet installer, put out a few internal fires and set her office back to rights after her impromptu stay on set.

By the time Erica's day was finished, she felt confident everything was back on track, which was a nice feeling.

But what wasn't a nice feeling was the fact that CJ hadn't tried to text or call her since leaving her this morning. True, he was on set and he probably had a full shooting schedule, but how hard was it to send a quick text?

No fixating allowed, that voice reminded her. *People will show their true intention if you let them.* If CJ wanted to call, he would.

And if he didn't…well, she'd have her answer about that, too.

Erica perched on the edge of her neatly made bed, fingers dancing across the keyboard of her laptop as she typed out invitations for Laura's bachelorette party.

With every chime signaling an email sent, her thoughts intermittently drifted against her will, pulling her back to memories of CJ. Her heart fluttered a little with a mix of hope and doubt, the night they'd shared looping in her mind like a highlight reel that refused to stop playing.

She shook her head, trying to refocus on the task at hand, but the monotony of typing names and addresses left too much room for wandering thoughts.

The phone lay next to her, its screen blank and unyielding. She willed it to light up with a notification, any small sign that CJ hadn't just vanished after their intimate encounter.

"Come on, Erica, keep it together," she muttered to herself, her gaze inadvertently straying to the device again. The silence from CJ was louder than any message tone, a silent symphony of rejection that filled the spaces around her.

"Focus," she whispered, her fingers resuming their earlier rhythm. She breezed through a few more invitations until another pause allowed doubt to creep in once more. Wasn't this exactly what she had feared? That the connection she'd felt, the laughter and shared secrets under the guise of night, were nothing but a well-rehearsed act?

Which she'd fallen for *again*?

The clock on the wall ticked away the time, and the sinking feeling in her stomach grew heavier with each passing hour. It wasn't just that she was possibly being ghosted; it was the creeping realization that she might have willingly played the fool in CJ's performance not once but twice.

"Screw him, then," she muttered, the words hollow as they hung in the air. Yet despite her resolve, her eyes betrayed her, glancing one last time at the silent phone before she turned off the bedside lamp.

The darkness of the room seemed to echo the silence from CJ, wrapping around her like a shroud. As sleep eluded her, Erica lay there, grappling with the nagging question that gnawed at her pride: Was she really that much of a sucker?

Chapter 11

The dust swirled around CJ's boots as he made his way to Mariposa, the weight of the production's future pressing on his shoulders. Sure, one might say it wasn't his problem if the production failed, but he believed in this project, and he'd be damned if he'd let it fail without at least trying to help.

I have an idea, CJ had said to Anna as she'd stared up at the blue skies, the lingering of acridity of smoke still in the air.

But Anna had looked despondent. *I hate to say it, but this was the nail in the coffin. We can't recoup this loss*, she'd said, her eyes still red from the smoke. *I just don't understand how this happened. A set fire? I'm at a loss.*

It had supposedly been an accident—bad luck—but it seemed this production was having more than its fair share of that level of catastrophe.

And then a wild idea had come to him. *What the hell? What do we have to lose?* He'd pitched his scheme to the director, who likely had been envisioning her career on its deathbed for the production's failure.

Anna, clearly feeling it was hopeless anyway, had waved him on. *Sure. Knock yourself out, CJ. Lord knows we could use a damn miracle.*

With each step, he ran through the potential pitch in his head now, aware that the entire project teetered on the brink of collapse. Under ordinary circumstances, he would've felt bad for the production but would've moved on without breaking a sweat. But this project had legs. He could feel it. It was more than just another Western in a crowded market—it had heart and grit.

He had to do whatever he could to save it from going under—and he knew just the person to ask for help.

Josh Colton, with his easy smile and lingering curiosity about the film industry, was sitting behind the reception desk when CJ walked into the cool lobby of the resort. The contrast between the calm interior and the chaotic set couldn't have been more pronounced. He knew it was a team effort, but he knew Erica helped keep this place running like a well-oiled machine.

"Hey, Josh," CJ began with an engaging smile. "Remember me?"

Josh smiled. "How could I forget? What brings you back? Need a room or something?"

"Actually, I'd like to ask a favor. I remember you mentioned an interest in the movie biz… Can we go to your office and talk a minute?"

"Hit me where I'm weak, why don't you?" Josh replied with an intrigued grin and motioned for CJ to follow him. As they walked into Josh's office, CJ caught Erica talking to staff, but she saw him right as Josh closed the door behind them.

"Okay, you got my attention. What's the favor?"

"I'll cut to the chase—a large portion of our set burned down last night. It was an accident, but the damage is cata-

strophic. This production has been hit with multiple wham-
mies, and this one—well, the director doesn't think we can
recover, but I do."

"How so?"

"By shifting locations while that portion of the set is
rebuilt."

"As much as I'd love to help, I'm not really sure how I
could. You're filming a Western, right?"

"True, but I recall you mentioning something about a
piece of the Mariposa property that's closed for a remodel
that just happens to have an old barn..."

"Yeah, that's true, but it's not safe out there, which is
why we have it closed off."

"I wouldn't worry about that part. All we need is the fa-
çade, and the set team will have it looking like it's straight
out of the history books," CJ assured quickly, preempting
any concerns. "And if there's so much as a scratch on anything, it's on me. I'll foot the bill."

"Are you sure you want to take that on?" Josh asked.

"I'm probably reckless—and if my manager was still
around, he'd make me stop—but I think that's why I want
to do this. I need to do something good for other people,
not just for myself, you know? And I've known Anna Wilson for a while, and she's the best of people. Her talent is
next level, but it's taken her a while to get a project like
this greenlit. I don't want to see it go down the toilet. Not
if I can help."

Josh nodded quietly, seeming to feel the shadow of Allison's death just as surely as CJ did but likely for different reasons. "I'm happy to help. We'll find a way to make it work."

Relief washed over CJ. "That would be amazing, Josh.

Truly. I mean, I know we don't know each other that well, but I mean it when I say that you're a good guy."

Josh chuckled, shaking his head. "Hey, don't go starting rumors. I've got a reputation to protect."

But Josh was a good man. CJ could see it. Not to mention Erica was an excellent judge of character, and he couldn't imagine she'd work for a family that was trash.

"I'll set up a dinner with the director and producer so y'all can meet and hash out the details. I really appreciate this, man. You're saving a lot of jobs."

Josh smiled, remembering, "Hey, since we're talking, I heard you have a horse-wrangler issue. I know a guy. Good with horses, reliable. He could fill in."

CJ's excitement was barely containable as he shook Josh's hand. Not only had he secured a temporary shooting location but also a lifeline for the horse scenes. He couldn't wait to share the news with Erica, to see the spark of hope relight in her eyes. This was more than a win for the production; it was a personal victory for CJ, a chance to prove his worth beyond doubt.

"Now that we've got that settled, mind if I grab your executive assistant for a minute?"

Josh said, "I don't mind, but good luck trying to find her. She's never in the same spot for long. I'm pretty sure she portals from one place to the other."

He chuckled and let himself out, immediately heading in the direction he'd seen Erica last.

Erica's steps faltered as she turned the corner and spotted CJ, leaning casually against the wall with his hands buried in the pockets of his faded jeans.

The sight of him was a jolt to her system, like an unexpected storm breaking the stillness of a summer day. Why was he here? Her heart took off, wings beating erratically against the cage of her ribs. She swallowed, schooling her expression into one of friendly professionalism.

"Erica," he said, pushing off the wall with a grace that made her stomach flip. His eyes locked onto hers, carrying that familiar spark of mischief she found so disarming.

"Why are you here?" she asked, her voice steady despite the fluttering within. "I thought your shooting schedule was tight."

"It was—it still is, but there's been a change in plans," he answered with a tone that seemed too casual for the concern knitting her brows together.

"A change? Like what kind of change?"

He ignored her question for a minute to gaze into her eyes. "Why do you get prettier each time I see you?" he murmured, as if perplexed by his own question.

She faltered, her voice catching in her throat as heat climbed her cheeks. How did he manage to make it feel like they were the only two people in the world?

But then she remembered. No calls, no texts…just silence. That unwelcome pattern crawled over her skin, leaving a trail of discomfort. She wasn't about to fall into his arms every time he found it convenient to be around her.

"Is everything okay?" Erica asked, trying for professionalism, even though her stomach muscles were trembling.

That seemed to shake CJ loose from the sensual fog, and he shook his head. "Actually, you're not going to believe this, but part of the set burnt down last night."

Erica's eyes bugged at the unexpected news. "Excuse me? Burnt down? Is everyone okay?"

"Everyone is fine aside from some scratchy throats and gritty eyes from the smoke. Thank God for the on-call fire engine. They were able to put it down pretty quick, but those facades go up fast. Doesn't take much to raze them to the ground, and *poof!* Millions of dollars gone."

"Oh God, that's awful," Erica said. "What part of the set went down?"

"The fire tore through the saloon," he answered, meeting her gaze. "It's all gone."

The saloon—their saloon—where beneath a pale moon, they'd crossed lines drawn in the sand of professionalism. Erica felt the sting of loss for a place that had become a private landmark in her memory.

"Wow, I..." She trailed off, her mind trying to piece together how this could have happened, especially considering how rigid safety protocols were on set. But then again, with everything else that had befallen the production, *safe* was perhaps not the right word.

"But there's a silver lining," CJ said, touching her elbow gently, grounding her back to the present. "Josh has agreed to allow filming to resume here while the set is rebuilt, so in a way, your resort is saving the production."

"He did what?" Erica repeated, shocked. "How'd you manage that?"

"When I was a guest, me and Josh started chitchatting, and he happened to mention that he'd always been fascinated by the movie business. So I capitalized on that fascination."

"I don't know how Laura is going to take that news," Erica said, shaking her head.

And speak of the devil.

"Oh my good gravy, Erica, brace yourself—my brother has volunteered the resort for a movie location." Laura's voice sliced through the low hum of resort activity as she approached, her expression a mix of bewilderment and burgeoning stress. Her hands fluttered to her chest, where her heart seemed to be pounding out an SOS. "Has he no idea how much strain that's going to put on the staff? On me?"

"Um, yes, CJ just told me," Erica replied, her voice soothing like a balm. "But don't worry, Laura. I'll handle everything." She laid a reassuring hand on her boss's arm, grounding her amid the swirl of unexpected news. "You just worry about your wedding stuff. Let me handle the resort extras."

Relief flooded Laura's expression even as she cast an apologetic look toward CJ. "I'm sorry. I'm sure it's terribly exciting to have a movie set on location, but right now, it's the last thing I can handle. This wedding prep is devouring every single one of my brain cells. If I had to juggle one more ball, I'd probably drop them all."

"I totally understand, and we appreciate your help more than you know. As I told Josh, Mariposa stepping up is definitely saving the production—and countless jobs."

That seemed to make Laura stand a little straighter with pride. "Well, I'm glad we can make it work." But to Erica, she said, "I'm sorry this is falling onto your plate. You already have so much."

"Well, you know what they say…if you want something done, give the task to a busy person," Erica said with a confident smile.

"True— Oh!" A sudden thought struck Laura like lightning, breaking through the overcast of her worries. "Willow RSVP'd! She'll be here for the bachelorette party. We'll need to arrange a room for her—one with a good view. She likes to watch the sunrise with her coffee."

"Of course. Willow will have a great room waiting," Erica promised, already mentally scanning the reservations to accommodate Laura's friend.

"Perfect—thanks!" And with a flutter of hands that mirrored the chaos of her mind, Laura dashed away to tackle some other emergent issue, leaving Erica and CJ alone once again.

"You're really the backbone of this place," CJ said with wonder in his voice.

Erica chuckled at his praise, but something still troubled her and she needed to talk about it.

"Come with me," Erica said to CJ, motioning with a tilt of her head toward the closed section of the resort.

The closed section, a forgotten corner of the resort that had seen better days, featured a large barn, broken-down stables and a rotting fence line that might've been built in the 1800s. Josh had plans to turn it into an outdoor amphitheater for outdoor concerts, but those plans were still in the early stages. In the meantime, it was cordoned off to guests for safety reasons.

She gestured to the area with a dubious look. "It's not much to look at. Are you sure the set department will be able to make it work?"

CJ surveyed the area with a critical eye, deciding. "It's perfect," he said, almost to himself. He turned back to her, a spark igniting in his gaze. "Our team can work wonders, Erica. You won't even recognize it in a few days."

"Camera-ready and safe?" She couldn't keep the skepticism from her voice, her brows knitting together as she imagined the scale of transformation required.

"Absolutely," he confirmed with a nod, his assurance as steady as the ground beneath their feet. "You'd be amazed what they can accomplish. An added bonus—Josh has a horse wrangler he can call in to replace the guy that was a no-show. Like I said, Mariposa is saving our production in more ways than one."

"Why are you so determined to make it work? I didn't think actors were this invested in the behind-the-scenes stuff."

"They aren't usually, but this production needs to get made and I have the means to make it happen. So I'm going to do what I can."

"Does that mean you need to renegotiate your contract to add producer credit?" she teased.

"Maybe if I still had a manager," he quipped, glancing away, reminding her that he was still dealing with the aftermath of Doug's actions. "But I'm good with being in the background for this. I believe in the production. The script is too good to let it die because of some bad luck."

"What if it's more than bad luck?" she ventured.

"Like someone is sabotaging the production?"

She nodded, but he didn't seem to believe it.

"No, this is just a case of coincidence gone bad. Nothing more. I'm sure of it, which is why I'm putting my money where my mouth's at. I've promised Josh that for any damages the production causes, I'll foot the bill."

Erica gasped. "CJ, that's financially reckless. I wouldn't make promises like that."

"I can afford it. It'll be okay," he assured her.

Erica watched him, noticing the way his confidence filled the space, as if he could already envision the final product. It was that vision, she realized, that made him so good at his job—and made him so damn sexy.

About that...

"CJ, if we're going to work side by side during this film shoot here, I need to say something, or it'll eat me alive."

Yet CJ had a different agenda. His gaze latched on to hers, his hand extending toward her. "I can't stop thinking about you," he confessed softly. "What spell has Erica Pike cast on me that turns me inside out and sidewise?"

Her eyes met his, her breath hitching in surprise, but she retorted smoothly, "Probably the same spell that has you forgetting how to use a phone for a quick text or call after hooking up with someone. You did it again, CJ—and I need to know what the hell is going on, or whatever this is between us...will have to be strictly professional going forward."

Chapter 12

CJ shifted uncomfortably, the Arizona sun casting long shadows that seemed to stretch out like accusatory fingers. Erica's expectant gaze held a blend of confusion and hurt, mirroring the tightness knotting his chest. "I've been swamped with the production," he started, the words tasting like ash on his tongue.

"Really?" Erica's eyebrow arched, skepticism etching her features. "Is that all there is to it? Because I'm a busy person, too, and I still manage to find time in my day to send a quick text if it's important."

He sighed, a hand raking through his hair as he met her probing gaze. Moments trickled by, each second heavy with an unspoken truth that he wasn't ready to share.

The fact was several times during a lull in production CJ had felt the lure of his phone, her number burning in his mind, but something—fear, perhaps, or a deeply ingrained sense of self-preservation—had stopped him every time.

But how was he supposed to say that without hurting her feelings?

Erica, sensing he was holding back, said, "Look, I'd rather an ugly truth than a pretty lie. Just be honest, please."

"You're right," he admitted, grappling with the unfamiliar weight of honesty. "I could've sent a quick text or made a short call, but I chose not to."

"Was it truly just about sex?" Erica asked.

"No," he answered quickly, "it was never just about sex. I like you, Erica. I mean, like, really like you."

"Okay, so why the radio silence after we hook up?" she asked, confused.

Yeah, CJ, why?

Frustration laced his tone, not only because of the awkward situation but because he couldn't really explain why he was acting like this.

"Here's the thing, I'm in LA and you're here. I can't do long-distance, and I would never expect you to leave what you have here just to follow me to California. So, I figure, why delay the inevitable, right? We had fun, it was great and I would be open to hanging out anytime I'm in town or vice versa. No strings, just good times. I mean, we're good together. Why not enjoy what we have when we have it?"

It sounded good in his head but felt hollow in his heart, and judging by the incredulous expression on Erica's face, she wasn't on board—and, worse, was insulted.

"Hang out?" Erica echoed, voice laced with disbelief. "You mean, be your 'Arizona girl'? Just a convenient hookup?" Her stance hardened, disappointment sharpening her words into knives. "Have you lost your mind? What gave you the impression that I would be open to such an arrangement?"

"I thought you might be open-minded to something a little unorthodox," he said stiffly, surprised at how red Erica's face had gotten.

"No, CJ. I won't settle for that—and frankly, I can't believe that you would even ask."

"Erica, I—" CJ began, but she cut him off.

"Thank you for letting me know where I stand. It helps to clear up some confusion for me. Fool me once, shame on you…fool me twice, shame on me. I should've learned from the first time. From this moment forward, we'll keep it professional. That's all." With those final words, she turned away, leaving him standing there feeling like a jackass and wishing he'd said something different.

But he couldn't lie to her. She deserved better than dishonesty just so he could get what he wanted. He watched her walk away, leaving him behind like a bad habit, and he wanted to run after her but remained rooted in place.

Nobody ever shared how doing the right thing sometimes felt like crap.

He returned to base camp with good news, but his stride gave away his irritation. Why did Erica have to be so damn stubborn? The win with the resort's location approval was a thin bandage over the gash in his personal feelings over Erica's decision to cut him off.

He had no doubt Erica could handle being professionally detached—he'd already seen her do it once before—but he hadn't liked it nor had he enjoyed the feeling of being on the wrong side of Erica Pike.

"Anna, Caroline!" he called out as he approached the bustling cluster of trailers, catching the director and the AD talking with the production manager. Their heads swiveled his way, eyes alight with curiosity. "We got the green light for the resort location."

"Seriously? Don't get my hopes up if you're just messing around."

"I wouldn't joke about something this serious," CJ said without his usual sense of humor. "It's all legit. I suggested we meet for dinner to talk over the logistics, but Josh Colton gave the thumbs-up and we're clear to start whenever we're ready."

Realizing this was real, Anna's mouth fell open, her surprise giving way to swift efficiency. She whipped out her phone, punching in the numbers with unbridled excitement. "This is huge, CJ! Caroline, while I'm sharing the news with the executive producer, you set up dinner with the resort reps for tomorrow. I want to get this moving as quickly as possible before anyone comes to their senses and rescinds their offer."

"On it," Caroline said, clapping CJ on the shoulder. "Good work. You never cease to surprise me. Did your friend Erica have anything to do with this?"

His friend. For some reason that made him wince, but he shook his head. "No, I talked with one of the owners. Josh Colton has a latent desire to be involved with the movie business. I just capitalized on it, but make sure the crews know we're going to be on private property and they need to be respectful. I don't want the Coltons to regret saving our asses."

Caroline sobered. "Absolutely. I'll make sure everyone's on their best behavior."

"Great. I'll leave the rest of the details up to you guys. I need a nap."

CJ made his way back to his trailer, feeling drained and irritated. As he walked, he went over the conversation he'd had with Erica in his mind, still trying to figure out why she was so insistent on cutting him off entirely. She wasn't even open to being his *friend*.

When he reached his trailer, he kicked off his shoes and flopped onto the couch with a heavy sigh. He closed his eyes and let out a long breath, trying to calm himself down. But no matter how hard he tried, he couldn't shake off the lingering feeling that he'd just lost something worth keeping.

He reached for his phone on the coffee table and scrolled through his contacts until he found Erica's number. He stared at the number, wondering if he ought to walk back his disastrous verbal vomit, but he doubted Erica would take the call even if he tried.

He tossed the phone and dropped back onto the couch.

When he woke up hours later, it was already dark outside. He groaned and rubbed at his face, feeling disoriented from the long nap. His stomach grumbled loudly, reminding him that he hadn't eaten since breakfast.

CJ got up and headed toward the small kitchenette in the corner of the trailer. He rummaged through the cabinets until he found some instant noodles and heated them up in the microwave.

It was too late to go anywhere, and the rest of the base camp were off doing their own thing for the night. Flicking on the tiny television, he resigned himself to mindless TV shows to distract himself from the reality that he might've screwed up something worth exploring.

If he could only pull his own head out of his ass to figure it out.

Erica stood before the full-length mirror, her reflection casting back an image of composure she didn't feel. The hurt still stung—a raw, uninvited guest lurking beneath the surface of her carefully applied makeup.

CJ's words echoed in her mind, a jarring note off-key from the reality of her professional life: "Like I would ever be his *Arizona* girl." She snorted indelicately. What the hell was he thinking?

What kind of woman did he take her for? Had she given off some kind of vibe that she'd be open to something so... *cheap*?

Ugh. Stop thinking about him.

She turned away, the hem of her short, slinky dress swishing against her thighs. Erica had chosen it not out of vanity but as armor, a declaration of her own self-worth in the face of someone who'd seen her as little more than a convenient diversion.

She was a woman of poise and intelligence, not just curves and legs—though the dress did accentuate them with a certain undeniable flair. *Eat your heart out, CJ Knight.*

Her phone buzzed on the dresser, a message from Josh lighting up the screen: Looking forward to tonight! It's going to be great having you there to finalize everything. Thanks!

Great was not the word she would have used. *Necessary*, perhaps. *Unavoidable*, definitely.

Josh was blissfully unaware of the undercurrents he was asking her to navigate—how could she explain to him or Laura the gravity of sitting across from CJ at dinner when she was working so hard to maintain the veneer that, indeed, everything was fine?

"Professionalism," she whispered to her reflection, a mantra to steel herself for the evening ahead. With one last glance, she ensured she was impenetrable to CJ's charm and determined to treat this as she would any business dinner with a VIP guest.

The restaurant's ambiance was impeccable, the kind of place where the lighting was always flattering and the waitstaff moved with an almost choreographed grace.

Personally, she would've preferred a burger joint, someplace where she could wear jeans and a T-shirt and eaten her weight in french fries, but Josh had wanted to make an impression, so Crimson Canyon Restaurant was the only choice.

As she entered, Erica felt eyes on her—not just CJ's, though his gaze was unavoidable. She drew in a breath and let the cool Sedona air settle her nerves.

"Erica, you look stunning," Josh greeted, all smiles and genuine appreciation. He guided her to the table with a hand at her back, utterly oblivious to the tension that knotted her stomach tight.

"Thank you, Josh," she replied, allowing a smile to grace her lips. It was easier with him because his intentions were clear and completely professional.

CJ's chair scraped against the terra-cotta tile as he rose to greet her, and Erica's pulse quickened against her will. Her entrance had drawn his attention immediately, his eyes tracing the silhouette of her dress—a subtle yet undeniable acknowledgment that she had, perhaps inadvertently, dressed to break his heart. She caught the brief hitch in his breath, a momentary lapse that betrayed his composure, and it gave her a private thrill.

"Erica," he began, the word hanging between them like a delicate thread.

"Good evening, CJ." Her voice was a cool drink of water, quenching any sparks before they could ignite.

CJ took the hint as Josh pulled Erica's seat out for her, and Erica sank gracefully into her chair with an appreciative smile.

"Right, so, introductions are in order—Josh Colton, I'm pleased to introduce our production's director, Anna Wilson, and our assistant director, Caroline Briggs."

"Pleasure," Josh said, grinning from ear to ear. "I gotta tell you—this is so exciting. My resort, immortalized in film…it's, well, pretty damn cool."

The table chuckled at Josh's unbridled enthusiasm, and Erica nodded, sharing a smile with Josh while wishing it wasn't CJ Knight's film that was making Josh's secret dream come true.

She shifted in her seat, the fabric of her dress clinging to her skin as if it, too, sensed the need to hold steady.

CJ's gaze darted to Erica as if pulled by a magnet, but he quickly looked away as if he didn't trust his gaze not to linger too long. Was he remembering what every inch of her bare skin tasted like? She smothered a smug smile, hoping he was squirming beneath that strained smile.

From the corner of her eye, she noticed Anna observing the silent exchange, an unreadable expression etched onto her intelligent features. Anna said nothing, but the slight tilt of her head and the faint narrowing of her eyes suggested she perceived more than she let on.

"Shall we order wine to start?" Erica suggested, directing the conversation back to the safety of business, allowing her to breathe easier—for the moment. "Crimson Canyon is known to carry some of the best wines in the world."

"Great idea," Josh agreed, nodding. "Any preference?"

"Surprise us," Anna said.

The clink of fine cutlery against porcelain and the murmured symphony of negotiation provided a backdrop to Erica's strained composure. Across the table, CJ leaned slightly toward her, his eyes searching for an opening.

"Erica, you are—"

"Please, let's keep this professional." She cut him off with a brief smile, her voice a low whisper edged with steel. She ignored CJ and offered, "Let's start with the Puligny-Montrachet Premier Cru, one of my favorite French wines."

"Sounds exotic," Caroline said. "I'm always down to try new things."

CJ took the hint and swallowed whatever compliment he'd started to offer. His expression flickered with disappointment before settling into a resigned nod.

He turned away, his attention reluctantly reclaimed by the discussion at hand, leaving Erica to exhale a silent breath she hadn't realized she was holding.

As the dinner wore on, plans were etched into reality with every stroke of a pen on a napkin, every handshake across the table.

The evening finally ended, everyone parted ways, their voices carrying promises of crews arriving with the first light, ready to transform the derelict section into a bustling film set for the next two weeks.

While Erica enjoyed seeing Josh so excited, she knew the filming would put a huge strain on the entire resort. Laura was more sensitive to the daily operations than Josh, but they'd make it work somehow.

And that included squashing her personal feelings about CJ.

In the solitude of her car, Erica allowed herself a moment to feel the pulse of pride for keeping her emotions under wrap, even when CJ looked like a delicious snack and smelled even better. She'd never considered herself prone to romantic whimsy, but CJ had a way of drawing out aspects of herself that she'd never known existed. She hadn't decided yet if that was a good thing or not.

But she held firm, clinging to her convictions like a shield.

This small victory was hers, a testament to her strength, yet it did nothing to soothe the hollow ache that lingered in her chest, a reminder that detachment came with its own cost.

Two weeks—that was all she needed to get through— and then she could get back to normal life.

Without CJ.

Chapter 13

Days later, CJ stepped onto the set with a low whistle, his gaze sweeping across the landscape that had come alive under the meticulous hands of the set builders. The barn, once a skeletal relic, stood robust and proud. Granted, it wouldn't stand up to a certified inspection, but for a filming facade, it was damn good.

The sagging fence line now stood straight, like it must've when it had first been built. He could almost hear the jangle of spurs and the distant whinnying of horses as he walked through the resurrected 1800s Wild West set that was supposed to represent the Buford Homestead, where an integral character, Clarissa, had been killed.

His chest swelled with a sense of pride and purpose— this was the distraction he needed; this was his world, away from the complicated web of conflicting feelings that Erica spun around him.

"Looks good, huh?" One of the builders tipped his hat in CJ's direction, pulling him from his reverie.

"Better than good," CJ replied, his voice laced with genuine admiration. "It's like stepping back in time. Great job."

With a nod to the builder, CJ turned his attention back to the set. Every detail, from the weathered signs to the strategically placed water barrels and hanging tack, transported him into the heart of a story waiting to be told. He squared his shoulders, determined to pour himself into the work, to live in the scenes they were about to shoot, if only to push the thought of Erica to the furthest corner of his mind.

The energy on the set was electric as everyone prepared for the first take of the day. Cameras rolled into position, actors donned their costumes, dialogues whispered under breaths as the final touches were applied. Then, with the call of "Action!" the scene came alive, gunslingers and townsfolk moving with rehearsed precision.

But just as CJ was about to utter his first line, Anna yelled, "Cut!" It sliced through the action abruptly as the light rig started to flicker and buzz ominously until it shorted with a sharp snap and the lights went down.

Even though it was daytime, filming on location still required lights to make sure the scene was properly lit, and losing the light rig had the power to grind everything to a stop.

"Damn it! Not again," Anna muttered, rubbing her temples. Crew members scurried about while the rigging crew assessed the situation. "What's happening to the rig?"

The key gaffer jogged over to Anna with a perplexed expression. "Sorry, Anna. We're trying to assess the situation now. We just need a few minutes. It's probably a loose wire or connection."

"Let's hope," Anna said, shaking her head, looking worried.

"Got a surge here," called out one of the electricians, his hands buried in a mess of wires. "Gonna need a few hours to sort this out."

Anna swore under her breath and rose from her director's chair, removing herself. "I'll be in my room trying to convince the executive producer not to shut us down," she said, walking away.

Frustration simmered in CJ's chest as he watched the crew disperse, some seeking refuge in the shade while others tinkered with their respective equipment, hoping for a quick fix. The momentum they had built up seemed to evaporate under the midday sun, and CJ couldn't help but feel a growing sense of apprehension. Mishaps were part of the job, sure, but this felt like an omen. Was this production cursed? He wasn't a spiritual guy, but maybe they ought to have a priest come out and sprinkle holy water on everything, just to be on the safe side.

CJ leaned against a post, his gaze wandering over the set. This was supposed to be smooth sailing after all the hurdles they had faced, yet here they were, stuck again. With a quiet sigh, he glanced up at the sky, silently willing the universe to cut them some slack, to let them tell their story without further interruption. But as the sun continued its relentless march across the heavens, CJ knew better than to rely on wishes. They needed action, solutions—and fast.

The clatter of tools and hushed conversations of the crew echoed around him. A thin layer of sweat lined his brow, not just from the heat but from the weight of responsibility that now rested squarely on his shoulders. His name—once a golden ticket in the industry—was the adhesive holding this project together. He had leveraged his reputation to secure the location and even promised his own funds as collateral for any damages incurred during their stay at the resort.

His jaw clenched at the thought. Failure was a luxury he couldn't afford.

In the midst of his silent brooding, movement caught his eye. Erica stood a short distance away, her profile illuminated by the soft glow of the afternoon sun. She was talking with Caroline, her hands animatedly shaping the air between them. For a moment, CJ found himself rooted to the spot, captivated by the familiar cadence of her gentle laughter. Should he say hello? Wouldn't it be impolite to just keep walking?

Taking an involuntary step forward, he hesitated when their eyes locked. Her smile faltered, and she turned abruptly back to Caroline, dismissing him without a word. The sting of rejection lanced through him, and with a scowl etched deep into his features, he spun on his heel and stalked back toward the center of the set where his costar, Jenny Oliver, was going over lines.

"Are they shutting down production?" she asked, pulling her sides from a hidden pocket in her voluminous muslin dress to fan herself. "God, it's freaking hot here."

"Yeah, probably. Anna left to talk with the higher-ups about the additional setback, but we might be able to salvage the day if the gaffers are able to get the lights back up and running."

Jenny didn't share the same sense of urgency, yawning as she continued to fan herself. "I swear I'll fire my agent if he sends me another period piece anytime soon. I'm going to suffocate under all these layers."

He chuckled. "Well, you make it look good," he said. Jenny preened beneath his praise, taking a brief moment to twirl in her skirts for his benefit. "Well, at least this part is fun," she said, grinning.

Like him, Jenny Oliver was a hot commodity around Hollywood right now. She had all the right tangibles— young, beautiful and talented—a triple threat when a lot of actors only had one or two of those attributes to offer.

But when out of character, she looked bored out of her skull and less than enamored with their desert location. "Well, if we're done for the day, I'm getting out of this torture device. Catch you tomorrow, CJ."

He waved and watched her swish her way to the wardrobe trailer so she could change, leaving CJ to wonder why he hadn't done the same. There was no reason to hang around if the day was done, but he felt a different level of responsibility for the production than before, and for some reason, he just wanted to check with his own eyes that only the lights were mysteriously affected.

In hindsight, his mental health might've been better if he had just followed Jenny's example.

As if the day hadn't already taken enough out of him, another setback lay in wait. Approaching the props table, his keen eye immediately spotted the disarray. Leather holsters had been slashed, glass bottles shattered and vintage playing cards scattered and torn—all integral to the barn scene they were slated to film next.

"What the...?" He muttered, bracketing his hands on his hips as frustration chewed on his composure. "How in the hell did this happen?" He motioned to the prop master, a veteran with more years under his belt than CJ had been alive, hustled over with a tight-lipped expression. "Did you see this?"

"Yeah, right about the same time the lights blew. I was just about to let Caroline know."

"How'd it happen?"

"No idea. They were fine this morning—each one logged in perfect condition in the prop book."

"So, someone managed to ruin important props, and no one saw them do it?"

"Appears that way, but I'm asking around. I'll find out what happened."

CJ nodded, reluctantly letting it go because what else could he do? With a heavy sigh, CJ surveyed the damage, an uncomfortable suspicion nagging at his brain. Was someone sabotaging this production?

"Rough day, huh?" The voice belonged to the new horse wrangler, a rugged man with easy confidence that seemed alien to CJ at that moment. He swiveled to greet the man who offered his hand. "Rein Granger—pleasure."

"Rein…" CJ repeated with a small smile. "It's a good thing you turned out to like horses, or else you might've found that name a hard act to live up to."

Rein grinned, as if used to a little ribbing about his name. "Lucky for me my family is four generations deep in horseflesh and ranching. This stuff's in my blood. Not sure how well I'd fare as a lawyer. Can't handle being caged in four walls for longer than a minute, which is why I work so well with the animals. Plus, they don't make a fuss about dirt on your knees."

CJ chuckled, envious of those kinds of deep roots. His family had been more nomadic in nature. They'd bounced from place to place throughout his childhood, but he'd always longed for a place to call home for longer than a year.

Probably the reason why he'd bought his house with his first big check. He'd paid up front so that no one could ever take it from him, no matter if his career dried up someday. Doug had given him hell at the time for not financing the house like most people, but he'd been adamant. He wanted something that would always be his until the time he decided to move on.

"You friends with the Coltons?" CJ asked.

"Yeah, me, Josh and Knox go way back. His old man was a bit of a jerk, but Josh is good stock. Hell, if I wasn't afraid that Josh might kick my ass from here to tomorrow for even looking sidewise, I might've tried shooting my shot with his sister Laura, but it wasn't meant to be, I guess."

CJ remembered a snippet of information from Erica, saying, "She's about to get married, I heard."

"Yeah, that door shut hard on my chances, but hey, what're ya gonna do, right? It is what it is."

CJ liked Rein's chill attitude. He could see why Josh had called him in. The man was a good fit. "Well, looks like we're down for the day," he said, dusting off the knees of his chaps. "What's there to do around town? Anything good?"

"Depends. Looking to wash the trail dust down with something stronger than whatever you've got stocked in that fancy room of yours?" The wrangler tilted his head toward the direction of Sedona. "I know a place that's good for toe-tapping music, good whiskey and a pretty girl or two."

CJ hesitated for a heartbeat. The rational part of his brain screamed to decline, to prepare for the next day's shoot, but rationality wasn't in the house any longer—not with Erica's obvious snub and the set's problems dogging him. "Sure," he found himself saying. "Why not?"

"Great. The place is called the Rattlesnake Pub. Don't let the name—or the look of it—scare you. It's where all the locals go to let off steam. Meet you there at nine tonight." But as Rein started to walk away, he spun on his heel to ask, "You ain't a sloppy drunk, right?"

CJ had to laugh at the bold question, but he answered, "Not that I can recall."

Rein grinned with approval. "Good. I hate babysitting grown men," he said before returning to finish up his duties.

The Rattlesnake Pub was a dive, its neon sign buzzing like an agitated hornet. Inside, the smell of stale beer and fried food contested for dominance, but the music was jumping, and it was filled wall-to-wall with people.

"What'd I tell ya?" Rein said, motioning for another round of whiskey. "This is where the real fun happens—not in those stuffy, gentrified places where a half-empty plate will run you a month's rent."

CJ downed the shot, elbows planting heavily on the sticky counter. The bartender, a woman with a no-nonsense look, slid a shot glass toward him without a word.

"Keep 'em coming," CJ said with a grin that he wasn't sure was real, the fiery gulp scalding his throat and offering a brief respite from his thoughts.

He didn't want to think about Erica, about the way she'd turned away from him, closing off whatever fragile connection they might have shared. So he drank. Each shot was a hammer blow to the barricade he'd built around her image in his mind, each one crumbling it further until he could no longer tell if he was trying to forget her or work up the courage to call her and beg for forgiveness.

"Slow down, Hollywood," Rein advised, downing his

own shot. "I told you I ain't babysitting a grown man. If you fall on your face, that's where you stay."

"Fair enough," CJ said, though the floor was probably where he belonged. The booze loosened his tongue enough to ask, "You got a girl or something?"

"Naww, I had an old lady, but she split when she realized I was never gonna make enough money to buy her that fancy house she was dreaming about."

"I'm sorry, man. That's rough."

Rein waved away CJ's condolences. "Everything happens for a reason."

CJ internalized that sentiment, wondering if that were true. He didn't want to ruin the mood by sourly pointing out that sometimes bad things happened randomly to good people because a bad person crossed their path. *End of story.* Like what'd happened with Allison Brewer. *Ahh, hell, don't go there. Not tonight.* Shoving Doug from his thoughts, he simply nodded as if he agreed, and moved on. "Hey, any chance you might've known the original wrangler who went MIA?"

"Kyle Jefferson? Yeah, I've heard of him. Decent guy. Not known for being a flake, that's for sure," Rein said. "He just didn't show up for work?"

"Yeah, that's the story. Rumor has it he knew the girl, Allison Brewer. Like, they dated or something."

"Well, I didn't know him *that* well, but I remember the name Allison Brewer. She's that poor girl who got killed by that rich guy?"

CJ nodded, admitting, "My manager was that rich guy."

"No shit." Rein breathed in surprise. "That must've been a shock."

"You can say that again," he quipped darkly, motioning for another round. "You think you know someone until they go and do something like that. Makes you realize you don't know much about anything."

Rein whistled low and commiseratively. "Amen to that." Seeming to want to switch subjects quickly before the mood completely soured, Rein asked, "Well, how about you? Is there a Mrs. Hollywood waiting for you back in LA?"

CJ barked a short laugh. "No, not even close. Currently the only other person in my house is a professional moocher who house-sits for me when I go on location. He's a decent guy, but I think he's more interested in *saying* he's an actor than actually pursuing a gig. But I don't mean to make him sound all that bad. He's cool—and he's kinda like my best friend. I mean, when you have a career like mine…you have to keep the people you trust close to you and keep everyone else out."

Rein chuckled. "I know the type." He paused a minute before asking, "What do you know about that hot executive assistant? I think her name's Erica…"

Red-hot territorial energy that he had no right to feel ripped through him. "What about her?" he asked, a little sharply.

"Chill, chill—I was just asking. She's probably too rich for my blood anyway. Are you two a thing?"

"Nope. I screwed that up. Big time. Twice." *Damn, enough alcohol*. At this rate he'd be giving away all his secrets by night's end. He knocked on the sticky bar with a derisive chuckle, admitting, "I think I ought to call it a night. I have an early call in the morning, and I can already tell it's going to be rough."

"Yeah, no problem. You need a ride?"

"No, I don't want you to leave on account of me. I'll catch an Uber or something."

"You sure?"

"Yeah, it's cool." CJ rose and the world swam, but he managed to walk stiff-legged out of the bar and into the cool night air. His vision blurred as he tried finding the Uber app, his fingers feeling fat and uncooperative. That whiskey must've been practically moonshine—and it was catching up to him faster than he realized.

He must've blacked out for a second because when he opened his eyes again, he'd definitely called someone to come and get him.

"I need a ride," he slurred, the world swaying in a nauseating dance. The chill of the night air slapped him but did little to sober his senses. There was no getting around the fact that he was drunk. "I'm outside the R-Rattlesnake Pub." He sat heavily on the curb before he fell down. "I'll be waiting."

He clicked off, fighting off the urge to barf his guts out.

It seemed like forever before he saw a car roll up, but as he struggled to his feet, he realized with drunken embarrassment he hadn't called Uber.

He'd called Erica.

Chapter 14

Erica's phone shattered the silence of the night with its insistent buzzing, a discordant sound that pulled her from the brink of sleep. Groggy eyes squinted at the screen, a name flashing in neon letters against the darkness: *CJ*. What on earth?

"I need—uh—ride," the voice slurred from the other end, words sloshing around like a dinghy in a storm. "Rattlesnake Pub."

Was he drunk?

She sat up, frowning. Rattlesnake Pub's background noise bled through the call, a cacophony of raucous music and laughter. Erica pinched the bridge of her nose, irritation sparking. Why was he calling her? Didn't he have an entourage of people at his beck and call for this kind of thing? It was on the tip of her tongue to hang up and go back to sleep, but she couldn't do it.

"All right, CJ. Stay put," she sighed, rolling out of bed and pulling on a pair of jeans. Duty gnawed at her conscience; no way could she leave him stranded. Anything could happen to the idiot, and then she'd feel like crap that she'd ignored his call.

The night air nipped at Erica's skin as she made her way

to the pub. She found CJ slumped over the curb, a lone figure on the cold cement. If half the people knew they were walking past an A-list celebrity they'd whip out their phones and record his sorry state for cash or bragging rights.

Hauling him to his feet was like trying to lift a sack of wet sand, but she managed, half dragging, half supporting him to her car.

"Good service," he mumbled with a drunken grin. "And you smell good. Can I say that? Is that allowed? 'Cause you do. You smell like coconut and lemons. Like a lemon pie."

Erica ignored his ramblings, even though his praise made her warm all over. It wasn't the first time CJ had complimented the scent of her skin, though under different circumstances.

It was too late to drive to the resort, so she'd just have to take him back to her place and he could have the sofa.

Thankfully her little house wasn't far, but getting CJ from the car to the house was like wrangling a hundred-eighty-pound toddler who didn't want to take a nap.

Finally she managed to deposit him onto the couch, his body sprawling with the grace of a felled tree. As Erica fumbled with his shoes, a mumble escaped his lips, raw and unguarded.

"I'm such an idiot," he groaned, his head lolling back. "Always screwing things up...she's practically perfect."

Could he be talking about her? How embarrassing would it be if he was rambling about someone else? Maybe his costar? Jenny Oliver was drop-dead gorgeous and younger than her by at least ten years.

His words stirred something in Erica, a memory of her grandmother's sage voice: *a drunk man's words are a sober man's thoughts*. The phrase hung in the air, heavy with truth. Was this remorse speaking? Her cheeks heated at the possibility that CJ felt a certain kind of way about her but, for whatever reasons, couldn't exactly act right.

She observed him, a mixture of exasperation and curiosity softening her features. The man had a knack for finding trouble, yet in this vulnerable state, it was hard not to feel a tug of empathy.

However, be that as it may, was she expected to simply absolve him each time he messed up just because he was stunted in the emotional-intelligence department?

"Forgive and forget?" she whispered to herself. No, that wasn't her style. *Say what you mean, mean what you say* was more her speed.

Yet as she watched him, a familiar ache twisted inside her, a reminder of what could have been. She'd be a liar if she didn't admit she'd imagined what life together might've looked like, even with their divergent career paths. Unlike CJ, she hadn't automatically assumed it would never work.

The night stretched on, punctuated by the uneven rhythm of his breathing and the restless turning of her own thoughts.

Erica padded over to the kitchen, the soft shuffle of her feet against the linoleum barely registering above CJ's rhythmic snoring. She filled a glass with water to the brim and grabbed two aspirin to head off the monster hangover that would be waiting for him when he woke up.

"Here, drink this," she coaxed, nudging the glass into his hands with a tenderness that surprised even her. "And take these."

"Wha…?" His voice was sandpaper on silk, words half-formed and slurred. Eyelids fluttered open, revealing blood-shot eyes that struggled to focus on the care she offered.

"Water. Aspirin. Trust me, you'll thank me later." Her tone brokered no argument, but it wasn't without warmth. She didn't envy him the migraine that awaited him.

He complied, the water spilling down his chin in his clumsy attempts. As he swallowed the pills, he muttered something indistinct, a mumble lost to the void between consciousness and oblivion. Erica retrieved the empty glass before it could slip from his grasp and end up a mess on her floor.

She draped a blanket over him, tucking the edges around his frame. His breaths came easier now, less like the gasps of a drowning man and more the steady tide of peaceful sleep.

Damn him for being a taboo snack she shouldn't want.

Still, she lingered, studying the way the moonlight danced across his features, casting shadows that played hide-and-seek with his stubble.

The corner of her mouth twitched upward—a reluctant smile for the drunken idiot who had somehow snuck into her heart despite every wall she put up. Even as her mind scolded her stupidity, her fingers brushed a lock of hair from his forehead, a silent concession to the feelings she fought so hard to deny.

"Good night, CJ," she whispered, the words spilling out like a secret meant only for the stars outside her window.

Once under her own covers, sleep proved elusive—her thoughts a jumbled mess, flipping endlessly between irritation and concern, frustration and something perilously close to longing.

Her dreams, when they finally claimed her, were a kaleidoscope of blurred faces and half-remembered touches, leaving her to wake in fits and starts, which only made the promise of morning something she wasn't looking forward to.

Sunlight invaded the room in sharp, accusing beams, prying Erica's eyelids open with the subtlety of a sledgehammer.

Despite feeling like dog poop, she rose, dressed in her running gear and padded into the living room with her tennis shoes in hand to find CJ sitting up, an awkward figure on her sofa.

"Morning, sunshine," she said with a derisive smile in her tone. "Rough night?"

"Hey," he rasped, voice gravelly, as he struggled to straighten up. His hair, a wild mess of dishevelment, stood defiantly in every direction, declaring the chaos of the night before. And yet if the situation were different between them, she'd climb his body like a monkey shimmying up a tree because even a hot mess, CJ was…well, hot.

"Christ, my head…" CJ pinched the bridge of his nose between thumb and forefinger, squinting up at her. "I, uh… how did I…?"

"Mix up calling an Uber with dialing my number? One's an app, buddy." Erica crossed her arms, leaning against the wall which felt oddly supportive. "I'd love to know the mechanics of that one myself."

"God, did you pick me up?" Shame shadowed his features, an apology forming in his bleary eyes before his lips could catch up.

"Looks like it." She kept her tone light, but her insides twisted. To see him unraveled, apologetic—it tugged at something within her she wasn't ready to examine too closely.

"Sorry," he mumbled, and the word seemed to fall from him, heavy with a regret that reached beyond last night's bad decisions. It hung in the air between them that Erica was quick to push away.

"Apology accepted," she replied as if it was really not a big deal, even though it was. "It's my job to look over the VIP guests, though I've never had one call me personally to be their DD."

"Erica, I don't—" He shook his head, as if to clear the cobwebs, then winced again, recoiling from the pain that movement surely caused. "Hell, I don't even know where to start. I've never done anything like this before."

"Don't worry about it," she said, waving away his apology as she dropped into a chair to lace up her tennis shoes. "The shower is yours. I'm going for a run. It should take me about an hour. K-Cups are on the counter if you want coffee."

CJ nodded, wincing at the movement. "Have a good run," he managed, before falling back against the couch, closing his eyes against the invading sunlight.

Erica chuckled to herself and headed out, thankful she wasn't suffering like CJ was, but it probably served him right. What was he thinking going into a strange bar without a good wingman?

As she was finishing her run, her watch dinged with a text message from CJ.

Thanks for picking me up. This time, I ordered an actual Uber to take me back to the resort so I don't mess up your morning routine any more than I already have.

Was that sharp disappointment that he'd split before she returned or relief that they didn't have to dance around the inevitable awkwardness?

Kinda felt like disappointment, but where was the sense in admitting that?

No, this was a good thing. Now she could go about her business like normal, without CJ in the way.

Yeah. Much better.

So why did she feel like all of the endorphins from her run were suddenly swirling down the drain?

The glaring lights of the set felt like needles in CJ's skull, the aftermath of last night punishing him with every step he took. Embarrassment clung to him like a second skin, the memory of waking up in Erica's house after mistakenly dialing her instead of managing to open a damn app replayed on an endless loop behind his bloodshot eyes. She must've thought he was a complete idiot after last night.

It wasn't even an understandable mistake. It was as if his subconscious had deliberately sabotaged him with that move.

"Places, everyone!" The voice cut through the fog in his head as he emerged from the makeup-and-wardrobe trailer, transformed into his character.

His hangover receded to the wings, upstaged by the adrenaline that came with performance. Lines poured out of him, smooth and rehearsed, the morning's shoot unfolding with the precision of a well-oiled machine.

This was what he knew and understood—whatever was happening with Erica might as well have been in a foreign language for all he could figure out.

But the moment the director called "Cut!" and the crew dispersed like ants to a dropped sugar cube, the sanctuary of his focus crumbled.

Except something else caught his attention as everyone else rushed to craft services for lunch.

The smell of sawdust and hot wires mingled as voices carried—a hushed, urgent conference between Anna and Caroline.

"Can you believe it?" Anna's words were wrapped in disbelief. "Someone actually messed with the electrical line. I thought it was just a coincidence, but it looks like it was deliberate. What the hell is happening?"

CJ's heart lurched, his stomach following suit as he realized the import of Anna's revelation. This wasn't just about forgotten lines or a prop misplaced; this was someone playing with lives—and it pissed him off.

Lunch became an afterthought as CJ waited for Caroline to leave. He wanted to talk to Anna alone.

"Anna," he said, his voice low and edged with the gravity of the situation, "what's going on?"

Her eyes, usually sharp with command, swam with unshed tears. She sighed, the sound heavy with the burden of potential ruin hanging over them. "If one more thing goes wrong, CJ...the execs—they'll shut us down. They're scared, and I can't blame them."

"Hey, we'll figure it out," CJ tried to infuse confidence into his words, the same kind he summoned for a difficult scene, but it sounded hollow even to his ears. "It's probably just someone being petty. You know how people can get when they don't get their way or something. I doubt anyone's trying to actively shut us down."

"Yeah, maybe." She gave a shaky laugh, the sound brittle enough to crack. "I need to…" Her gaze darted away, landing on something unseen. "Handle something." With a swipe under her eyes, she excused herself, promising to return before it was time to roll cameras, but CJ got a bad feeling.

There were no rewrites in real life, no second takes to fix the dumpster-fire turn their production had taken. It wasn't fair. Anna had worked so hard to make this film happen, and now? It was falling apart faster than anyone could patch it back together.

CJ's gaze snagged on Jenny openly flirting with Rein.

Rein, the epitome of rural charm in denim and leather, caught CJ's eye across the lot and shot him a conspiratorial wink before his attention snapped back to Jenny.

Good for him, he thought. Though Rein ought to be careful—Jenny had a way of chewing men up and leaving them on the side of the road for dead.

Watching them was like peering through a window at a scene he wasn't part of, one where laughter came easy and regrets didn't linger like stale cigarette smoke.

A pang of something—a mix of envy and a wishful longing—twisted in his chest.

Why couldn't it be like that between him and Erica?

His tongue twisted into knots and his words tripped over themselves whenever she was close enough to touch. He wanted to say it out loud, to unravel the tangle of *I'm sorry* and *I can't help it* that knotted inside him, but history had taught him that he was more likely to choke on the truth than to speak it.

Shaking his head, he turned away from the duo. His

still-sour stomach made the idea of lunch a queasy one. He bypassed the craft services table and went looking for the key gaffer. He had questions only the man in charge of the lighting department could answer.

He found him quickly enough, still working while everyone else was enjoying carne asada tacos.

"Hey," CJ started, his approach cautious. "I heard about the wires. What happened?"

The gaffer grunted, a noncommittal sound that hovered in the air between them. CJ could practically see the thoughts flicker behind the man's eyes—calculations and concerns etched deeper than the lines of age and experience.

"Your guess is as good as mine. Someone messed with the lines. Cut a few clean through."

"Any idea why someone would do that?" CJ asked, frowning.

"Kid," the gaffer began, his tone flat as the plains, "why people do this kind of stuff is above my pay grade."

"Right, sorry," CJ said, feeling like a trespasser and an annoyance, but he couldn't help himself. "Any clue who might—" CJ tried again, only to be cut off by a slicing hand gesture.

"Look, I lay cables, not traps. Got no business sniffing out sabotage," the man stated flatly. His gaze slid away, signaling the end of the conversation.

"Sure, sure," CJ said, backing off, but a different question needled his brain—was the key gaffer the one deliberately sabotaging the production? He didn't like to think that was possible, but suspicion clung to his thoughts even as he walked to the barn.

He needed a minute to regroup, get his head on straight.

But the threat of potential sabotage hummed in his ears, a discordant sound that refused to be ignored. He was no detective, no hero in some gritty thriller—he was just an actor caught in a plot twist that felt far too real.

And it made him feel useless. All he could do was throw money at the problem, and that didn't seem to be solving it.

The script pages felt heavy in his pocket, a reminder of the work still ahead. But as he rounded the corner, he stopped dead, the wrinkles of concern smoothing out at the sight of Erica.

She sat alone on a bale of hay, munching a sandwich while the sun painted her in hues of gold and amber.

The sight of her was a jolt to his system, like coffee after a night of bad decisions. He hovered there, one foot half-turned toward her, the other itching to bolt. To join or not to join, that was the question hammering through his veins.

Hey, Erica, he could say and maybe this time get it right. Or maybe he'd just trip over his tongue again and add another layer of awkward to their already patchy history.

He watched her laugh at something only she knew, the sound silent to him but loud in his imagination. It was a private moment, one he had no right to interrupt. Was she texting someone else? A different guy?

Not your business.

CJ spun on his heel, leaving Erica to her business.

"Lines," he whispered to himself, the word a feeble shield against the swell of emotions threatening to capsize him once again.

It was the script he needed to focus on—being someone else was about the only thing he understood these days.

Chapter 15

The Buford Homestead loomed like a grizzled sentinel of the past, the setting sun casting long, eerie shadows through its weathered beams. The Colton barn had been transformed into something Erica hardly recognized, as real as if it'd been taken from a page of history and plunked down on the property, and she was stunned at the high production value of every detail.

When Anna had invited her to watch this particular scene, Erica had been tempted to decline with the excuse of too much work on her plate already poised on her tongue. But she'd accepted the offer with secret eagerness that should've been a red flag.

And now she was here. The set was alive with motion as everyone prepared for the big scene.

Erica, her mind muddled with lists and plans for Laura's bachelorette bash, stepped onto the film set, a buzz of anticipation zipping through her veins. She had told herself that this was just another task, another box to check—behind-the-scenes access, nothing more. Yet as the director shouted "Action!" and CJ burst into a brutal fight scene with his on-screen nemesis, her pulse quickened.

She watched, utterly absorbed, as CJ grappled and

lunged with the ferocity of a warrior. The sound of their grunts as they strained against one another in a brutal dance of coordinated savagery was mesmerizing in a way she wasn't ashamed to admit had her enthralled.

Each calculated swing, each deft maneuver was poetry in motion, and the duality she'd once seen in him melted away, leaving only the artistry of his craft. Her heart hammered a rhythmic tribute to his every move—the clash of fists, the controlled aggression a ballet of bruising encounters. It took her breath away.

It wasn't hard to see why the man commanded the box office.

And then it was over.

"Cut!" The director's voice sliced through the charged air, and like waking from a trance, Erica blinked back into reality. The actors relaxed, shoulders drooping with fatigue but faces aglow with the thrill of the scene well done. They knew they'd nailed it, and their confidence was contagious. Erica jumped from her chair beside the director and ran up to CJ, gushing.

"Wow, CJ, that was…incredible," she found herself saying, the words tumbling out in a rush of admiration she hadn't anticipated. CJ turned toward her, a smile cracking the rugged facade of his character.

He wiped at the sweat dripping down his face, grinning. "There's nothing quite like getting your ass kicked for authenticity, right?" He chuckled, rubbing a hand along his jaw, where a darkening bruise bloomed like a storm cloud. He rolled up a sleeve, revealing a tapestry of scars like battle honors, each one a story etched in skin. "Months with the fight coordinator to make it look this good. But, man, the bruises were real."

Her laughter bubbled up, genuine and bright. "You wear them like medals."

"Only the brave get wounded in battle," he replied with a wink.

This was a world she couldn't fathom, but CJ made it look like it was just another day at the office. "Well, that was incredible," she said, unable to hide her enthusiasm. "To be honest, I've never been one for violence in movies, but seeing it from this angle... I have a newfound appreciation for all of the work that goes into making them."

"I'm glad you came," CJ said, holding her smile with one of his own. "I—"

Just then, the moment shattered as a loud crash boomed, a cacophony of splintering wood and chaos. Instinctively, Erica flinched, and the world tilted violently. She felt a solid body collide with hers, sending them both sprawling to the ground—a jarring thud that stole the air from her lungs.

"Erica!" CJ's voice was sharp with concern, close to her ear.

As the dust settled, she realized how narrowly disaster had missed her, an unkind game of chance played with falling timber. A shiver raced down her spine, her heart pounding a frenetic drumbeat against her rib cage.

"Are you okay?" CJ's eyes searched hers, the playful light extinguished, replaced by a flicker of something raw and protective.

"Y-Yeah," she stammered, her voice barely above a whisper, the brush with mortality still echoing in her bones. "I'm fine."

At least, she thought she was. She blinked against the plume of dust clogging the air from the shattered wood, coughing against the scratch in her lungs. "What happened?"

"Erica, you're bleeding!" The urgency in CJ's voice cut through the ringing in her ears as she tried to make sense of the chaos around them.

Shards of sunlight pierced the dust-laden air, revealing a scene punctuated by frantic movement and sharp shouts. Crew members darted about, their faces etched with concern, but none so viscerally alarmed as CJ, whose hands hovered over her, unsure where to touch without causing more harm.

"Let me see," he said, his tone softer now, guiding her gaze to her arm. Erica's eyes followed, and what she saw sucked the breath from her lungs—a splinter of wood, jagged and unyielding, protruding from her flesh. A bloom of crimson marred her skin, painting a vivid contrast against the pale fabric of her blouse.

"God, that looks bad." CJ's face was pale, a ghostly echo of his usual confidence.

"Doesn't feel great, either," she managed, shock weaving its numbing spell through her veins. Her voice sounded distant, like it belonged to someone else, someone watching this unfold from afar.

Had she really just been skewered like a cube of beef?

"Get a medic here—now!" someone bellowed, and within moments, the set's first aid team swarmed in, their practiced hands working with an efficiency that only amplified the gravity of the situation.

"Looks like we need to get you to a hospital," one of the

medics announced after a cursory examination, his voice a calm anchor amid the storm.

"I'm going with her," CJ stated, the words falling like a decree. His hand found hers, a lifeline in the chaos, grip firm and unwavering.

"Thank you," she whispered, feeling the tremble in her fingers mirrored by his own.

As they loaded her onto a stretcher, the wail of approaching sirens crescendoed into the frenetic action, the ambulance emerging as some semblance of order. Laura and Josh appeared on its heels, their faces etched with worry.

"Erica!" Laura's voice broke as she caught sight of her, hooked to an IV and a bandage carefully wound around the bleeding wound.

"Hey, I'm all right," Erica tried to reassure her, words tumbling out brittle and hollow. But was she all right? She had a piece of wood in her arm.

"Move back, give her some space!" a paramedic instructed as they wheeled her toward the waiting ambulance, the urgency displacing comfort.

Laura reached for Erica's hand, squeezing it in a silent promise of solidarity. "I'm coming with you," she declared, eyes locked with Erica's in a fierce pact.

CJ stepped aside, the lines of his jaw tense, and nodded. "I'll follow behind."

Erica felt the world shrink to the space of her own heartbeat—fast, insistent, alive.

One minute she'd been riding a high, and the next she'd narrowly cheated being squashed like a bug and heading to the hospital to have what felt like a tree trunk removed from her arm.

Life was weird.

She pressed a hand to her forehead, trying to steady the swirl of dizziness that threatened to pull her under.

"Really, I'm fine," she insisted, her voice betraying her with a quiver as she fought against the wave of lightheadedness. The metallic taste of fear lingered at the back of her throat.

Laura was at her side in an instant, her presence like the steadfast push of a lighthouse beam through fog. "No way am I letting you go alone," Laura said firmly, edging CJ out with a protective maternal fire burning in her eyes. The strength in her voice was the kind that could part a sea of chaos.

CJ's face, etched with lines of concern, tightened, but he stepped aside. "All right," he conceded, the word dragged from him like a weight. He turned to the cluster of people gathered around, their faces a blur to Erica's strained focus. "Josh, can you—"

"Already on it," Josh cut in, his tone all business as he volunteered himself for duty, motioning to the others nursing their own wounds. "We'll follow the ambulance."

Erica watched through the ambulance's open doors as Josh rounded up the rest of the walking wounded, including CJ, who cast a last look back at her—the gleam of his eyes a silent vow to see her soon.

As the paramedics secured Erica for the journey, the chatter and chaos of the set became distant, like listening to the ocean from inside a shell. The barn, now a skeleton of danger, stood ominously quiet in the background.

"Let's call it a night," someone called out, their voice

slicing through the murk of Erica's thoughts. "Shut every-thing down until we know it's safe."

One by one, lights snapped off, the glow of the day's filming fading into a stark reality. Actors, crew, every-one—their movements slowed, subdued by the near miss that hung over them all.

"Take care of her." CJ spoke softly to Laura, relinquish-ing his place beside Erica as if passing a baton in a race they were all running together.

"Like she's my own," Laura replied, her grip on Erica's hand a lifeline anchoring her to the moment.

The ambulance doors closed with a definitive thud, seal-ing away the outside world. The engine hummed to life, its rhythm syncing with Erica's racing pulse, a shared ca-dence as they pulled away from what might have been a final scene.

And only then did Erica blissfully pass out.

CJ's heart pounded a brutal rhythm against his rib cage, while his hands clutched the steering wheel until his knuck-les whitened, each turn and stoplight a frustrating delay. He hadn't given Josh the option to drive, even though it was Josh's town and not his. He couldn't handle the thought of not being able to drive as fast as his anxiety demanded to get to Erica.

With each passing moment, Erica's pained face flashed behind his eyelids, a stark image that drowned out all thoughts of the chaotic film set he'd just torn away from.

"Damn it, move!" he muttered under his breath, urging the traffic to part like some petulant sea before his mount-ing desperation. He couldn't shake the image of Anna's face, either, pale with dread as she went to share the news with the higher-ups. The production was hemorrhaging money and trust, but none of it weighed on him now—not with Erica's well-being hanging in the balance.

The hospital loomed ahead, a beacon in the approaching dusk, its fluorescent lights harsh against the dimming day. CJ skidded into the parking lot, nearly colliding with a shopping cart left carelessly by the curb. The sting of his seat belt cutting across his chest went unnoticed as he bolted from the car, barely registering Josh's strained voice calling after him.

"Easy, CJ! She'll be okay," Josh said, but CJ was already threading through the sliding doors of the emergency room, his eyes scanning for any sign of her.

"Family only beyond this point," a stern-faced nurse blocked his path, but CJ's frantic gaze and the bandages peeking from beneath his sleeve spoke volumes. A flicker of sympathy crossed her face, and she stepped aside with a resigned sigh. "Make it quick."

Inside, the sterile scent of disinfectant mixed with the metallic tang of blood. The relentless beeping of monitors played counterpoint to the shuffle of shoes and low murmur of voices. There she was—Erica, his compass in the storm, laid out before him with medical staff orbiting her like planets around a sun. Her arm, marred by the jagged wood shard, seemed so small amid the white sheets.

Thankfully, it must've been a slow day in the ER because a doctor was already talking with Erica when he arrived.

"Hmm, that's quite a souvenir. What happened?"

"We're not sure. One minute everything was fine and the

next, a portion of the barn had collapsed. When the dust and the shock settled, I saw this in my arm," Erica explained.

CJ walked in, going straight to Erica's side, daring anyone to tell him to leave. He shared additional information. "Hi, I'm CJ Knight. The accident happened while on set. She's right—a piece of the barn just collapsed, and we have no idea how it happened."

The doctor eyed CJ. "You look injured yourself."

"Just scrapes and bruises. There are a few people who got hit during the collapse, but Erica took the brunt of it."

The doctor nodded, returning to Erica. "Well, it's in there pretty deep. Given the nature of your injury, I'm going to recommend surgery to remove the debris," he explained, his voice clinical yet not unkind. "The nurses will go ahead and prep you. Once you're under, it shouldn't take long to patch you up."

"Sounds like a piece of cake," Erica said, but her voice trembled.

The doctor removed his gloves and threw them away, leaving to make room for the nurses to do their thing.

A kindly nurse appeared with a soft, round face and a gentle disposition. "Sounds like surgery is in order. The good news is it'll feel like you blinked and then it'll all be over. However, standard protocol requires us to ask—could you be pregnant?"

Erica blinked and shook her head. "No, I don't think so."

But the nurse made an apologetic expression as she said, "Well, we'll just run a quick test to be sure, and then we'll be able to prep you for surgery."

CJ's fingers threaded through Erica's, holding on, willing his heart to stop beating like a wild thing. He couldn't stop replaying the scene in his head or freaking out over how Erica could've died.

"Hey," she whispered, squeezing his hand back. "I'm tougher than I look. It'll be fine."

"Yeah, I know you are. I just… I'm so sorry, Erica," he said, feeling responsible for her injury. "I'm going to find out what happened, and I swear, if someone did this on purpose, there'll be hell to pay."

But Erica was less bloodthirsty, saying, "I'm sure it was just a freak accident. Don't work yourself into a lather over this."

The nurse returned then, her face etched with lines of concern. She hesitated, eyeing CJ before settling on Erica, the weight of unsaid words hanging between them. "Erica, there's something we need to discuss privately," she said, voice low and steady.

Perplexed, Erica looked to CJ in apology, saying, "Can you give us a minute?"

"Yeah, sure, of course," CJ said, releasing Erica's hand. Every instinct screamed for him to stay, yet he found himself stepping back, seeming to retreat to an area where he wasn't privy to the whispered secrets between patient and healer. But he could still hear the hushed tones of the conversation. Was it wrong? Probably. Did he care? Not really. He felt territorially protective over Erica in ways he couldn't explain and definitely couldn't fight.

"Um, well, seems you actually are pregnant, Miss Pike," the nurse said with a small, rueful chuckle. "I hope this is good, unexpected news, but it does change the plan to put you under general anesthesia."

CJ's breath caught in his chest. *Pregnant?*

Erica seemed just as shocked. "I'm sorry, I think I have dust in my ears… Did you say I'm pregnant? Are you sure?"

"Yes, the blood test is conclusive. Not far along but definitely pregnant. Due to this, we can't risk general anesthesia," the nurse continued, her words wrapped in professional warmth. "Local anesthetic—it's safer for a baby in the first trimester during the procedure. The danger of miscarriage is small, but the doctor won't want to risk it."

CJ's heart hammered against his rib cage, a frenzied drummer too loud in the quiet corridor. Pregnant? The world seemed to twist beneath him, reality skewing into a shape he couldn't recognize. He stumbled backward, the taut wire inside him snapping, sending his senses reeling.

Footsteps rang hollow on linoleum as he shuffled to the waiting room, the pulsing thrum of his pulse drowning out the world around him. Each step felt like wading through molasses, time stretching and bending like a surreal painting.

He collapsed onto the closest chair, the plastic cool and unforgiving beneath him. The weight of the revelation pressed down, each breath heavier than the last. Was the child his? A storm of possibility raged in his mind, every thought a flash of lightning with no thunder to follow.

Josh found him and immediately started asking questions. "How's Erica?"

CJ snapped out of his funk to nod, answering on autopilot. "She's good. They're going to use local anesthesia to pull the wood free and then sew up her injury."

Looking relieved, Josh said, "That's good. Everyone else seems okay, too. Erica's injury seems the most severe, but man, that scared the shit out of me."

"You and me both," he murmured.

"I need to head back to the resort, start the insurance paperwork. I'll catch an Uber so you can stay here if you want."

CJ nodded, appreciating Josh's willingness to catch a ride without him. He couldn't fathom leaving Erica's side, not when he knew she was pregnant.

The baby might not be yours—calm down. That voice of reason seemed almost defensive, but there was something in his gut that told him no, that baby was his. Erica didn't sleep around. He knew that much about her. Plus, the nurse said she was in her first trimester, which was early from what he understood about babies—which, admittedly, wasn't a lot.

So what did that mean for them?

He didn't have answers—only more questions.

And the only person who could help him answer those questions was about to go into surgery to have a big shard of wood removed from her body.

He slumped down in the hard plastic chair, feeling out of his element...and scared.

Chapter 16

Erica's heart lurched, a tiny paper boat caught in a tempestuous sea—*pregnant*. The word echoed in her skull, bouncing off the insides like a rogue pinball. She barely had time to wrap her mind around the life-altering revelation before the sterile tang of the hospital nudged her back to the present.

"All right, Miss Pike, we're ready for you," a nurse said, her voice a calm contrast to the storm inside Erica.

She nodded mutely as she was wheeled down the antiseptic corridor, harsh lights flickering overhead like a staccato rhythm to the chaos in her chest. The operating room loomed, a frigid cave of clinical precision where her arm would be freed from the jagged invader that had punctured her skin. A part of her wished she'd been able to just go to sleep and wake up with all of this a weird dream, but the reality was far more jarring.

"Deep breaths, Erica," the doctor instructed, his tone professional yet oddly soothing. "We'll have that wood out in no time."

And true to his word, the procedure unfolded with a stark simplicity that belied the complexity of her thoughts. A few well-placed stitches, a whisper of relief as the offending wood was extracted—a minor victory overshadowed by the reality of a new life growing inside her. Before she could grapple with the magnitude of it all, she was being patched up, handed a prescription and sent on her way.

"Take it easy with this arm, avoid any heavy lifting and make sure to take your antibiotics as prescribed," the doctor advised, ticking off each point on his fingers.

"Thank you," Erica managed, forcing a smile through numb lips.

When she emerged into the lobby, the sight of CJ waiting, his posture radiating concern, seemed to anchor her. His eyes met hers, and without a word, he was at her side, handling her with the delicate care one might use for a precious, yet fragile, artifact.

"You didn't have to—"

"Hush," he said. "I'm driving you," he said in a tone brooking no argument, as if she were silly for suggesting otherwise. She didn't have the desire to argue and simply nodded.

He helped her gently into his car, the silence between them thick with the unsaid. Every glance he cast her way felt heavy with words they weren't ready to speak, every touch a silent vow of support she wasn't sure how to receive.

No less than three days ago, she'd tersely cut off any semblance of even friendship with CJ, drawing a professional boundary between them that he wasn't welcome to cross.

Now he was her baby daddy.

So much for keeping it professional, she thought wryly.

"When we get to your place, you're going to rest," CJ said, firmly in control. "I know that goes against your personality but… I mean, there are other things to consider now."

Dancing around the elephant. Fun times.

But CJ's hand found hers, tentative yet steady, a tangible connection amid the dizzying and rapidly changing reality between them and she clung to him.

"Thanks," she breathed—not just for the ride, but for the silent understanding, for the presence that didn't press or pry, only offered temporary sanctuary, which she sorely needed.

CJ's car rolled to a stop outside Erica's place, and CJ was already out and opening her door before she could gather her thoughts.

"Careful," he murmured, his hands ghosting around her as if she were a soap bubble ready to pop.

"CJ, I'm not made of glass," she murmured but stepped gingerly onto the pavement, her injured arm cradled protectively against her.

Inside, the living room greeted her with its familiar comfort, everything as she liked her environment to be after a long day at work. How would she fit a baby into her space? She had so many breakables and collectibles that weren't exactly baby-friendly.

CJ guided her to the sofa, piling cushions with an exactness that didn't match his usual easygoing nature. He moved through her space, straightening, adjusting, doing anything but standing still.

"Thanks," she managed, sinking into the pillowed cloud.

"Water? Food?" CJ asked, hovering close, his restlessness palpable.

Oh gosh, if he didn't stop hovering she'd lose what was left of her frayed sanity.

"Sit, please," Erica said, her voice thin but insistent. He

obeyed, perching on the edge of an armchair like a bird too anxious to roost.

Silence stretched between them, filled only by the ticking clock and their shared unease. Erica took a shaky breath, feeling the weight of revelation balloon within her.

"We might as well get to the heart of the current situation. I didn't know," she started, her gaze locked on her hands, twisting in her lap. "About the…pregnancy." The word felt foreign on her tongue, like she was talking about someone else's situation instead of her own. "I mean, I… wasn't in the right time in my cycle and… I, well, I just…"

Frustration made her stumble on the truth of the matter until she finally blurted, "Okay, we should've been more careful, but neither of us were thinking clearly, obviously."

"So… I'm safe to assume…"

"Yes, CJ. It's yours," she said, the words brittle but true. "I haven't been with anyone else since—you know, before you left."

His expression shifted, the questions now replaced by a dawning comprehension that she caught at the same time. Good gravy, that meant she'd already been pregnant when they'd hooked up a second time on the movie set.

"Wow" was all he managed, the monosyllable heavy with a thousand unspoken thoughts.

"Wow," she echoed, a laugh bubbling up from her nerves like fizz in a shaken soda can.

The room seemed to breathe around them, the walls echoing back their astonishment as if to say, *Yes, this is really happening*, and neither knew what to say.

CJ's descent onto the sofa sent a plume of air rushing from beneath the cushions, a testament to the gravity of the situation that anchored him next to her. His mouth opened and closed, a fish gasping for comprehension in an ocean of responsibility.

"Guess we can't keep things professional now, huh?" Erica's voice, a frayed thread, tried to weave humor into the heavy fabric of reality.

He managed a strangled sound—half laugh, half sigh—before springing up as if the couch were a launchpad to fatherhood. "We'll need to schedule your checkups, get prenatal vitamins and—oh, foot rubs? Is that a thing? I've heard pregnant women have feet issues. Probably from carrying around another person all day. I'll have a masseuse brought in to rub your feet every day—"

"Stop," she pleaded, the word a hand raised against the barrage of his well-meaning torrent. "Just sit with me. Please."

Her plea reached him through the static of his panic, and he paused, the frenetic energy in his eyes softening. "Right. Sorry." He folded back down beside her, his presence a solid, reassuring weight. "I'm just out of my depth, and I don't want to keep screwing things up. I'm sorry, Erica. I—I don't even know what else to say."

Erica understood. "Can you hold me?" she asked.

CJ scooted forward and enveloped his arms around her, drawing her close. Erica's tension melted into the warmth between them. Her exhale filled the space, a sound rich with relief and the faintest echo of hope, even though she just wanted to shut her brain down for a bleeding second.

"Thank you," she whispered into the fabric of his shirt, the texture against her cheek grounding her in this new, shared existence. They didn't need to solve every problem right this second. What she needed right now was CJ and a quiet moment.

The rest could wait.

After a long while, Erica disentangled herself from CJ's arms and rose with an offer to make them something to eat, to which CJ could only stare with incredulity, returning with an adamant, "The hell you are. If anything, I'll order us something, because I'm not much of a cook, but you're not lifting a finger tonight."

"CJ, don't be ridiculous. I'm not broken—and before you come back with 'But you're pregnant!' women have been having babies for a very long time, and I feel mostly fine, so stop worrying."

"Be that as it may, you're carrying my baby, and I don't feel comfortable with you overdoing it on my watch. At least wait until I leave," he added with a subtle return of his usual humor.

She chuckled with acquiescence. "Okay, that's fair. Tonight I will not lift a finger and you can handle everything. And if you're offering to order takeout, I'd love a burger with all of the trimmings. I'm actually starving."

Relieved to have a purpose, CJ jumped on her request, and within minutes, he'd placed two orders for the best burgers Sedona could offer and promised the delivery driver a ridiculous tip if he could get it here within thirty minutes or less. Being rich had its perks.

But now that he'd finished that one task, he was left to wonder what to do next. He was still a nervous ball of energy and yet feeling totally useless at the same time.

Erica sighed, sensing the tension inside him, though

she must've misinterpreted his anxiety, saying, "CJ, I'm not expecting you to drop to your knee and promise me forever. We're both adults. We can handle this situation between us without placing any relationship expectations on the table, okay?"

But it wasn't okay and that wasn't why he was nervous. "What if I want a relationship with you, Erica?" he blurted before he could stop himself. At her widened stare, he rushed to clarify. "Okay, I know I'm being super erratic right now, but I like you...and I can't imagine anyone I'd rather have a baby with, but every time I try to say the right thing, somehow my foot ends up in my mouth and I screw it all up."

"CJ..." Erica's gaze darted away, as if uncomfortable with his admission, and he felt like an idiot for blurting out something so raw. "I just think we should take things slow for now...we're both running on shock right now. Neither of us should be making big decisions in the wake of our discovery. Let's just...let it rest for a minute, okay?"

That made sense, even if it deflated his sails a bit. His grand gesture had fallen embarrassingly flat, but her advice was more logical, forcing him to nod glumly. "Yeah, of course," he said.

But Erica saw how her advice had landed and softened the blow, adding, "Let's just...take our time with this." Erica's fingers traced the fabric of the cushion, her gaze fixed on some distant point of contemplation. "I'm not saying no to figuring it out together. I just don't want us to do something rash because of... Well, because of this."

CJ blew out a short breath, taking a minute to settle his nerves. She was right. Nothing had to be solved or sorted out today. What mattered was that Erica was safe, the baby was safe and they had at least eight months, give or take, to figure out the rest.

The food arrived, and CJ enjoyed a good, solid meal that also helped settle his thoughts and put him back on track. As much as the news that Erica was pregnant was huge, he had another issue to deal with, and it couldn't wait.

"Are you sure you're going to be all right?" He double-checked with Erica as they cleaned up after dinner.

"I'm totally fine," she assured him. "I need to call Laura and let her know what's going on, but I plan to be at work tomorrow."

Even though CJ would rather she stay home and rest, he knew that was asking a lot. "Light duty, right?" he suggested.

"Yes, I'll take it easy."

"Okay, then I'll trust you to keep your word on that. I have to talk to Anna about the production. Last I saw, she was heading to make a call to the execs, and I don't think it was going to be a good conversation after the barn practically fell on us."

Erica frowned. "CJ…there might be some truth to the suspicion that someone is trying to stop the production. I don't think you can chalk up all of these incidents to bad luck or coincidence."

CJ agreed. "The key gaffer admitted that someone had cut the wires to the lighting rig a few days ago. It was a miracle it didn't catch fire again."

"Do you think that's what happened to the saloon at the original location?"

"Seems likely. All it takes is a single spark, and every-thing goes up in flames."

Erica shuddered. "Why would someone want to sabotage a big production? That's a lot of jobs and a lot of money on the line."

"I don't know, but I think it's time to start asking different questions," he said, grabbing his keys. "I need to talk to Anna before she's an entire wine bottle deep in depression. This production was her baby."

At the mention of *baby*, they both paused, then laughed awkwardly as CJ admitted, "It's weird to think, huh?"

"Yeah," she nodded, smiling. "I guess we'll get used to it eventually."

He was struck by how incredibly beautiful she was, and he reached for her gently. "Can I kiss you good-night?" he asked.

Erica answered with a slow nod, her gaze meeting his boldly. He didn't waste a minute in pressing his lips against hers, his tongue darting to lightly taste, sending a thrill hurtling through his nerve endings. They were electric together—was it any wonder they'd made a baby?

He could've spent all night kissing her, but time was his enemy right now. Regretfully pulling away, CJ said his goodbyes and left for the resort, switching gears.

Time to figure out what the hell was going on and why someone was deliberately trying to kill any hope for the production.

Chapter 17

CJ's hand hovered over the door, a sense of dread settling in his stomach like an unwanted guest as he knocked softly on Anna's room at Mariposa Resort. When the door creaked open, there she was: silhouette slumped against the sunset bleeding through the curtains, wine glass cradled like a fragile hope in her hand. Her eyes, usually sharp as sea glass, were now glassy and rimmed red, telling him more than words could about the day's toll.

"Anna?" His voice tiptoed into the room. "You okay?"

She managed a wobbly smile that didn't reach her eyes, shaking her head as she tipped the bottle, filling her glass. "Drink?" she asked, voice flat, the word hanging awkwardly between them.

"No, thanks," CJ declined, the weight of her gaze pulling him closer. "The execs—what did they say?"

There it was, the dam breaking behind her eyes as she swallowed hard, fresh tears pooling. "They've pulled the plug, CJ. It's over," she whispered, her voice a ghost of defeat. "Too many accidents…we've become an insurance nightmare."

His throat tightened, watching her crumble. Anna, the unshakable force behind their project, now reduced to this—a woman questioning her own resolve. Goddamn, if he got his hands on whoever was responsible for this mess, he'd catch a murder charge.

"Maybe they're right," she muttered, a tear betraying her and rolling down her cheek. "I can't... I don't want anyone else getting hurt because of me." Her hand paused mid-wipe, and her bleary eyes sought his. "Erica? How is she?"

"Erica's..." CJ started, then hesitated, the irony of the situation twisting his lips into a half smile. "She's fine. Actually, she's pregnant. And—I'm the father."

For a moment, Anna looked as if he'd slapped her with a dead fish. "Excuse me? What? You two? I didn't even realize..."

"Neither did we," CJ admitted, scratching the back of his neck with an uneasy chuckle. "I mean, it was nothing official between us, but I guess things have changed now."

Raising her glass in a trembling salute, Anna offered a watery "Mazel tov" before pushing herself up from the chair, her legs shaky as newborn foals. "Sorry, CJ, I'm terrible company right now. I have to find the courage to tell the rest of the cast and crew that we're done, and so far, it wasn't in the wine bottle and now all I want is to go to bed."

CJ understood. "Yeah, of course. But Anna, before you tell anyone, give me twenty-four hours, okay? Let me talk to someone...higher up."

Her laugh was bitter, devoid of humor. "You think you can turn this around? Be my guest."

"Promise me," he insisted, holding her gaze.

"Fine," she sighed, half-defeated. "Knock yourself out, hero. I'll be here, trying to sleep away this damn nightmare."

And with that, she turned away, leaving CJ grappling with the wreckage of their dreams and the new life forming amid the chaos.

Sunrise found CJ with his duffel slung over one shoulder, the crisp morning air biting at his cheeks as he strode across the dew-speckled grass of Mariposa Resort.

He squinted against the early light, a crease forming between his brows—a physical manifestation of the resolve hardening within him. It wasn't just about saving the production now; it was about proving himself, about stepping up when everything seemed to crumble.

He slid into the driver's seat of the rental car, the fabric cool and unwelcoming beneath him. The engine hummed to life, a soft, steady purr that seemed at odds with the turmoil churning in his gut. He had a quick flight to LA already booked, and he had a meeting slated for thirty minutes after he landed.

As the vehicle rolled out onto the open road, CJ's thumb hovered over his phone screen, a message drafted but not yet sent. The words felt heavy, each letter weighted with a significance he'd never dealt with before. With a flick of his thumb, the message shot through the digital ether:

Hey Erica, heading to LA to sort some things out. Back tomorrow. —CJ

It was simple, almost too simple, but beneath the surface, there was so much more going on. He wasn't just letting her know about his whereabouts; he was laying down the first brick on the path to reliability, to being present. He released a shaky breath, never before realizing how he'd always been the one to disappear first, laughing off conflict and adopting a "chill" attitude that often translated into the guy who couldn't be caught.

The car ate miles of asphalt as he drove to the airport. His thoughts drifted to Erica, their unplanned intertwining of lives, and the small, budding existence that now linked them forever. He didn't voice it, didn't even shape the thought clearly in his mind, but somewhere deep inside, a silent vow formed—a whisper of commitment to the future and to the family he never knew he wanted until now.

But first, he had to figure out what the hell was going on with the people who signed the checks. If being an A-list celebrity didn't afford you the chance to champion a good cause, what good was it?

Time to make his celebrity status work for him, instead of working for his status.

The ping of Erica's phone was a welcome distraction, her thumb swiping the screen as CJ's text tumbled across it. Had she been holding her breath, wondering if he would text her before leaving town again? Maybe. The fact that he had felt like a step in the right direction, small though it was.

Grinning to herself, she pocketed the device and slipped through the back offices, her pace brisk and her mind focused with the news she knew she had to share.

But as she rounded the corner toward Laura's office, she halted mid-stride at the unexpected visitor chatting casually with both Laura and Josh.

Matthew Bennett? *Good lord, does that mean he accepted the wedding invitation?*

Matthew, a Colton stepcousin, with his sportsman physique and a head full of cropped dark brown hair that somehow managed to look effortlessly windswept, was a wild card in Erica's book. Unfortunately Matthew was connected to family drama. It wasn't his fault, but no one knew for sure where his true allegiances landed. Money always had a tendency to muddy the waters, in Erica's experience.

Golden-brown eyes flicked her way, a spark of recognition igniting within their depths.

"Erica!" Laura's voice, laced with something more than greeting, pulled Erica from her appraisal.

In an instant, professionalism cloaked her like a second skin, her smile stretching as she crossed the threshold into the buzzing office. She read the room—the subtle shifts, the tension riding on the undercurrents of conversation—and knew this was not the time for her news.

"Matthew, Josh," she greeted, nodding at each in turn.

Josh smiled with genuine relief. "I was so relieved when CJ let us know that you're okay. I can't believe the barn failed like that."

"What happened?" Matthew asked with a confused frown. "An accident at the resort?"

Josh looked reluctant to share, but answered, "There's a film shooting on location here. There was a small mishap. Thankfully everyone was okay, except for Erica. She took a piece of wood to the arm."

"Sounds terrible. Are you sure you're okay?" Matthew asked.

"Nothing a few stitches and a round of antibiotics can't handle," Erica replied with a quick smile.

Laura shared a look with Josh, just as Matthew said,

"Hmm, that could be a liability issue. Have you had the lawyers look into the ramification of an accident like that caused by filming?"

"We don't know that it was caused by the filming," Laura clarified quickly. "It was the old barn in the closed section of the resort. It might've been unstable from the start. We're having it inspected to determine the cause of the accident."

Matthew nodded. "Good idea. In the meantime, I'm assuming filming is shut down until it's been deemed safe?"

Erica wanted to glare at Matthew for poking his nose where it didn't belong—they had the situation well in hand and didn't need Matthew's two cents—but her expression remained professionally neutral.

Laura offered a brief smile. "All in hand. Hey, Josh why don't you give Matthew a tour of the resort, show him some of our newest attractions."

"Great idea," Josh said, gesturing for Matthew to follow.

As the men exited, their footsteps a fading beat against the floor, Erica turned to Laura, with an incredulous expression. "Who appointed him the OSHA representative?" she joked.

Laura pursed her lips in annoyance. "Honestly, when I sent the invitation, I didn't expect him to accept. I only let him know about the wedding out of courtesy, and now he's here thinking he can have an opinion on how we run Mariposa."

"Stepcousin, right?" Erica said, affirming her memory.

"Yes," Laura said. "I mean, I'm sure he means well, but right now, I just want him to zip it. Anyway…" She shook off the last few minutes and returned to Erica, "How are you? Are you sure you're okay?"

"I'm totally fine," she assured Laura. "They didn't even have to knock me out to stitch me up. Honestly, I probably could've saved myself a trip to the hospital if I'd just pulled it out myself and smeared some antibacterial ointment on it."

"Good God, no. You absolutely needed to be seen by a doctor, but I'm glad you're okay. I was so worried."

The silence settled like a heavy blanket between them, the absent hum of office chatter leaving room for Erica's racing heart to fill the space.

"However," Erica said, taking a steadying breath. "Laura," she began, the words slipping out with a tremulous certainty, "something else was discovered while at the hospital."

"Something else?" Laura repeated with a confused frown. "What do you mean?"

"So, as it turns out… I'm eleven weeks pregnant."

Laura's face lost color as if the news had physically struck her, her lips parting in a silent gasp. "Eleven weeks?" Laura gasped.

"Yep."

"Eleven— Oh God, are you telling me…" Laura finally found her voice, a mix of disbelief and concern. "It's CJ's baby, isn't it?"

Erica nodded, her own surprise at the situation still fresh, "Yeah, sure is."

A groan escaped Laura, her hand flying up to her face. "How?" She dropped her hand to clarify at Erica's blush. "I mean, I know *how*, but you're the last person I'd ever suspect would find themselves pregnant from a one-night stand."

"You and me both, sister," Erica quipped, shaking her

head. "But life has a way of humbling you when you least expect it."

"You can say that again." Laura took a minute, trying to find her footing in the conversation. "Okay, are you... I mean, do you feel—okay?"

"Okay? I don't know." Erica forced a laugh, attempting to slice through the tension. "Ask again in a few days." She flexed her fingers, the bandaged arm a visual reminder of her vulnerability.

"Yeah, I get that," Laura said but quickly switched gears as only Laura could. "Well, okay, it is what it is. No more lifting or—"

"Hey, I'm fine," Erica cut in, the firmness in her voice belying her inner turmoil. "Really. Just because I have to go easy on the arm doesn't mean I've turned into glass. You and CJ both are trying to put me in a padded bubble, and that's not necessary."

Laura studied her, the corners of her mouth twitching upward in a hesitant smile. "You'd hate that, wouldn't you? Being treated like you're fragile?"

"More than anything," Erica confirmed with a nod, grateful for the understanding that always seemed to anchor their friendship.

Laura's concern etched deeper lines into her forehead as she leaned forward, the creak of her chair breaking the tense silence. "You know, I could always pass on the bachelorette-party planning to someone else," she offered, her voice soft but insistent.

Erica shook her head with a determination that surprised even herself. "No way. The plans are set, everything's ticking along like clockwork. I'm not letting anyone snatch this from me—it's going to be epic."

Laura grinned. "It was probably a stupid offer."

"It kinda was," Erica said with a wink. "But your heart is in the right place." Back to business, Erica said, "Willow flies in tomorrow, right?"

"Yeah, and I should be psyched to see her, but…" Laura's voice trailed off, her eyes darting to the window, where chaos seemed just a pane away.

"Hey," Erica said, her tone firmer than she intended, "this storm will blow over. And your wedding? It's okay to be over the moon about it—no guilt allowed."

A smile flickered across Laura's face, the first genuine one since the bombshell news. It was moments like these that reminded Erica why she'd go to the ends of the earth for her friend.

"You're right," Laura said with a small, guilty snicker. "I'm super excited. And you know what—it's going to be fine. Everything is going to work out for you and for me. Do you hear that, universe?" She shook her finger at the ceiling as if chastising a listening deity. "I'm manifesting total bliss, and that's that."

Erica laughed, her voice bouncing off the office walls. "Well, there you have it, folks. But now I've got work to do." She paused, throwing a playful wink Laura's way. "Enjoy your time with the relatives."

With that, she exited Laura's office, leaving behind an echo of her laughter. Her heart felt oddly buoyant despite the looming life-altering shift ahead of her.

Was pregnant euphoria a thing?

Note to self: buy book on pregnancy.

Heading down the halls, her heels clicked sharply as she went.

When everything else was out of whack—routine always felt right.

Chapter 18

CJ's sneakers slapped the sunbaked pavement as he hustled through a maze of trailers and cables, the LA heat clinging to him like a second skin. The studio lot buzzed with an undercurrent of tension, electric and alive, a far cry from the calm serenity of the resort.

Funny how he never really noticed how this environment was a recipe for anxiety. He'd always attributed that tension in his body as excitement, but now it felt different. Was this the impending "Dad Effect" happening? He'd have to untangle that later. For now, he had to focus on the situation facing the production.

"Mr. Knight?" A young PA with a headset that seemed too large for her head flagged him down, her eyes scanning a clipboard as if it held the secrets of the universe. "Mr. Greene is ready for you on the fourth floor."

"Thanks," CJ grunted, taking the stairs two at a time, the thud of his heartbeat keeping pace with his ascent. He was taking a huge chance, but he felt he had to do it.

The door to the executive's office swung open with a decisive push, revealing a space that screamed power—the kind of room where dreams were made or shattered on a whim. There, behind a desk that could double as a small aircraft carrier, sat the man himself: Harold Greene, the notorious executive whose fair handshake was as legendary as his ruthless business tactics.

The fact that Mr. Greene had taken CJ's request to meet spoke volumes about his star power, but CJ wasn't naive— Mr. Greene liked money, and he liked making it. And right now, that was CJ's superpower. The minute CJ stopped being box office gold, the man would forget he existed. So, with that knowledge, CJ figured he might as well "make hay while the sun shone" and use whatever advantage he had to save the production.

"Harold," CJ began, going straight to the point, "you can't just pull the plug over a couple of hiccups. *Waterworld* tanked—literally—and they still finished shooting."

"No chitchat first? Okay, I respect that." Greene leaned back, his chair creaking in protest. "CJ, unless you've got Costner's deep pockets and are willing to sink twenty-two mil into this sinking ship, I suggest you let it go," he said. "This production is going to turn into an albatross around your neck if you're not careful."

But CJ wasn't going to do that. Maybe it was his stubborn belief in the underdog or his sense of fair play, but he couldn't let it go. "Let's get down to brass tacks. I know for a fact you have a handful of pet projects that aren't going to make a dime domestically and you're not pulling the plug on them. So, why this production? This feels personal. You aren't giving Anna a fair chance. What's the real reason— because I smell a steaming pile of bull, and you can't convince me it's a bed of roses."

Harold's gaze narrowed. "Say it with your whole chest. What are you implying?"

"Not implying, I'm pointing out the obvious. Every film has its setbacks. Hell, what's happened so far on this production is literally small potatoes, but you've got Anna dancing on a wire, threatening to the pull the plug at every turn. You're being an ass, and I want to know why."

He was taking a risk. Harold Greene had the power to crush his career if he chose, but CJ was banking on the fact that he also knew that the man was a straight shooter and respected bold moves.

A moment passed between them until Greene sighed, shaking his head. "It's not personal, CJ. Maybe the project was just too damn ambitious, and maybe Anna wasn't the right call," Greene said, toying with a pen between his fingers. "And if it seems like I've been riding her throughout this production, it's because I actually want her to succeed. I think she's very talented and deserves a shot."

"So, why are you shutting down the movie?"

"Look, the insurance companies are getting real skittish about insuring productions with problems. Sure, no one was badly hurt, but there have been too many incidents that could've been bad. No one's going to rally behind a film shoot that someone died on. It's just facts. I'd rather cut my losses than deal with the potential of a tragedy."

Might as well go big and tell Greene what he suspected. "Someone's messing with us, Harold. The key gaffer found the wires cut to the main lighting rig, and I'm willing to bet that someone created the dangerous situation with the barn. The owner of the resort is having the structure examined as well as the set crew."

"Sabotage? Why?"

"Hell if I know, but it feels personal."

"But you don't have any proof of that, correct?"

"I mean, we have proof someone cut the wires," CJ said.

"That's not enough. Shit happens on a production. The wires could've been accidentally compromised. What's the motive? I know you want to find a reason to make this more than it is, but you don't have to. Look, if it's about your paycheck, don't sweat it. Doug might've been a twisted guy, but he negotiated a tight contract. You'll get your cash either way."

Just the mention of Doug was a trigger for CJ. "Damn it, Harold, it's not about the money!" CJ's words echoed off the walls, his frustration palpable.

"All right, all right." Greene raised his hands in a calming gesture, clearly mistaking CJ's passion for desperation. "Take it easy, CJ. We'll make sure you're taken care of."

CJ's stomach churned, acid bubbling like a caustic critique. The money talk? It was white noise, a static hum in the background of a much bigger picture. He wasn't some mercenary actor, flipping roles for a quick buck; this was about the art, the story that needed to be told.

"Listen to me," CJ said, his voice low and tight with urgency. "You think I'm here rattling cans for change? This is bigger than a paycheck."

Greene sat back, the chair creaking under the shift of his weight, eyes wide with a flicker of uncertainty. Maybe he hadn't seen this kind of fire before—not from someone like CJ.

"Anna's vision for this film…it's groundbreaking. And I won't stand by while you choke it with red tape." CJ's words were a punch, direct and unflinching.

"Groundbreaking?" Greene echoed, skepticism pulling down his mouth. But CJ could see it—the crack in the exec's smooth facade, the hint that maybe, just maybe, he got it. "C'mon, it's a Western period drama. Let's not make it to be more than it is."

"If that's all you see about Anna's vision, you've got it all wrong. The historical aspect of the film is just the vehicle for the theme of human grit required to shape new worlds and survive the violence of new beginnings. I'm telling you, this script has *Oscar-worthy* written all over it."

Greene chuckled wryly. "If I had a dollar for every time someone has pitched that to me... I wouldn't need my studio paycheck to pay for my next ex-wife."

"Yeah, well, when it's coming from me, it means something."

"Of course," Greene said, his tone placating. But CJ wasn't having it.

"If you don't have the stones to see this through, I'll do it. If it takes every dime I've got, I'll bankroll it myself." The words spilled out, a reckless promise, but they carried a weight of truth that anchored them firmly in the room.

Greene's face froze, his usual slick composure slipping like ice underfoot. "CJ, what are you doing? Are you serious?"

"Watch me." Without another word, CJ turned on his heel, strides eating up the plush carpet as he headed for the door.

Behind him, the silence was loud—a stunned quiet that felt like the aftermath of a scene well played. But this wasn't a performance. This was real, raw, and CJ was all in.

As the office door clicked shut behind him, CJ's pulse thrummed a victory beat. He might have shocked the big shot in the suit, but more importantly, he had just bet on the one thing he believed in more than anything: the movie, Anna's vision, their shared dream.

He might've just done the stupidest, most reckless thing in his life.

And he had a kid on the way.

Erica was threading her way between the bustling halls when she sensed someone trailing her. She turned to find Matthew, his approach casual but his eyes intent.

"Erica!" he called out, a practiced smile spreading across his face as he quickened his pace to match hers. "I've been hoping to catch you for a moment."

"Matthew," she responded, her voice even but her mind racing. She didn't have time for idle chitchat, especially not with a Colton hanger-on. Still, politeness won over. "What can I do for you?"

Matthew leaned in, his eyes sparkling with intrigue. "I have to admit I'm fascinated by all this movie-business intrigue that's been going on here at the resort. What really happened at the barn?" he asked, his voice dropping to a conspiratorial whisper as if they were buddies and Erica was going to spill secrets.

Erica's guard went up immediately. For one, she wasn't going to share resort business with anyone, much less someone who was simply a stepcousin with a tentative claim to the family resort. And two, she wasn't the sort of person to gossip.

"There's really no intrigue. Just a minor issue with one of the set pieces," she replied evasively. "It was really nothing."

"Nothing? I heard you had to go to the hospital," Matthew

returned with a quizzical expression. "Doesn't sound like nothing to me. What kind of safety protocols were in place?"

Erica forced a short laugh at his query. "It was nothing so dramatic. All I needed was a few stitches. It was more of a setback for the production than for me."

"So, they're going to keep filming?"

"I would assume so," Erica said with a short, pleasant smile that was her standard operating procedure for anyone difficult. "It was just bad luck," she offered with a dismissive wave. "These things happen sometimes in big productions." She hoped her explanation would end his probing.

"Sure, sure," Matthew said, nodding, though his brow remained furrowed with concern—or was it something else? He switched gears, sliding into even darker territory. "And Allison Brewer's murder...that must have been tough on everyone here."

The mention of Allison sent a prickling discomfort down Erica's spine. She forced a tight-lipped smile, the shadow of the tragedy too heavy to lift with pleasantries.

"Absolutely tragic, yes. But we're all trying to move forward." Her words came out more clipped than she intended, but Matthew's relentless digging was wearing thin on her patience.

"Of course, of course," he murmured, his gaze drifting past her as if trying to unearth secrets from the very air, which as far as she was concerned, weren't his business. She also knew Laura wouldn't appreciate him digging like this, either.

"Sorry, Matthew, I need to handle something," Erica cut in, seizing the chance to escape. "Excuse me."

As she walked away, her thoughts churned with suspicion. Matthew's intense interest didn't sit right. She couldn't shake the feeling that his inquiries were more than mere curiosity. *Talk to Laura*, she reminded herself mentally, already anticipating the next item on her never-ending list of tasks.

Later, finding a rare pocket of stillness in the outdoor spa area, Erica slumped into a chair. Enclosed by high hedges, the world seemed to fall away, leaving only the hum of distant activity. Exhaustion weighed her eyelids down like anchors.

Pregnant, she reminded herself, the word alien yet full of consequence. She placed a hand over her belly, the future stirring there as imperceptible as a whisper. Hard to believe a baby was growing in there when her pants weren't even tight yet.

"Life's curveball," she muttered, her heart thrumming with a mix of anxiety and wonder at what lay ahead.

Could CJ be part of this new chapter? The idea of integrating their wildly different worlds seemed as plausible as mixing oil with water. He belonged to the glitz and glamor; she to the quiet routine of her small-town life. And she liked her life, just as much as she was sure CJ liked his—so who had to be the one to give something up?

"Movie stars don't do diaper duty," she whispered, the reality pinching her heart.

A glance at her watch jolted her back to the present. With a resigned sigh, she straightened up and brushed off the invisible crumbs of fatigue. There was no time for rest, not when duty called. She pushed herself up, the promise of an early night's sleep dangling before her like a carrot on a stick. Dinner, then bed—that was the plan, and she intended to stick to it.

Chapter 19

The crunch of gravel under tires announced CJ's return before he even killed the engine. Erica watched from the porch, arms wrapped tight around her midsection. The last rays of the setting sun caught on his wind-tousled hair as he stepped out of the car with a briskness that didn't quite reach his eyes.

Her instant joy at seeing him dimmed at the seriousness in his gaze.

"Hey." His voice carried across the yard like a pebble skimming water, all surface energy. "We need to talk."

She nodded, her own reply snagged in the dryness of her throat. Her gaze lingered on the lines of tension drawn tight across his forehead as they settled into the living room. He paced, then stopped abruptly, facing her.

"Is everything okay?" she asked.

CJ shook his head, frustrated. "Let's just say the meeting wasn't as productive as I'd hoped."

"What happened?"

They stepped inside the house before CJ admitted, "Harold Greene seemed pretty adamant that he had no choice but to shut down the production, but he's got to be lying to me," he started, scratching the back of his neck, going straight to the headline. "So, I did the only thing I felt I had to, and I took on the production financing myself."

The words hung between them as Erica visibly balked at the announcement. "I'm sorry, what? Financing? CJ, that's…" She hesitated, the walls of support she wanted to offer him cracking under the weight of her worry that he'd just done something incredibly brash. "Can you…afford that?"

CJ didn't shy away from the question. "Um, well, I don't know. I mean, I have money in accounts and whatnot, but Doug handled all that stuff with my accountant, so I guess I'll have to find out the details. Maybe use my house as collateral if need be, but I feel it had to be done. Besides, I think I'll make back my investment. Anna's film is Oscar-worthy. I believe in it."

"CJ, that's incredibly risky," she murmured, wondering how to handle this news. On one hand, it wasn't her business how he spent his money, but on the other, this could be an indication of future behavior that could prove problematic for a new father that made her feel uncomfortable. Was he going to do this kind of thing whenever things didn't go his way? He couldn't possibly think that throwing money at a problem was the only way to handle a situation that wasn't to his liking.

"I know, but the production's being shut down over such small things," he shot back as if that was enough to justify his action. "I mean, it's sabotage and it's not Anna's fault, but Greene is acting like everything that's happened is because she's not capable of handling the production. You've met Anna—does she seem incapable of handling the job?"

"No, not at all," she murmured, but she wasn't a fair

judge of what made a good director. "But CJ, maybe you shouldn't have jumped into such deep waters before checking the depth. Taking on a movie production that could cost millions without even finding out if you could write a check that big? I… I mean, I can't even fathom doing something so rash."

"Good thing I can swim," he quipped darkly with a flicker of a smile, but Erica didn't think now was the time for flippant remarks.

The silence stretched, a taut string ready to snap. Erica breathed through her nose, forced calm into her lungs. *Okay, regroup. Take a minute to process before saying something you regret.* She reached out, fingers brushing his. An attempt to bridge the chasm yawning open in the room. There was no doubting his ambition, his drive. But at what cost?

"Let's just…sit on this for a night, okay? I ordered pizza, thought you might be hungry after jet-setting to Southern California and back in a day," she said, gesturing to the pie waiting for them.

A true smile replaced the tension in his jaw as he nodded, reaching for her. "I am hungry—for the pizza and for you," he said, pulling her to him. They hadn't exactly worked out what they were to each other yet, but Erica willingly went into his arms, sinking into the pleasure of his touch.

"Thanks for being there for me," he murmured, pressing a kiss against her forehead, the tension leaving his body. "Let's eat."

Erica didn't push back with her misgivings, choosing to let it go for now, but a part of her worried she was only kicking a can down the road. She would never bank her financial future on a decision made in the heat of the moment, but CJ just did.

CJ, as if moving on, gleefully grabbed a slice of pizza and bit into it with relish. "Oh yeah, that's good stuff. Good call, Erica. Good call."

She smiled and grabbed a slice, but her smile felt pasted on. Sometimes love felt like a leap into a void, and tonight, the ground beneath them seemed perilously thin.

By the time they were finished with the pizza and cleaned up, Erica felt CJ's hope that she might invite him to stay the night, but she couldn't bring herself to do it. She could only pretend for so long before she said what was bothering her, and that would probably ruin the night. Instead she kissed him soundly and sent him on his way with a promise to see him tomorrow.

CJ, obviously perplexed by her decision to send him back to his own room at the resort, left without pressing the issue, and Erica was grateful.

The door closed behind him with soft click, a quiet thunder in her chest. She stood alone, surrounded by the aftermath of their conversation, the pizza sitting heavily in her stomach.

A past lover had once accused her of being too rigid in her own ways, too set in her belief that her way was always the right way. Was she doing it again? Or was she right to question CJ's actions when a baby was in their future?

In bed, the sheets were cold, and it took a minute to warm up, reminding her that she'd practically kicked CJ out when he could've been there wrapping her in his warmth. The clock ticked away the seconds, each one a heartbeat of doubt. Erica turned onto her side, then her back, then her side again, a restless dance with the shadows. She hated not having the answers.

Was she being too rigid? It wasn't her decision to make about his finances, but they were a team, weren't they? A partnership meant diving together, not watching one plunge while the other stood safely on solid ground.

She could manage on her own; her independence was not a question. Yet the notion of CJ's recklessness, the ease with which he gambled their future on a roll of dice gnawed at her. Trust was a fragile thing, and tonight it felt as if he'd tossed it into the wind, leaving her to catch the pieces.

With a sigh, she punched the pillow, seeking comfort in its softness. Sleep would come eventually, but peace was another matter—a puzzle whose pieces didn't quite fit in the darkness of the room.

The following day, Erica rose and rushed to get to the resort, eager to cling to her routine. Sunlight filtered through the office blinds, casting long stripes across the floor as she shuffled papers on her desk with a mechanical rhythm, trying to immerse herself in the mundane tasks at hand. But the echoes of last night's conversation with CJ reverberated in her mind, each note of his voice a reminder of the rift growing between them that he had no clue was forming because she didn't speak up.

"Erica? You got a minute?" Josh's voice, usually the epitome of calm, held an edge that cut through her concentration.

"Sure," she responded, pushing aside her concerns as she rose from the chair. Her footsteps were silent against the carpet as she followed Josh into Laura's office.

Laura sat behind her desk, her athletic frame rigid, the tension in her posture telegraphing the seriousness of the moment. The usual warmth in her blue eyes was replaced by a stormier hue.

"Close the door, please," Laura said, her fingers drumming an anxious beat on the wooden surface.

Erica did as asked, the soft snick of the latch amplifying the knot in her stomach. Josh leaned against the wall, arms crossed, his expression grave. She took a seat, bracing herself for the impending disclosure.

"We just got word from the investigator," Josh began, his gaze fixed on Erica. "About the barn collapse."

"Okay…" Erica prompted, her heart picking up speed.

"Two support beams were tampered with," he continued, the words dropping like stones into the silence. "Deliberately weakened."

"Damn it," Erica breathed, wishing for different news. "Who would do such a thing?" she managed to ask.

"That's what we need to figure out," Laura said, worry etching lines around her eyes. "We can't let this get out. Not yet. We don't want to cause a panic."

"Of course," Erica agreed, feeling the weight of the secret settle on her shoulders. "Are you going to allow the production to continue on the property?"

"That's the question. I want to help, but it seems the production has a bigger problem than their location. Someone could've been seriously hurt," Laura said. "As it is, I hate that you were collateral damage in whatever beef this person has against the film crew or the production itself."

"I'm fine, Laura," she assured her boss, but this news

only deepened her concern that CJ had taken on more than he could chew.

However, given this new information, Erica felt it prudent to share her own concerns. "There's something else," Erica ventured, the image of Matthew's intense golden-brown eyes flashing before her. "Matthew has been asking questions. About the resort, the accident. It made me uneasy. I feel he deliberately waited until I was alone to ask me questions that he should've been asking you or Josh."

"Matthew?" Laura's tone sharpened with surprise. "Why would he—"

"Family drama." Josh's interruption was clipped. "You know how it is with the Bennetts. Always some undercurrents."

"Maybe I shouldn't have invited him to the wedding?" Laura's expression was troubled. "I just hadn't wanted to seem rude, but honestly, the whole situation with Glenna and Dad…and now Matthew…it's another thing that seems more like a burden than anything else."

"I mean, you had to invite Dad and Glenna. Like it or not, they're family, which means Glenna's nephew is family, too. Maybe his questions were just part of a curious mind and nothing more."

"Maybe," Laura agreed, but her frown remained. "Thanks for telling us. I'm sorry he made you uncomfortable. We'll talk to him about going to other people about resort issues."

"I don't want to create more drama, but it seemed prudent to share," Erica said. At Laura's nod, she felt okay to switch gears since she was there. "Everything is set for the bachelorette party. Willow is arriving tonight, and her room is ready. Was there anything else you needed me to put on my calendar for today?"

"No—you've been amazing, my rock, as always," Laura said, smiling with genuine appreciation. "Thank you, Erica."

Erica smiled and let herself out, leaving Laura and Josh to work out the problem with Matthew. Even though she should probably keep the information to herself, she felt compelled to share with CJ what the investigator had discovered, especially since he'd just agreed to take on the production.

It was one thing to suspect foul play, another entirely to confirm it with cut beams and obvious evil intent.

But was she betraying Laura and Josh's confidence by sharing that information? Was it her place?

"Can't keep secrets," she muttered to herself. The words came out gritty, like sand against her teeth. She knew what she had to do, no matter how much it twisted her insides. She reached for her phone, thumb hovering over CJ's contact.

Hey, she typed, then paused. Her thumb hesitated, then pressed with determination. We need to talk. It's urgent.

The message sent. There was no taking it back now. Erica sat there, her heart drumming a frantic beat, waiting for CJ's response.

This felt like a big move, a momentous decision to share information that wasn't exactly hers to share but could affect CJ's future.

And hers, by proxy.

She'd never been a rule-breaker by nature, and doing it now didn't give her a thrill. If anything, she felt sick to her stomach, but she couldn't in good conscience let CJ leverage everything he had on something that could end up costing him everything.

Maybe even his life.

Chapter 20

CJ knocked sharply on the door of Anna's bungalow, his thoughts churning from the news Erica had just shared with him in confidence.

Anna, looking better than the last time he'd seen her, was on her laptop when he entered. "We have to talk," he said, getting straight to the point. "I've got information that you're going to want to hear, and you'd better stay sitting down because it's a doozy."

"What's going on?" Anna asked.

"Someone's trying to tank the movie, Anna." CJ's words were like flint striking steel, ready to ignite. "And if that wasn't a big enough pile of bullshit to shovel, the fact that they nearly took out Erica makes me see red."

"What do you mean? How do you know this? I haven't heard from the loss and mitigation team doing the report."

"The Coltons ran a private investigation and found two support beams had been deliberately cut, which means none of the shit that's been happening has been accidental."

Anna's hand flew to her mouth, her breath hitching. "You're serious?"

"Deadly, but there's more." He recounted the confrontation at Harold Greene's office and how he'd thrown caution to the wind, vowing to keep the production afloat with his own funds when Greene refused to back down.

"Oh, CJ!" Anna gasped, her shock reverberating in the small room. "You did what?"

"Maybe I've lost it," CJ admitted, his hands flexing as if grasping for solutions that weren't there. "But I can't let it go under. Not now."

"God, CJ," she breathed, shaking her head. Her disbelief was a punch to the gut, but there was no turning back.

CJ searched Anna's gaze, needing pure honesty. "Tell me, do we pack it up? Or do you want to keep going? Because I'm in it for the long haul if you are."

"Are you sure?" Anna asked, uncertain. "We're talking a lot of money on the line. Can you...afford it?"

He chuckled ruefully, shaking his head. "I guess we'll find out. But I need to know this is what you want, too. This is your project Anna—I'm just trying to see it through."

Anna held his gaze, seeming to waver, but when determination replaced her anxiety, he knew they were going for it. "If you're in, I'm in. Thank you for believing in the project, CJ."

"Then it's settled." CJ nodded, the weight of his decision settling on his shoulders like a mantle. "But before we do anything, we find the bastard behind this. Let me take care of that part. You handle getting the crew back in working order. We're behind schedule, and we need to make up the deficit."

"Look at you—you're a natural producer," she teased with a smile as he let himself out.

Exiting the bungalow, CJ didn't pause as he dialed his accountant. The ring sounded like a countdown to a bomb going off.

"Hey, it's CJ. Look, I need to free up some capital. Put my Malibu place up as collateral."

"Are you insane?" The accountant's voice crackled through the phone, incredulous and sharp.

"Completely," CJ shot back, a wry grin tugging at his lips despite the gravity of the situation.

His accountant launched into a tirade of reasons why this was financially irresponsible, but CJ cut him off. "Just prep the paperwork. I'll be in touch."

Hey, it's only money, right?

Ending the call, CJ immediately dialed his attorney next, the numbers familiar under his touch.

"Draw up the contracts. I'm stepping in for Harold Greene for the Anna Wilson project."

"Christ, CJ, that'll ruffle feathers. What are you doing? This could be professional suicide. Think this through."

"Let 'em ruffle." CJ's response was curt, final. Greene wanted to see how far he'd go to see this project through? *Watch and learn, buddy.* CJ had stubbornness in spades.

He ended the call and stared out across the resort, the sprawling landscape a testament to grandeur and ambition. His heart raced, adrenaline and resolve fueling him. He'd made his play, laid his life's work on the line, and now he needed to talk to Erica.

CJ's stride was purposeful as he closed the distance between himself and Erica, who he found doing her usual rounds, being the busy bee that he'd come to recognize as part of her personality.

"Hey," he breathed out, his voice tinged with the remnants of chaos from the morning's revelations. "Thanks for digging into that barn mess. I appreciate you sharing the information. I needed to let Anna know. We've got to clean house before we move forward."

"CJ, about that… I'm happy to help however I can, but I have to tell you that I'm intensely uncomfortable with how recklessly you've jumped into this new role as producer. Do you even know the first thing about being a producer?"

"No, but I've always been more of a trial-by-fire kind of learner. I'll figure it out."

"Before you lose your damn shirt?" she countered with a touch of exasperation.

CJ shifted, pushing his hand through his hair, irritated that Erica was being a giant wet blanket when he needed her support. "It'll be fine. The movie's half-shot anyway. All I'm doing is ensuring it gets finished. Besides, once I find out who the clown is that's been sabotaging the production, it'll be smooth sailing."

"Has any movie in the history of moviemaking ever been 'smooth sailing,' as you put it? C'mon, CJ, I feel you need to take a step back and think this through."

CJ stiffened. "I thought you'd be more supportive. I'm doing what's right, not just what's right for me."

She recoiled slightly, words catching in her throat. "I am supporting you," she said, softer now. "But I'm also worried. You're playing a dangerous game with…well, a future that includes more than just you."

That last part jabbed him hard. Was she implying that he wouldn't be a good dad because of this? He needed space before he said something he regretted.

"Got it. Thanks." His response came out sharper than he'd intended. When she blinked at his tone, he tried to soften his delivery with a noncommittal, "Let's talk later? Dinner?"

"Sure," she agreed, but her smile didn't quite reach her eyes. He turned on his heel, leaving her standing there with her concerns hanging like a heavy curtain between them.

He couldn't think about that right now. He had a long list of people to interview if he was going to figure out who was responsible for the sabotage.

The day aged, the sun climbing to its peak and then bowing gracefully toward the horizon as CJ sat across from crew member after crew member with each team lead. Questions fired, answers dissected. Then he met a production assistant—a guy with shifty eyes and a story that didn't add up.

"Name?" CJ demanded, not bothering with pleasantries.

"Rick Dennies," the PA mumbled, shifting uncomfortably under the scrutiny.

The production manager checked his roster, frowning. "Who brought you on, Rick?" he asked. "I don't see you on my list of new hires."

"Can't say. Hired over the phone." Rick's gaze darted away, then back again, a flicker of guilt passing through his expression.

"Cut the crap," CJ insisted. "How the hell did you end up on this production?"

"I..." he stuttered, clearly no criminal mastermind as he blanked on a convincing lie before admitting, "I mean, I got hired over the phone and was told when to show up. My credentials showed up in the mail with a wad of cash."

The production manager balked. "Are you kidding me? That's not how we hire people. What the hell?"

CJ knew he was looking at the problem. "Ever work on a movie set before?"

"No, but I got skills—handyman stuff."

"Skill enough to cut a wire, but not enough to know that you're cutting through a support beam, I'm guessing."

Rick started to deny the implication, but he wasn't smart enough to come up with anything that quick. A look of defiance hardened his features as he shrugged as if he didn't care if he was caught or not. "Whatever."

"Yeah, whatever. You could've killed a woman when your stupid stunt nearly brought the barn down on her head."

At that, Rick shifted his gaze. "Look, I needed the work, and this seemed easy enough. Besides, y'all got enough money to spare with all your rich cars and houses. No one needs your Hollywood bullshit anyway. But no one was supposed to get hurt. I was just supposed to mess things up a bit."

"Yeah, well, you nearly got someone killed." CJ glared, barely able to throttle down the white-hot rage that burned up his throat. "And you burnt down an entire set."

"Didn't mean for any harm," Rick stammered, hands fumbling. "Just some trouble is all. Got paid cash to stir things up."

"By who?" The question hung heavy, loaded with the threat of unspoken consequences. Both the production manager and CJ pressed for details, but Rick wasn't exactly a fount of information.

"Like I said, never saw a face. Just instructions, cash and when to show up for work. Once I was on set, no one asked me any questions. It was easy to go unnoticed."

"Jesus." CJ scrubbed his face with both hands, feeling the edges of control fray. "Remind me to beef up security. I want everyone to get new ID badges and lock this set down. No one is present unless they've been cleared to be there."

The production manager nodded, grabbing Rick. "You're coming with me until the police can come and get you."

Rick jerked his arm out of the production manager's grip, but when CJ jumped up with a snarl, just begging him for a reason, Rick wisely backed down and agreed to go quietly.

But CJ's adrenaline was pumping through his veins, needing an outlet. They might've found the gun but not the person behind the trigger. Who the hell was going to such lengths to sabotage the film? Was it Harold Greene?

As much as he wanted to pin this on Harold, it didn't seem his style.

But if not him, who?

Was he supposed to wear the hat of actor, producer and now detective?

So be it.

He wasn't stopping until he had answers, a finished film and the satisfaction of knowing he hadn't quit—for any reason.

As the sun dipped below the horizon, casting a fiery glow upon the resort, Erica's phone buzzed against the smooth marble countertop. She snatched it up, heart lurching before she registered CJ's name on the screen. A breath she hadn't realized she'd been holding escaped in a rush when his message popped up, a simple: Can't make dinner. Rain check?

Oh, thank God. She was a coward to avoid the conversation they needed to have, but a complex knot of frustration and relief tightened in her chest.

CJ's reckless decision to fund a sinking ship of a production gave her stomach a queasy feeling that had nothing to do with the tiny fluttering human growing there.

"None of my business," she muttered to herself, even as the murmur felt like a lie. The truth was that everything CJ did was her business now, whether she liked it or not. But dwelling on it wouldn't solve anything. Instead she craved the comfort of logistics and lists—things she could manage, things she could control.

"Erica! Look who's here!" Laura's voice, vibrant and clear, cut through Erica's brooding.

Willow burst into the lobby, her arrival a spectacle of energy that seemed to make the air buzz. Laura enveloped her friend in a boisterous embrace that made Willow's luggage topple forgotten to the side. Their laughter echoed, bouncing off the walls and filling the space with warmth.

"Finally, the party can start!" Willow declared, grinning from ear to ear.

"Wouldn't dream of starting without you," Laura shot back, her blue eyes twinkling. "Oh my God, please tell me you are ready for an epic night of catching up because you are not sleeping a wink until I've completely caught you up to the events in my life."

"Babe, it's what I live for. Let's do this. I'm yours for approximately two weeks and then I have to regretfully return to my life, but until then…let's pretend we're back in college and have the metabolisms of our college selves."

"Deal." Laura and Willow hooked pinky fingers in a secret handshake that looked like something teenagers would do and then pealed into laugher at their shared inside joke.

The sight of them, so carefree and excited, acted like a balm to Erica's frayed nerves. For a moment she allowed herself to bask in their joy, letting the tension seep out of her shoulders. The bachelorette-party preparations—a tangled web of decorations and schedules—flashed through her mind. It was just the kind of distraction she needed, a project to immerse herself in fully.

"All right, you two, let's get you settled in," Erica chimed in, stepping forward to help Willow with her bags. "We've got a bachelorette party to throw and only forty-eight hours to do it."

"Lead the way, party queen," Willow teased, looping her arm through Laura's as they headed toward the accommodations.

"Trust me," Laura replied, beaming at Erica, "we're in good hands with Erica in charge."

She smiled with appreciation for the sweet vote of confidence and made for the party zone, her steps quick and purposeful. The balloon arch mocked her with its limpness, half-inflated balloons sagging like the worries she tried to keep at bay.

She snapped instructions at the decorators, her hands deftly twisting a stray balloon into place. With each pump of the helium tank, her confidence swelled. This was her realm, the orderly world where shades of pink and gold obeyed her command.

"Make sure those balloons are smiling by the time guests arrive," Erica directed, her tone leaving no room for anything less than perfection. The party coordinator, a clipboard clutched in her arms, scurried over to Erica, rattling off updates.

"Got it. Check on the cake...chocolate, not vanilla. Confirm the caterer's menu...no shellfish—Laura's allergic. And the punch...make sure they are clearly marked *alcoholic* and *nonalcoholic*." Erica recited the list as if it were the litany that kept chaos at bay. "This bachelorette bash must go down without a hitch. Laura deserves the best."

"Absolutely," the coordinator affirmed, her pen flying across the checklist with each of Erica's crisp confirmations.

Satisfied, Erica surveyed the space, noting the twinkle lights woven through the trellises that promised an evening of enchantment. It was all coming together—every detail crafted with care, every corner curated for celebration. This was control, something painfully absent when it came to CJ and how he handled his life. Here she could shape the outcome, mold it with her own two hands.

"Thank you," she said, offering a rare smile to the team. "You're making magic happen."

Flushed with the success of a plan in motion, Erica gathered her things, ready to call it a night. As she strode toward the exit, a hushed urgency from a nearby hallway tugged at her attention. She slowed her pace, ears straining to catch the fragmented whispers that bounced off the walls.

"The merger with Sharpe Enterprises—not likely," a male voice grumbled, the words sharp and clipped with tension.

Erica leaned against the wall, frowning at the unknown voice. "It's a bad investment...murder and accidents...insurance nightmare," another muttered, the weight of concern heavy in his tone.

Erica's pulse hammered a frantic rhythm in against her wrist. Whoever it was must've been talking about Allison's murder, for sure. She didn't know anything about a merger, though. She melted into the shadows, hoping to catch another fragment but whoever had been talking was gone.

A merger? Erica knew a little bit about the Colton family issues—a tangled mess that had started with Laura and Josh's father, Clive, and involved a lot of money disagreements—but Erica made it a point to stay out of that side of the Colton business.

However, that phone call...didn't sound good. Not only were they referencing Allison's murder but the more recent accidents on the set, which made Erica wonder if someone was capitalizing on the resort's bad luck or creating bad luck for their own purpose.

She checked her watch. Laura was likely already gone with Willow to party like they were back in college, and she hated to ruin the night with something like this. Perhaps it could wait until after the bachelorette party.

Yes, she decided, settling her nerves, whatever that was...could wait. It wasn't as if she had much more than a snippet of conversation to share, which honestly could end up being nothing.

Which was an excellent reason why eavesdropping was a bad idea, and she didn't know what was wrong with her.

This situation with CJ had her running backward for the first time in her life, and she didn't like it.

Not one bit.

Chapter 21

CJ leaned against the sun-warmed terra-cotta railing that bordered Mariposa's main courtyard, his gaze tracking the flurry of crew members dismantling the final shot of the day.

The golden hour light dripped over the scene like warm honey, casting long shadows that swayed in rhythm with the palm fronds above. He exhaled a sigh of relief, his chest unclenching for what felt like the first time in weeks. With the bad apple in custody, the air seemed lighter, almost effervescent with newfound optimism.

And it felt good.

"Cut! That's a wrap!" he heard the director call out, the words sounding in his heart like a victory chant.

"Finally," CJ murmured to himself, a smile tugging at the corners of his mouth. Hard to remember when his biggest challenge had been learning his lines. Now he had an entire production on his shoulders, on top of his usual performance.

He pushed off the railing and walked toward the resort's main building, where Erica would be immersed in her own brand of chaos. As he navigated through the labyrinth of hibiscus bushes and trickling fountains, he rehearsed the lines in his head, planning to dissolve any lingering doubts she harbored about his new role as producer now that he felt more secure in the production.

"Erica, hey," he called out, entering the whirlwind of the impending party that looked lavish enough to host a celebrity.

She was a vision of efficiency, her fingers flying over a tablet screen while simultaneously barking orders to the staff swirling around her. Her focus was laser sharp, not a single detail slipping past her vigilant eyes. Erica was a marvel to watch in action. He ought to pick her brain about how to make his production more efficient, he thought with a private chuckle.

"Can it wait, CJ?" Erica didn't look up, her voice clipped with the stress of imminent celebration.

"Actually, I just wanted to—"

"Listen, I'm drowning in party prep here," she interrupted, finally glancing up, her eyes reflecting the storm of responsibility on her shoulders. "There's a mountain of things to sort, and I've got half an hour to move Everest."

"Sure, sure," CJ conceded, taking in her frazzled state. He knew better than to add to her burden. "Just wanted to let you know today on set went smooth. Like, baby-bottom smooth. Not a single mishap."

"Thank heavens for small miracles," she sighed, a ghost of a smile flickering across her face.

"I think I make a pretty good detective, actually," he teased, coaxing a small smile from Erica before she returned to her tablet.

"Hey, want to be my plus-one tonight?" Erica asked,

not looking up from her device. "It's a bachelorette party, but it's co-ed."

"Me? Hanging with my baby mama at Arizona's hottest party?" He raised an eyebrow, his mouth curving into an unexpected grin. "Wouldn't miss it for the world."

But Erica blanched and immediately shushed him with a panicked look. "*Ixnay* on the *abybay* stuff," she said, dropping adorably into Pig Latin, which oddly delighted him.

"You never cease to amaze me, Erica Pike," he murmured, reaching out to snatch her close, ignoring her protest and enjoying the immediate blush in her cheeks. "I don't care who knows that you're carrying my *abybay*. I'll shout it to the world if you give me half the chance."

She melted against him. "That's not fair," she said breathlessly as his mouth hovered dangerously close to hers. "The hormones are playing Ping-Pong with my brain."

"Good," he returned with a silky chuckle. "Just the way I like you," he said before sealing his mouth to hers. He reluctantly released her, loving the way she softened against him like her bones suddenly evaporated. "See you tonight, boss lady," CJ said with a grin, leaving her to her business.

But even as he walked to his room, each step took him further away from that happy place he'd been basking in. Was Erica working too hard? Should pregnant women be pushing themselves with such a punishing schedule? Or was he worrying about nothing and creating one more thing for them to argue about?

Frowning, he muttered to himself. "I need to trust her." If Erica needed a break, she'd take one. She wouldn't do anything to hurt the baby. Besides, it wasn't his place to dictate how she ran her life, even if she was carrying his precious cargo.

A baby. His baby. A whole body shiver followed the thought. *Wild how things turn out…*

After showering and changing, CJ returned to the section of the resort cordoned off for the private party and whistled low and appreciatively at the stunning view. The sun dipped lower, splashing the sky with hues of tangerine and lavender, shadows lengthening across the manicured grass. The guests began to arrive, their laughter and chatter mingling with the soft strains of music floating on the breeze. Laura Colton emerged from her private bungalow, radiant in an off-white summer dress that swayed with her every step.

But it was Erica who stole his breath.

Her elegant frame was sheathed in a pale lavender dress that dusted her knees and hung on her shoulders with thin spaghetti straps. Her beautiful dark hair tumbled down her back in loose waves that made him want to bury his nose in the thick mass of it. His mouth hungered for the taste of her lips and his fingers itched to palm her belly and hold her close.

Erica saw him and quickly joined him with a radiant smile. "What do you think?"

"I think it might be rude to outshine the bride-to-be at her own party," he said, bending down to brush a soft kiss across her lips. "But you're a vision."

"Oh gosh," Erica gasped softly, blushing beneath the compliment, but she recovered with an appreciative "You look pretty good yourself," as she smoothed his silk tie.

"Well, I will say this—if you ever leave Mariposa, you

have a career in celebrity parties. This is better than any Hollywood party I've ever been to."

Erica grinned. "I actually do enjoy party planning. It's stressful but relaxing at the same time. I don't know…it's hard to explain, but I really enjoy this part."

The party, much like the woman it celebrated, seemed to shimmer with an effortless charm. Within an hour the party was in full swing, everyone laughing and having a great time.

But just when the caterers brought out a huge cake, a ripple went through the crowd, a discordant murmur that CJ felt somehow in his bones.

The atmosphere had shifted—subtly at first, like the soft encroachment of a shadow before darkness falls. CJ's senses pricked as laughter soured into confusion, the clinks of glasses halting mid-toast. The first guest staggered, hand clutching their stomach as if an invisible fist had landed and then another. More people started to moan and look sickly, clinging to tables and chairs, some barfing their guts out.

What was happening?

"Erica?" CJ called out, scanning the crowd for her familiar form. His voice cut through the growing murmur, sharp with concern.

She was doubled over, one hand pressed to her stomach, the other supporting herself against a table. Her face was ghostly pale, a stark contrast to the vibrant colors of the party around her. CJ's heart plummeted, dread coiling in his gut as he rushed to her side, sidestepping a man who crumpled to the grass like a puppet with its strings cut.

"What's wrong?" he asked, the urgency of the situation

dawning. There were too many people sick at once for this to be an accident.

"Someone call an ambulance!" The command was torn from his throat as he reached Erica, his hands hovering, afraid that touching her might somehow make it worse.

"Oh my God, the baby," she gasped out, eyes wide and brimming with shared fear.

"It's going to be okay, Erica," he promised, but a thin sheen of sweat had popped along his forehead at the realization that someone had poisoned either the food or the punch, something that could reach the most amount of people at this party.

And Erica had ingested something contaminated...

Around them, the party descended into chaos. Bodies slumped onto tables or lay writhing on the ground, the sound of coughing and retching punctuating the air. Staff scrambled to help, their faces masks of terror and uncertainty.

"Help's on the way," someone shouted, a disembodied voice amid the cacophony as he held Erica, refusing to let her go until a medical professional wrenched her from his hands.

Sirens wailed in the distance, the sound slicing through the pandemonium.

The paramedics arrived, a flurry of motion and urgency. Erica was lifted onto a stretcher, her form small and vulnerable beneath the stark lights. CJ followed, feet numb, every step an echo of the fear pounding through him.

"Will she be okay? She's pregnant," he said, his voice a stranger's in his ears—strained, raw.

"Sir, we'll do everything we can," a paramedic answered, not unkind but distant, focused.

The ambulance doors closed behind Erica with a thud that resounded like a verdict. CJ watched as the vehicle lurched into motion and Erica was trundled off to the hospital for the second time since knowing her. If the situation were different, it might even be funny, but there was nothing to laugh about right now.

His mind raced, images of the day's successful shoot dissolving into the horror of the present. Was it connected? Another sabotage attempt? His jaw clenched at the thought, anger and worry a tangled knot in his chest.

Laura's friend Willow was one of the people who was also transported, along with a handful of other guests, but Laura found CJ with an offer to ride with her to the hospital.

At the hospital, their party overwhelmed the emergency room as the staff put a rush on the toxicology report, and it wasn't long before doctors discovered the culprit: ipecac syrup.

Both CJ and Laura breathed a sigh of relief as the attending doctor took a minute to explain.

"In most cases, not lethal, but definitely enough to make people very sick. Most of the patients in your party will be released as soon as they finish a round of electrolytes, but we'd like to keep Miss Pike a little longer to make sure nothing affected her pregnancy."

Laura nodded vigorously. "Yes, of course. Thank you, Doctor." She waited a beat for the doctor to go on his way before turning to CJ, tears brimming in her eyes. "I don't understand why this is happening. First the barn and now this? Why?"

Maybe it was a rhetorical question and her last nerve had just frayed beneath the strain, but CJ felt compelled to share what he knew so far. "I don't know if this is related to the stuff happening on the set, but we caught the person who sabotaged the barn and he's currently still in custody. I'm sorry about your party. It was truly beautiful before all the throwing up started."

Laura stared for a minute before a bubble of near hysterical laughter follow. "It was, wasn't it? Oh God, I don't know if this is a sign or—"

She was cut off by the sound of the man Erica had previously whispered into his ear was Laura's fiancé, and Laura sank into his arms, openly sobbing as he held her, crooning softly.

The man took a minute to calm his bride and then briefly introduced himself to CJ. "Noah Steele. Can someone tell me what the hell is going on?"

Laura hiccuped and wiped at her eyes, offering a watery introduction. "Noah, this is CJ Knight, Erica's...uh, friend. I don't know what you guys are—I'm sorry. My brain isn't working right now," she said, apologizing. "He's here for Erica."

CJ shook Noah's hand. "The doc said someone dosed something with ipecac syrup. My money's on the punch. I doubt anyone would've noticed, and judging by how many people were sick, it was the easiest way to get to as many people as possible."

"Sounds about right." To his lady, Noah said, "I'm going to have everything bagged and tagged and have it tested. Are you okay?"

Laura nodded, her lip trembling. "I never drank any of

the punch. I was still nursing a hangover from last night with Willow, and my stomach wasn't up to anything that sugary. I was sticking to water until it was time to do the champagne toast."

"That decision may have saved your guts," CJ quipped. "Some of your guests got hit harder than others. You're going to need to call in a professional cleaning team to get the smell out of your courtyard."

Laura's gaze flew to Noah. "This is the worst timing, and I'm not talking about my bachelorette party."

"I know, honey. We'll talk about it later. Let's get you home," he said, wrapping an arm protectively around Laura, but she stopped, putting her keys in CJ's hands with a simple "I trust you" before leaving with her fiancé.

CJ found Erica lying in an emergency room bed in a plain cotton gown, hooked to an IV just as a nurse was running a Doppler over her stomach. The quick flutter of a fast heartbeat filled the room.

"All good in there," the nurse announced with a smile. "Mama might feel like dog dirt, but baby is snug and safe and none the wiser for your little adventure."

Erica gave a wan but relieved smile. "Thank God."

The nurse looked to CJ in question. "Are you Daddy?"

"Yes," he answered, going to hold Erica's hand. "Everything... Nothing's wrong with the baby after all that?"

"Nope. Babies are surprisingly resilient. Mama just needs a little rest and some extra fluids. Then the doctor will probably release you."

The nurse rolled up her Doppler unit and stuck it into her pocket before leaving them alone, pulling the curtain for privacy.

"Hey," Erica murmured, voice hoarse but fierce. "Is everyone okay?"

Still thinking of others even when she's laid up worse than the rest. God, he loved this woman. He smoothed her hair. "Everyone is fine. Toxicology came back as ipecac syrup. Nonlethal, but definitely going to make you miserable."

Erica frowned. "Ipecac? Why? I can't understand why anyone would do that."

"I don't know, but her fiancé—I'm taking it he's a cop or something? He's going to collect everything and have it tested, though he's pretty sure it was in the punch."

Erica blanched in distress. "I thought it tasted funny, but I figured it was just my taste buds being weird because of the baby. I didn't even think to have it thrown out and made fresh. Damn it," she muttered, looking frustrated with herself.

"Hey, don't you do dare do that. This is not your fault, and I won't let you take that on," he said firmly. "Someone was a royal dick and poisoned an entire party. You can't plan for that kind of contingency."

Erica blinked back the shine in her eyes, nodding. "You're right. I just feel bad for Laura."

"Yeah, me, too, but she seems like she can rally and she's got a good support system. Honestly, I'm more worried about you. This is the second time you've landed in the hospital and I'm afraid what a third might look like."

"Fair point. My insurance hasn't even crunched the numbers on the first visit yet," she tossed out with a dry chuckle. Her smile faded rapidly as she continued, "I'm not one to believe in omens or anything, but since Allison... Well, Mariposa just hasn't felt right. It's like there's this dark fog hanging over the resort. I can't shake off this nagging thought…could it somehow be connected?"

CJ didn't believe in ghosts, but he knew bad energy existed. However, he had a feeling whatever was happening had less to do with the supernatural and more to do with someone working on their own agenda.

The question was…who was it and what did they want?

Chapter 22

The sterile scent of the hospital still clung to Erica's skin as she shuffled through the sliding doors, her arm looped gently through CJ's. He'd insisted on driving her home in Laura's car, a sturdy SUV that smelled faintly of citrus and expensive perfume.

"Home sweet home," CJ announced with a forced cheerfulness as he guided her inside her quiet house.

"I can take it from here," Erica murmured, but CJ's expression left no room for argument.

"Like hell you can. I'm not leaving you alone. Doc said to rest, and I'm here to enforce it."

"Are you sure?" Erica asked. "I feel the bulk of our relationship has been punctuated by you having to take care of me, and honestly, I don't know how I feel about that. I'm not used to being the one needing care. I've always been self-sufficient and independent. This whole 'damsel in distress' gig is outside of my comfort zone, and I don't know how to act."

That was probably the most honest statement she'd made to CJ about herself, and it made her feel vulnerable but it was par for the course. Nothing between them had been typical for her relationships, and maybe that was why he made her feel things she'd never felt before.

Still, all that raw emotion was hard to manage when you were used to compartmentalizing everything into neat, tidy boxes.

CJ's gaze softened with understanding as he gently knuckled her cheek. "I like that you give me the opportunity to take care of you. I've never been the one who was riding in on a white horse to save the day, but I like when it's you I'm saving."

Erica's heart swelled with absolute love for this man even though she couldn't quite explain how she'd fallen so quickly and so hard. Maybe it had something to do with the tiny human growing inside her, but she wanted to fall asleep in CJ's arms and wake up every morning seeing his sleepy face. But how would that work given their completely different lifestyles?

Tonight was not the night to solve that dilemma. She sank into his arms, loving how safe and secure she felt within the cove of his embrace and simply enjoyed the pleasure of his touch.

"I'm tired," she admitted against his chest.

"Then it's time to tuck you into bed," CJ decided, grasping her hand and walking toward her bedroom. She flicked her bedside lamp, bathing the room in a soft glow as she undressed and slid into the sheets, thankful to be home.

Within moments, CJ had stripped and joined her.

Erica had never felt comfortable inviting men over to stay at her place. She'd had her share of noncommittal hookups, but she'd never invited them to sleep over and cuddle.

If anything, the idea of seeing them again in the morning had made her want to run away.

Except with CJ, she wanted him to stay. She felt safe with him, but there was so much they still needed to figure out.

"You have the loudest silence," he murmured, as if feeling the questions in her head roll off her skin and bounce off his forehead as he held her. "What are you thinking?"

She sighed. "Too many browsers to share right now. All I do know is that right here, right now, I feel safe and content, and that's enough."

CJ's arms tightened around her. "Good."

The twilight hours passed in a blur of soft pillows and even softer silences, their bodies entwined in the sanctuary of Erica's bed.

"When I thought I might lose you…and the baby…" The words cracked, heavy with unspoken fears. "I couldn't think straight. It scared me."

She turned to face him, the moonlight casting a silver glow across his features. "Everything turned out okay," she said, aiming for reassurance, but her voice wavered, betraying her. She'd been scared, too.

"This time. But look at what just happened. Poisoned, for Christ's sake." CJ propped himself up on one elbow, his gaze searching hers. "I mean, this is like something out of a movie—which feels totally weird for someone like me to say, but it's true. I've never known an actual person who's been poisoned before because it just doesn't happen."

"Yeah, tell me about it," she agreed, the admission tasting bitter on her tongue. It should've been a sick joke, but reality bore down on her with all its weight. Who would do such a thing? "I still can't wrap my head around it. I don't know who would want to hurt the Coltons. As far as I know, the community loves the family and the resort. I mean, the family always pours so much into the community, and they take pride in offering something of value to the area. It doesn't make sense to me why anyone would target them."

"Do you think someone was targeting Laura specifically?" CJ asked.

Erica frowned, perplexed. "I can't imagine why or who would do that. Laura is an absolute sweetheart, and I'm not just saying that because she's my boss. She's genuinely nice."

CJ wondered out loud, "If it's not targeted toward the family, maybe it was connected to the movie? I mean, it feels like a stretch, but I've never been on a movie like this where everything that can and will go wrong has, only to find out that someone was actively sabotaging the production."

"Yeah, but didn't you say the guy responsible for all the mishaps was in custody?" Erica asked.

"Yes, but we still don't know who hired him to do all that crap. We found the gun, not the person behind the trigger, and that's what worries me."

"It seems unlikely the two events are connected, though," Erica said. "I mean, the first incident happened out in the desert, not at the resort."

"That's what keeps tripping me up, too," he admitted, releasing a long sigh. "Hell, one thing this situation has shown me is that I wasn't cut out to be a detective."

"I don't know…you've done pretty well so far," she said with admiration in her tone.

He chuckled. "Well, I'll be happy to return to what I'm really good at. Although I'm not going to lie, I actually enjoy the producing gig. The level of control is something I've never had in a production, and it's been refreshing."

"Do you think you might want to do more producing?"

"I don't know—maybe. We'll see when this production finally wraps without a body count."

She smiled, enjoying the quiet conversation that finally felt real between them. Maybe there was a future together if they could hold on to this moment and turn it into something worth keeping.

The staccato clap of the slateboard pierced the air, and CJ nodded to the director. "Action!" Anna shouted, setting the scene in motion. It felt good to return to his character without the burden of worrying about the lights getting shut off because some corporate dickhead wanted to play games.

Everything was going smoothly, all scenes working as they should, and it looked as if they might be able to break for lunch early if they kept this pace, but just as they were knee-deep in the next scene, Anna's voice cut through the action like a hot knife through butter. CJ looked up in surprise only to see Harold Greene standing beside Anna, her expression pensive.

CJ's hand curled into a tight fist at his side, a visceral reminder that this intrusion was unwelcome as Anna waved him over.

"CJ, Mr. Greene would like to have a quick word with you," Anna said, civil but annoyed at the disruption when they'd been doing so well. CJ didn't blame her, and seeing as he was the one paying the bill, he wasn't interested in interrupting their flow.

"Harold," CJ greeted coolly, his voice betraying none of the irritation that buzzed under his skin like a live wire.

"Let's talk." Harold's tone brooked no argument, yet CJ stood his ground.

"Sorry—we're on a tight schedule and can't break just yet. I'll catch up with you during lunch." CJ turned his back on Harold, signaling the end of their exchange—for now.

As the crew resumed their orchestrated dance around the set, CJ's thoughts churned with wary curiosity. What the hell was Greene doing here?

Lunchtime descended upon the set like a curtain call, and CJ found himself face-to-face with Harold once more, the midday sun casting sharp shadows on the ground between them. He folded his arms across his chest, an unspoken barrier erected against whatever onslaught Harold had planned.

"Look, CJ," Harold began, leaning forward as if to press his words physically onto CJ. "You've made your point. I get it. You want to be taken seriously and this project seems like the perfect vehicle to make that happen, but you're in over your head. Get out before the legal sharks come circling. It's not just about signing checks. The studio will bury this production so deep, it'll never have a chance at picking up a distributor if you hold this line."

"And why would they do that, Harold?" CJ countered with a calm he didn't feel. "Unless you made it that way? Which would fly in the face of your claims that this wasn't personal, it was business."

"And I stand by that—there's nothing personal about

my decision to cut the funding. This set was a liability, and someone was going to get hurt. Sometimes you have to cut your losses. If you're truly serious about wanting to produce, you'll learn that."

CJ's jaw tightened, his resolve hardening like concrete. "You're wrong."

"Wrong about what?"

"This production. You're so hung up on the numbers you haven't taken the time to think about why this film needs to be made. It tells a story that hasn't been told yet, and if you don't have the balls to see it made, I will. Pretty simple."

"Is it worth losing everything?" Harold's challenge hung in the air, weighted with threat and condescension. "Because that's where you're headed. You think you're being all noble, but your cause is flimsy. Look, there will be other movies, better movies than this one, but if you burn your bridges, that ain't gonna happen. You hear me?"

Harold's eyes narrowed, but CJ didn't flinch. This was a battle of wills, and CJ was not about to surrender the field. He couldn't explain it—he couldn't back down. He knew what was at stake, but he couldn't let it go.

CJ tilted his head, scrutinizing Harold's rigid stance, the man's fingers drumming an impatient tattoo on the aluminum table. The tension in those digits fascinated CJ, a silent metronome to their standoff.

"Here's some news for you," CJ said, his words slicing through the hum of lunchtime banter and clinking utensils. "We caught the jerk creating all the problems on set—and since he's been gone, it's been smooth sailing."

Harold's rhythm faltered, his forehead crinkling. "What are you talking about?"

"Someone's been causing trouble on set. Deliberately," CJ clarified, the corners of his mouth lifting just so, savoring the flicker of bewilderment that danced across Harold's face. "And guess what? They were paid for it. The bigger question is who paid him? But I don't have to figure that out. I'm sure the detective on the case will dig into the *why*s and *how*s."

"Paid?" Harold echoed, his voice hollow, disbelief etching lines around his eyes deep as canyons. "I had no idea…"

Something about that raw surprise gnawed at CJ's certainty, like a gust of wind threatening to snuff out a flame. A part of him didn't want to believe Harold was involved, but then another part had questioned simply because he'd been so quick to shut the production down, almost as if he'd planned it that way.

But Harold's genuine shock was something of a surprise and he looked concerned about the information. "You're sure?"

"Without a doubt. The guy confessed—down to the dollar amount he was paid in cash to make trouble. You didn't know anything about that, right?"

Harold scowled. "That's a stupid question—of course not. I'm not a criminal, and I don't hire criminals to do my dirty work."

CJ sensed truth in that statement. Harold Greene was known as a hard-ass but never a shady guy, which was why he'd been surprised at how seemingly eager Harold had been to shut down the production for petty reasons.

Maybe Harold was just a tight-fisted investor and not a villain, which made him wonder all over again who might have cause to get their hands dirty on this. "Do you know anyone who might gain from the production getting shut down?"

"Not off-hand, but you can bet your ass I'm going to find out," Harold said, and CJ believed him. "Look, when I say it isn't personal, I mean it. But I may have pulled the trigger too fast, and I'm willing to concede that point."

"Thanks," CJ said grudgingly accepting Harold's version of an apology, but he didn't want to relinquish his producer spot now that he'd experienced how it felt to have some control of a project he believed in. "I appreciate that."

"With that said, listen when I say you don't want to tangle with the suits over this project. However, before you get that look in your eye, let me talk to the studio and see what we can do together, okay? I like that you've got balls, even if you're willing to put them in a vise just to make a point."

"What are you proposing?"

"I can bring you on as an official producer—not the executive producer, though. But you'll still have a seat at the table when major decisions are being made without having to throw your career and livelihood in the chipper to see it done. Sound fair?"

It did sound fair, but was he ready to give up the seat at the head of the table? Was his ego driving the train, or was he leveling up in his career?

With a baby on the way, he needed to figure it out before he made a decision that affected his future family in a bad way.

Chapter 23

Erica's fingers danced across the keyboard with a vigor that had been absent for far too long. The soft clack of keys was a welcome sound after days of rest at home, punctuated only by the occasional concerned call from friends and colleagues.

The only saving grace had been CJ's solid form curled against her every night. She felt safe with him beside her and enjoyed some of the best sleep of her life, which was interesting, considering she'd never been much of a cuddler.

However, happy to be back to her routine, even if everyone had balked at her announcement that she was returning only a few days after being poisoned. They meant well, but the walls closed in on her if she stayed still for too long. She needed the resort's pulse, the hum of activity to ground her—to remind her life was moving forward.

Besides, when it was quiet the questions that didn't have answers started to crowd her brain and panic followed.

"Erica." Laura's voice sliced through the rhythm, carrying a note of reproach. "I really wish you would've taken at least a week off."

Shaking her head, Erica swiveled in her chair to face Laura. "Rest is a cage," she declared, the intensity of her gaze saying more than words could. "I need to work, need to feel useful."

Laura sighed, the lines of worry that were etched around her eyes deepening. But Erica wouldn't be argued with when her mind was made up.

"Fine," Laura conceded, "but you're taking a lunch break. Dani's in town. You haven't seen her since she arrived, have you?"

"No, not yet. How's she doing?"

"Great! Of course, she missed all of the excitement—and by *excitement* I mean when someone tried to kill everyone at my bachelorette party."

"To be fair, the doc said ipecac syrup isn't lethal," Erica countered trying to lighten the reality. "Do you have any disgruntled boyfriends we should know about?"

Laura barked a short laugh, shaking her head. "Not that I'm aware of, but who knows?" She motioned for Erica to finish up. "Let's go. I'm starving and teetering on the edge of a low blood sugar attack where I turn into an entirely different person."

While she didn't want to break her pace, the thought of fresh air and friendly faces was appealing. "Well, we can't have that," Erica replied with a fake shudder, already saving her document and logging off her computer. "I'm ready when you are."

The bistro was a riot of smells and sounds, a kaleidoscope of life buzzing around them as they sat at a wrought-iron table under the shade of a sprawling elm. Dani's laughter, light and carefree, wove through the conversation like a bright ribbon.

"Glenna's coming to the wedding, then?" Erica asked,

spearing a cherry tomato with her fork. It burst with flavor as she popped it into her mouth. "That's unfortunate."

"Tell me about it," Laura grimaced, swirling her iced tea with a straw. "But Clive would throw a fit if we didn't invite her."

The fact that Laura called her father by his given name spoke volumes about how she felt about him, but she still felt obligated to observe certain social expectations. If it were Erica, she'd tell the old fart to pound sand. Clive Colton wasn't exactly vying for humanitarian of the year, and Erica was glad none of his kids seemed to inherit his personality deficits.

"Have you ever considered doing a DNA test to make sure you're even related?" Erica said, half-joking. "Your mother must've been a saint to put up with him."

"Trust me, the thought has occurred to me." Laura sighed. "But yeah, my mom, may she rest in peace, had to have been serving some kind of spiritual penance to put up with that man." She shared a short look with Dani, even though they had different mothers. "Clive has a knack for tricking people into believing he's a decent human being."

"So what happened with Glenna?" Dani quipped. "She's not exactly Mother Teresa."

"That's karma in action, I think," Laura answered with a small laugh. "Either way, they're peas in a pod, and I hope they live a long and unhappy life together."

"Laura, that's not like you to be so salty," Dani chided, although it was tongue-in-cheek. No one was up for championing either Clive or Glenna.

"What can I say? The well is almost bone dry for sympathy and magnanimity for people who don't deserve. But

I'm not about to create more gossip by not inviting them. I'll just try to pretend they aren't there."

Dani nodded, her brow creasing ever so slightly. "Keeping up appearances is such an emotional drain."

"Speaking of appearances—" Erica leaned in, her voice dropping an octave "—did you ever find out why Matthew Bennett was so interested in what's happening at the resort?"

Dani's eyes widened, a spark of concern igniting within their dark depths. "Matthew? Glenna's son? What was he asking about?"

"He was just real interested in stuff that I felt was none of his business," Erica said. "It made me uncomfortable, like he wanted me to share inner financial workings of the resort just because he's peripherally related to the Coltons."

Laura's expression of distaste mirrored Erica's. "Yeah, I'm not sharing that information with anyone who isn't on legal paperwork—and even then, it's on a need-to-know basis."

"Maybe he's just curious," Dani offered, trying to lighten the mood, though her light brown eyes betrayed her unease. "I've never gotten the vibe from Matthew that he was cut from the same cloth as his aunt."

"Maybe," Erica allowed, but her gut told her there was more to it than mere curiosity. "But with everything that's been happening…seems prudent to circle the wagons."

"Amen to that," Lauren agreed with an exhale, shoulders slumped as she toyed with the rim of her glass. "We need this merger. Sharpe Enterprises could turn things around for Mariposa."

"Is it really that bad?" Dani asked, concerned.

A furrow dug deep between Laura's brows, etching

worry into her skin like a map of all the resort's troubles. Erica reached across the table, a silent offer of solidarity that Laura grasped like a lifeline. "Negotiations have been brutal," Laura continued, the words spilling out heavier than lead. "And now this most recent situation has made the investors twitchy. I just don't know how this turns in our favor, and it scares me."

"Hey." Erica squeezed Laura's hand. "I wish there was more I could do." Helplessness gnawed at her, a hungry rat in the cellar of her capabilities. This was a game played in boardrooms and on balance sheets, far from her expertise.

Dani bit her lip, the line of her jaw taut as a bowstring. "Is there *anything* we can do?" she asked.

"Right now, it's a waiting game," Laura replied with a resigned shrug.

The conversation paused, a momentary ceasefire in their battle against worry, and Laura straightened up, armor back in place. "Enough about stuff that makes us sad," she announced, turning to Erica. "And how about you and CJ? How are things on that front?"

Heat crept into Erica's cheeks, unbidden and undeniable. "I'm…falling for him," she confessed, the words tumbling out in a rush. "Harder and faster than I ever expected, and I don't know how I feel about that, honestly."

"Is it because of the distance?" Laura asked.

"I want to say no, but it's definitely a consideration. I'm not about to start jetting off to LA every other weekend when the life I love is here."

"But a baby changes things, right?" Laura countered.

"Yeah, it does."

"I would imagine compromise is key," Laura offered with a knowing look.

"Compromise," Erica echoed, tasting the word, finding it both sweet and sour. The future unfurled before her, a path forked and formidable. One thing was clear: standing still wasn't an option, but picking the wrong path...would be devastating.

CJ's boots crunched on the gravel path leading to Anna's bungalow as dusk painted the sky in strokes of burnt orange and fading blue. He'd been turning over the day's events like a well-worn coin in his pocket, the edges blurred from too much handling. The weight of Harold's offer and the future of the film balanced precariously on his mind's edge.

"Hey," he said, rapping a knuckle against her door frame.

Anna appeared, waving him in. "CJ," she greeted, a smile touching her lips, but she looked preoccupied. "After today's shoot, I'd half expect you to be dead asleep. Great emotional depth, though. I just saw the dailies, and you never fail to impress me with your performance."

"Thanks," he said, appreciating her praise, but he needed to talk about the business end of the production. "Do you have a minute? I've got some stuff to hash out."

Her expression sobered as she nodded. "Of course." She stepped aside, granting him entry into the sanctuary of her temporary home. "What's going on?"

"Harold wants to come back on board, but it means I have to step down, though he offered me a producer credit. I don't know what the right decision is. Things have been going pretty good, and I like to think I had something to do with that. But it could also be coincidence and more a consequence of kicking out the bad apple."

"Which happened because of you," she reminded him. "Don't sell yourself short, CJ. You've really stepped up in ways I never could've imagined."

CJ cracked a smile, needing to hear the outside validation. He never imagined his sense of self might be as fragile as it seemed these days, but he really felt the weight of every decision like never before. "Do you think I should take the deal? Let Harold back in even when he'd been willing to trash everything we've worked so hard to create?"

Anna perched on the edge of the coffee table, her fingers laced together, a portrait of poise. Yet something flickered behind her eyes—a fleeting storm cloud skimming across a clear sky. "I don't know, CJ," she said, the words smooth but her voice betraying a tremor, like a violin string quivering after the note has died. "I've been so grateful for your help in keeping us going, but I can't deny I worried we might be kicking a bigger problem down the road without the studio's backing."

The distribution dilemma. CJ nodded. "Yeah, I know what you mean. I'd hoped a solution would just magically present itself, but something tells me that's not likely to happen."

She shook her head. "No, not likely," she agreed.

CJ looked to Anna. "Harold looked shocked when I told him about the sabotage, and I think it was genuine—which then got me to thinking…if not Harold, who would want to shut us down? Could it be personal? Some beef someone has with you?"

Anna hesitated, a mere second, but enough for him to

catch it—the look, quick as a thief in the night, that dashed through her gaze. "Personal?" she echoed, a practiced innocence to her question.

"Maybe something over a different production?" CJ ventured, treading lightly on the edge of her privacy. He wasn't one to pry into locked chests, but the stakes were high, and trust was the currency they were short on.

But the moment passed, and Anna shook her head, baffled, assuring him, "No enemies that I know of. Your guess is as good as mine."

"You're right—it could be totally random. Some crackpot with too much money and an active imagination. Lord knows the movie business draws them out like bees to honey," CJ said, though his gut twisted with doubt, intuition gnawing at him. He could push, but instead he chose to let it go. Sometimes the unsaid spoke volumes, and he was learning to listen.

"CJ, Harold has the connections," Anna started, returning to the real issue at hand. "Fighting the studio now...it's like trying to swim upstream. It might feel noble, but you'll just tire yourself out. If Harold is willing to come back, I think you should let him."

He nodded slowly, the weight of her logic settling over him like a heavy cloak.

"Sometimes I forget it's not just about the art," he admitted, dragging a hand down his face. The reality of it all made his head throb. "Erica's expecting, and I can't—"

"Play the high-stakes game?" Anna interjected with understanding.

"Exactly." CJ straightened, a rueful smile tugging at the corners of his mouth. "You're right. As much as it galls me to admit it, Harold's got the clout we need. But taking a step down after I made such a big decision, feels like…failure."

"No, that's your ego talking. Don't let pride sour a good thing," she advised. "Besides, it's not that simple anymore, right? Having a child…it shifts your universe. Trust me."

CJ couldn't help but chuckle, the sound more baffled than amused. "Yeah, I'm starting to realize that. The little bugger isn't even here yet, and I feel like every decision has to be made with a different level of diligence, which is way out outside of my comfort zone."

Anna nodded. "The decisions you make now? They'll ripple outward, touch everything and everyone you care about, which is why I think it's not a good idea to hold the course if Harold is willing to step back in play."

"You're probably right." CJ exhaled, a silent acknowledgment of the truth in her caution. "Guess it's time to start thinking long-term, huh?"

"Long-term," she echoed, her lips curving in a knowing smile.

With a final nod, CJ pushed away from the door frame, feeling the gravity of the moment settle into his bones.

Stepping out into the cool evening air, CJ felt the weight of his conversation with Anna cling to him like a second skin. The crunch of gravel under his boots seemed unusually loud in the quiet that enveloped Mariposa's bungalow-lined path. Each step was deliberate, a staccato rhythm to the beat of his troubled thoughts.

The sky hung heavy with stars, something he appreciated about the Arizona nights that he never got to enjoy back home with the LA smog.

Once upon a time, he'd ribbed Landon mercilessly for

his lackadaisical approach to life, but now the mirror turned its unforgiving gaze onto him. What had he been doing all these years if not dressing up fear as freedom?

Change meant risk, and risk was a language he'd thought he spoke fluently. Yet there it was—the potential cost laid bare by Anna's gentle wisdom. It wasn't just about the film anymore; it was about Erica, their unborn child and the kind of life he wanted to carve out for them.

A chuckle escaped him, dissipating into the night. "Commitment," he murmured, rolling the concept around in his mind like a foreign coin. This was no longer just about contracts and deals—it was about the heartbeats that would rely on his decisions.

"Scared, CJ?" he challenged the darkness, daring it to answer. The silence was his reply, an uncomfortable truth settling in his chest. Perhaps he had been chasing shadows when all this time, what he truly needed was shining right in front of him.

"Damn." He breathed out, stopping mid-stride. Was he really contemplating diving headfirst into the biggest role of his life? Father. Partner. Steadfast anchor.

"Or maybe it's damn time," he declared, louder this time, a decisive edge to his tone. With that, CJ spun on his heel to ride with Erica back to her place. He was ready to re-write the script of his own life.

Which meant giving Harold his decision.

Chapter 24

The morning sun had barely crested the horizon when Erica's pulse spiked at the sight of police cars reflecting off the terra-cotta walls of Mariposa Resort.

As she and CJ pulled into the drive, their arrival was swallowed by the commotion—a cluster of police officers, a pair of agitated resort managers, Josh and Laura, and on the fringes, a vulture-like reporter snapping photos and scribbling furiously in a notepad.

"Something's wrong," Erica muttered, her gaze darting to her bosses, speaking in hushed tones, their expressions strained as they talked with police.

CJ reached for her hand, his own grip tight with concern. "Should I stay?"

"No, it's okay," she assured him, motioning him on. "You'll be late for set."

He hesitated, his brows knitting together in that way that said he wanted to argue, but she squeezed his hand, a silent plea. "It's probably nothing. I'll fill you in at lunch, okay?"

"Okay," he relented, reluctance etched across his face as he turned toward the growing daylight and the promise of work, leaving her to deal with whatever this mess was.

Erica approached the scene, her heart thudding erratically, each beat a question mark pulsating through her veins. She caught Laura's eye just as the latter finally managed to peel away from an officer's questioning gaze.

"Erica," Laura breathed, the edges of her usually poised demeanor fraying like worn fabric. "It's bad."

"What's going on?" Erica asked, almost afraid to know.

"A guest was attacked." Laura's words tumbled out in a hurried torrent. "Someone hid in her closet, tried to— Well, she fought them off. They ran, but she left at four this morning—couldn't stay another minute—and I can't blame her, but I just can't believe it happened at all. We've never had a security breach like this before."

"What about the security footage?" Erica asked, her mind already racing through protocols and contingencies.

"Malfunctioned. Nothing recorded." Laura's hands were shaking, the tremors of responsibility and fear intermingling in a visible dance. "Can you believe that luck? Of all days for it to go on the fritz!"

"Damn it," Erica swore, unable to process the absurdly bad luck.

"And that's not all. More guests are checking out. They're scared," Laura continued, her voice quivering on the edge of tears. "And that stupid reporter over there is writing all of this down, like we need one goddamn more brick to fall on us right now."

"Hey," Erica said, her tone softening as she reached out to steady Laura's trembling shoulders. "These things, they happen. We'll get through it."

Laura nodded, her eyes glassy with unshed tears. "I've never felt so helpless."

"Neither have I," Erica admitted, her gaze drifting over

the tranquil grounds that now harbored an undercurrent of menace. "But we won't let this break us. Not now, not ever."

"But this feels like the nail in the coffin for the Sharpe merger. As if people getting poisoned on our watch wasn't bad enough, now this? We might as well close the damn doors."

"No, we'll find a way out of this," Erica assured Laura, but the words tasted hollow. If it looked pretty bleak from Erica's point of view, she could only imagine how it looked from Laura's.

By the time the officers finished taking statements, photographing the room for evidence and collecting any trace evidence that might've been left behind, it was noon and Erica was ready for a break. Her nerves were stretched tight, and she wanted nothing more than to fall into CJ's arms and forget everything for a minute.

But then he said something completely aggravating, and her raw nerves couldn't handle the additional stress.

"Excuse me?" Erica said, hoping her strident tone communicated that he better rephrase his statement before she bit his head off like a female praying mantis during mating season.

"I don't want you here alone after dark anymore," CJ stated firmly as they sat across from each other in the resort's secluded garden, the scent of flowering flora doing little to sweeten his sour mood.

Erica stiffened at his words, her spine a rigid line against the ironwork chair. "I can take care of myself, CJ," she said, her voice edged with a frost that belied the warm desert air. "I don't need anyone treating me like I need protecting."

CJ ran a hand through his hair, a gesture of exasperation

that did not go unnoticed. "It's not about that, Erica. It's just—what if this guy is still out there? Waiting?"

"Then we'll handle it," Erica replied curtly, unwilling to let fear dictate her movements, even as an involuntary shiver traced her spine.

"Handle it? Erica, come on! What's the plan? Hurt his feelings with harsh words?" CJ leaned forward, the muscles in his jaw ticking. "This isn't some script we can rewrite. This is real life. LA might be a jungle, but at least there you know where the danger lurks."

"LA, safer than here? That's rich." The scoff slipped out before she could catch it, her arms crossing over her chest in defiance.

"Damn it, I'm serious!" he barked, his cheeks flaring. "I can't... If anything happened to you or—" His voice cracked, the unfinished thought hanging heavy between them like the thick desert heat. "I'm not okay with you taking unnecessary risks for a dumb job. It's not worth it."

"A dumb job?" she repeated, insulted. "You think my job is dumb just because I don't make millions like you? Is that how you feel?"

"No, I'm not saying that," he said, shaking his head. But she wasn't convinced and frankly, she wanted to slap a knot on his entitled head for even thinking it.

Their gazes locked, a silent battle of wills, until Erica finally broke away, looking out over the sunlit grounds. She hated the feeling of being caged, of having decisions made for her.

CJ checked his phone, swearing beneath his breath. "I have to get back to set. We'll talk more about this later."

"Well, I don't know what else needs to be said," Erica said, rising stiffly and walking away.

Yet as she walked the familiar paths later that day, her senses were heightened, betraying her inner turmoil. The rustle of palm fronds, the whisper of sand beneath her shoes—every sound had her head snapping around in search of shadows that danced just beyond sight.

"Pull yourself together," she muttered under her breath, chiding herself for the adrenaline that quickened her pulse. She was jumpier than a jack rabbit in a room full of coyotes.

By the end of the long day, Erica was ready to put the events behind her. She was mentally and physically exhausted and just wanted to soak in a warm bath.

The dimming light cast long shadows across the path, turning benign shapes into lurking threats. She quickened her pace, the soft scrape of her shoes against gravel seeming to echo like something out of a horror movie.

A sudden flicker of movement caught her eye—a blur at the edge of her vision—and her heart leapt into her throat. With a start, she twisted around, the keys now a cold lump in her clenched fist.

"Easy there," came a low voice as Roland Hargreaves, the square-jawed head of security, stepped out from the twilight's embrace, hands raised in a calming gesture. "Just me, making sure everything's locked down tight."

"Roland," she exhaled, relief flooding through her, though it couldn't wash away the lingering disquiet. "You nearly gave me a heart attack."

"Sorry 'bout that." His eyes, a steady presence, scanned the area. "Can't be too careful, not after today."

Erica nodded, her gaze drifting over the tranquil facade of the resort, a stark contrast to the turmoil inside her. "Never thought we'd see more trouble like this here," she murmured, more to herself than to Roland.

"First time for everything, I guess," he said, though he seemed just as troubled as everyone else, perhaps more so as head of security.

"Let's hope it's the last," she said, forcing a hopeful smile.

Before heading for the parking lot, she paused by a Saguaro cactus, a shiver tickling her spine as she glanced around. Not one for superstition, Erica still found herself muttering, "Allison, if you're the one causing all this trouble, please stop." But then she realized how stupid she was being, talking to thin air and was thankful no one saw her. *Come on, Erica, ghosts and goblins? Grow up.*

"Ready?" CJ's voice cut through her reverie, firm yet laced with concern. He stood there, resolute in the fading light, his presence both an anchor and a reminder of their earlier spat.

Even as she wanted to tell him he ought to stay at his own bungalow tonight, her insides softened at the sight of him, rippling with protective energy, brooking no argument. His hand reached for hers, fingers intertwining in with hers, a silent vow that her safety wasn't an option.

They walked to the car together, his steps shadowing hers, and despite the tension that hummed between them like a live wire, Erica was silently awed by the tender feelings spreading throughout her body at the knowledge that CJ wasn't going anywhere.

Even if she wasn't being the easiest person to be around.

And that meant something—more than she realized.

Her entire life she'd spent cultivating a persona that was efficient, easy to get along with—a problem solver.

And if you were always the one with the solution, you couldn't afford being the problem, which meant her feelings were often shelved for the sake of calming tempers.

She didn't have to hide her feelings with CJ—and he didn't expect her to fix everything.

For tonight, she could let someone else take care of things. Starting with, "I'd really love to soak in a warm bath and forget this day happened," she said, meeting his gaze.

CJ's expression softened as the tension between them broke. "Then a bath is exactly what you shall have."

CJ's fingers drummed an impatient beat on his thigh, the sound inaudible over the clamor of the crew dismantling the barn set. Sawdust and the smell of fresh paint hung heavy in the air as they worked to erase any sign that they had ever been there. The resort shimmered with the last golden rays of the setting sun, a serene backdrop to the controlled chaos before him.

"Watch it with that beam!" he snapped more harshly than he'd intended as a couple of grips navigated a large piece of scenery past him.

"Sorry, Mr. Knight," one mumbled, ducking his head.

"Damn it," CJ muttered under his breath, raking a hand through his hair. He hadn't meant to bark; it was the gnawing concern for Erica nipping at his conscience that made him short-tempered.

He ought to be excited that they were able to return to their original location, but he couldn't focus when all he could think about was Erica being left at the resort without him.

The police were still clueless about the attacker, and every shadow seemed suspect. Yet Erica's pride wouldn't hear of any suggestions that removed her from the resort. So, he said nothing, even though concern twisted his guts and left him on edge.

"Hey, CJ, you heading out with us tonight?" Caroline called out, snapping CJ from his thoughts, her clipboard in hand.

"Not tonight. Got a flight to catch back to LA," he said with a half-hearted smile. "Tying up loose ends with the studio."

"All right, we'll see you when you get back."

He nodded, watching as the final pieces of the set were carted off, leaving nothing but memories and dust motes dancing in the waning light.

Hours later, CJ sat across from Harold in the latter's sleek Los Angeles office, the city lights a glittering mosaic far below. He tried to ignore the tightness in his chest as he listened to Harold lay out the terms of his new position. Associate Producer. It felt like a demotion, but the paycheck that came with it was anything but.

"Your accountant can breathe easy now, huh?" Harold joked, a smile playing on his lips.

"Guess I won't be joining the ranks of the houseless in Malibu," CJ quipped back, but he hadn't been worried.

Harold's expression softened, picking up on the dissonance. "Look, CJ," he began, leaning forward earnestly, "sometimes, holding out for the right shot is worth more than a quick jump at a big win. You're sharp. You'll get your chance to shine, and when you do, I want to be there, seeing you do it the right way."

CJ absorbed the words, their unexpected weight grounding some of the tension inside him. Maybe this wasn't surrender but a strategic retreat. Harold wasn't just handing down orders; he was offering wisdom.

"Thanks, Harold. I'll remember that," he said, a genuine note of gratitude threading through his voice. But even as Harold seemed in a general good mood, there was something that seemed to preoccupy him as he fidgeted with his gold-plated pen, spinning it between his fingers. "Was there something else?" he asked.

Harold sighed and set the pen down, meeting CJ's gaze with a hint of sheepishness. "It's about Anna," he confessed, the words coming out almost reluctantly. "Got some chatter in my ear a while back. Should've known better than to listen to that crap."

"Someone was badmouthing Anna?" CJ raised an eyebrow, feeling a protective twinge. "What'd they say?"

He waved away the details. "Doesn't matter. I usually toss that stuff straight into the trash bin in my mind. But this time… I don't know, it got to me. I think that's why I wasn't willing to listen to what you were saying about the production."

"Who was doing the chirping?" CJ asked, his curiosity piqued. He couldn't help but wonder if there was a connection to their earlier problems on set.

"It's not a good idea to name names in this business," Harold said, frowning. "But it's got me to thinking."

"Is it possible that whoever was doing the talking might've had motive to sabotage the set?"

Harold tapped his chin, considering. "Seems unlikely, but I suppose anything is possible."

"Would you look into it?" CJ pressed, needing an answer. "They might've thought it wasn't a big deal tampering with the set, but Erica was hurt—she could've been killed when that barn collapsed."

"I agree," Harold affirmed, his tone final. "No one's pulling that crap on my set and getting away with it."

CJ stepped out of Harold's sleek office, the polished chrome door clicking shut behind him. Relief was a cool shadow slipping across his mind, knowing Harold would dig into the underbelly of their troubles.

But as he strode down the corridor, lined with movie posters boasting bold titles and brighter stars, a nagging concern twisted in his gut.

Erica.

Her image flashed before him—those fierce eyes that didn't just look at you but through you, seeing past the facade.

"Damn it," CJ muttered, raking a hand through his hair as he pushed through the exit, sunlight glaring down like an interrogation lamp.

Was she tucked away safely between the manicured hedges and blossoming bougainvillea? Or was there someone watching her every move, waiting for the moment to strike?

Outside, CJ slid into his car, the leather seat hugging him like a promise of control he wasn't sure he had. He fired up the engine, the purr a low growl that usually set his pulse thrumming with power. Today it was just noise.

"Erica, you'd better stay safe," he muttered, a plea to the universe to keep his baby mama from harm while he was away.

Honestly, he couldn't get back to Arizona fast enough— back to the woman he'd fallen for at some point when he hadn't been paying attention.

Chapter 25

Erica spotted her first. The slender figure of Glenna Bennett Colton wound through the hazy midmorning light across Mariposa Resort's manicured lawn. The air was thick with the scent of blooming jasmine, but Erica's nose wrinkled as if she could already catch a whiff of the tension that followed Glenna like a second shadow.

"Looks like trouble," Erica murmured under her breath, her gaze tracking Glenna's determined stride toward the main office. Laura, standing beside Erica at the reception desk, stiffened visibly, her fingers tightening around a stack of brochures.

"Of all the times I do not need this," Laura said with a heavy sigh. "All right, time to put my professional face on and see what we owe to the *pleasure* of this unexpected visit."

Erica followed Laura as they caught up with Glenna as she paused to inspect a rose bush as if she had a degree in botany and it was her job to police everyone's garden. "Good morning, Glenna. This is a surprise," Laura said, forcing a smile.

"Surprises keep life interesting, don't you think?" Glenna said. "Darling, your roses look a little wilty. Have the gardener water morning and night to combat this arid desert climate. Poor things are positively droopy. I'm sure your guests aren't keen to pay VIP prices for hostel-level greenery."

Laura forced a tight smile. "I'll mention it to the groundskeeper."

"Excellent." Glenna's gaze was sharp, and she had that look about her—the one that said she'd come for more than idle chitchat—and Erica wasn't wrong. "I heard about the... incident," she began, her voice dipped in concern that felt as real as fool's gold.

"The incident?" Laura repeated, playing dumb. "What incident would that be?"

"Well, how many have there been that you can't recall which one I'm referencing? Obviously I'm talking about the assault on a guest. It was all over the newspaper. Front page, even. So embarrassing for the family. How did that happen?"

You nasty old windbag, Erica thought privately but kept her mouth shut. Glenna was purposefully poking at Laura to create a reaction.

"Yes, that was unfortunate, but we're trying to move forward," Laura said quickly, a practiced smile plastered on her face. Her blue eyes, however, shot daggers that didn't quite match the diplomacy of her tone.

"Unfortunate?" Glenna echoed, arching an eyebrow so perfectly sculpted it could have been drawn on by a master artist. "I'd hardly call a brutal assault on a guest as simply *unfortunate*—and from what I read, the papers seemed to agree. Have they found the assailant yet?"

"Not yet but they're still looking," Laura answered, clasping her hands in front of her, probably to stop herself from punching her snotty stepmother in the mouth. "I'm sure they'll find who did it, and we'll move forward with pressing charges."

"Newspapers tend to exaggerate," Erica interjected, unable to help herself. "It's how they sell copies."

"Or perhaps they're reporting genuine concerns." Glenna's voice took on a weighted quality as her gaze flicked past Erica with annoyance before returning to Laura. "Your father is worried, you know. He thinks—"

"Clive needn't worry," Laura interjected, her words clipped. "Everything is under control."

"Darling," Glenna said reproachfully, "must you insist on calling him by his name? He's your father, not the janitor."

Laura responded with a tight-lipped smile—which, judging by the subtle twist of Glenna's lips, had the desired effect. Glenna knew full well of the strained relationship between her husband and all of his children, which should say something about the man's character, but Glenna was cut from the same cloth.

"Still," Glenna continued, undeterred, "safety isn't something we can afford to be lax about. It's bad for business. Bad for the family name." Her lips curved into a smile that didn't quite reach her eyes—a smile that seemed to carry a heavier message than mere familial concern.

Laura nodded, her expression schooled into one of polite acknowledgment. "Of course, Glenna. We're all committed to safety here at Mariposa."

"Are we?" Glenna asked, her tone light but her implication heavy as lead. "Because I'd hate for any more...unpleasantness to affect your big day."

"Thank you for your concern," Laura said finally, her voice steady despite the storm raging in her eyes. "We'll make sure everything is up to standard."

"Good." Glenna gave a curt nod, her message delivered, the battle lines drawn without a single shot fired. "That's all I wanted to hear."

Josh appeared, as if summoned by an emotional bat signal sent up by Laura and Erica was glad for the intervention.

"Glenna, what a surprise," he began, the timbre of his voice threading through the tense atmosphere. "If we'd known you were coming we would've planned for lunch."

"Oh, I can't stay…just stopping in after reading that terrible article about the assault to show my support. Honestly, I was just telling Laura that situations like that should've never happened here. There's a standard, a reputation to uphold, and all it takes is a few bad slips and everything goes down the tubes. I'd hate to see that happen."

"Rest assured, we've not only increased our security personnel but replaced the faulty camera. It seems a rodent gnawed through the wiring—an unfortunate mishap, but not something we could've foreseen."

Glenna's nod was slow, her green eyes scrutinizing as she briefly examined a manicured nail. "I see. Though it does make one wonder—how often are these equipment checks done? With vermin being a concern, perhaps regular inspections should be more…meticulous."

"We don't have vermin," Laura retorted, a flash of temper showing.

Erica clenched her jaw, the muscles twitching as she bit back a retort. Her role here was support, not confrontation, no matter how much Glenna's honeyed barbs made her want to start swinging. She sucked in a breath through her nose, letting the scent of the resort's flowering jasmine calm the storm within.

"Your input is noted," Josh replied with an unflappable smile. His stance remained relaxed, yet there was something in his gaze—a glint of steel—that suggested he was no pushover.

"Right then, so happy to know that someone capable is at the helm. Laura, darling," she said, her voice wrapped in velvet concern. "You look absolutely exhausted. It's simply not flattering for a bride-to-be to appear so…worn."

Laura's blue eyes narrowed just a fraction. She forced a neutral expression, her athletic frame tense. "Thank you for thinking of me, Glenna, but I'm fine."

"Nonetheless," Glenna persisted, digging through her designer bag with bony fingers, "I must insist. Here—" she said, finally producing a crisp business card. "My nutritionist. A vitamin infusion works wonders. You should give it a try."

Erica could barely suppress the snort that threatened to escape her; Glenna's suggestion was almost comical, considering the woman looked more in need of a solid meal than anyone else in the room.

"Can't wait for the wedding. It will be quite the event to see." Glenna's laughter tinkled like glass about to shatter, and with that, her heels were clicking a staccato farewell down the path to her car.

"That woman," Laura growled, "is the devil in designer clothes. She's practically gleefully rubbing her hands at the thought of us failing."

"Don't let her get to you," Josh murmured, placing a

hand lightly on Laura's shoulder. "If the Sharpe merger falls through, we'll find something else. She's not getting her hands on Mariposa, okay?"

Laura's gaze met his, a silent acknowledgment passing between them. The weight of his words seemed to settle her, the rigidity in her stance easing ever so slightly. Erica watched, her own fists unclenching, the battle lines drawn yet again in the sand of their desert rose.

"I know. You're right," Laura said with a resolute nod. "She just caught me off my game with everything going on."

"Hey, we're all in this together, right?" Erica finally found her voice, though it sounded thin even to her own ears. Her gaze flitted between Laura and Josh, seeking some sign of assurance that wasn't reflected in the tight lines of Laura's posture.

The silence stretched, taut as a bowstring, before Laura managed a tighter nod, though it seemed more for her own benefit than anyone else's. "Absolutely," she said, but the word lacked its usual conviction.

But a different worry infiltrated her thoughts. Was it possible things were worse off at the resort than Erica knew?

Her job. Her livelihood. It wasn't just a paycheck—it was the sun-soaked mornings greeting guests, the laughter echoing from the poolside, the scent of salt and citrus that permeated the air. To lose that... Her heart skipped a beat at the thought.

Laura drew a deep breath and forced a smile, returning to business. "Erica, did you manage to get the police report from the bachelorette party?"

"It's on your desk," Erica said, watching as Laura left to

handle the insurance claim for the people affected by the incident, leaving Josh and Erica behind.

Josh seemed to sense Erica's disquiet and said cheerfully, "Don't worry—it's going to work out," and then went on his way, leaving Erica to wonder if everyone was in a state of denial or they were deliberately trying to keep everyone in the dark.

For the first time, the possibility of being jobless gnawed at Erica's gut.

CJ slumped into the producer's chair, the weight of endless days pressing down on his shoulders like a leaden shroud. His scenes were finished, and he was just waiting for his production assistant to take him back to base camp for the day.

The desert sun beat down mercilessly, but its searing touch was a mere whisper compared to the fatigue that clawed at his insides. Every muscle in his body screamed for rest, for the sweet surrender to sleep that seemed as elusive as a mirage in the vast Arizona landscape.

"Hey," Anna said, her voice slicing through the haze of exhaustion. She plopped down beside him, concern etching lines into her normally smooth forehead. "You're looking more beat than an old rug. You okay?"

He forced a grin that felt more like a grimace. "Burning the candle at both ends takes its toll, but nothing a good night's sleep won't fix." The lie tasted bitter on his tongue, but admitting weakness wasn't in CJ's script. Besides, this was all temporary. Soon enough the shoot would be finished, and he could take a break, though he wasn't sure in which zip code he'd land.

Anna's gaze lingered on him, sharp and assessing. She leaned in, close enough that he could catch the faint scent of lavender from her hair. "You can't keep doing this to yourself. You're human, not some machine. Caroline tells me that you're driving out to Sedona every night after the set wraps instead of returning to base camp."

There was no denying it. "Erica needs me. Can't have her alone in Sedona—not now. Not to mention the woman seems to be a magnet for accidents. Two emergency room visits—and I'm sure as hell not going to let a third happen. I'm half tempted to hire an on-call doctor just to follow her around and make sure she doesn't trip and fall down a well or something."

Anna chuckled. "I've never seen you so protective before. I like it. It's a nice change."

Tired as he was, he shared a smile. He was changing and while it right, it was still a challenge not to fall back on old habits but he supposed that was normal.

"Ever thought about bringing her here? Your trailer is pretty nice," Anna suggested. "Switch it up a bit. Might do you both some good."

"Maybe," he said, wondering if Erica would be open to "glamping" in his trailer, though he rather enjoyed getting away from everything associated with the movie business at the end of the night. Cuddling up with Erica at the end of a long night was the most normal he'd felt in ages, and he wasn't sure he was ready to give that up just yet for the convenience of a shorter commute to work.

Anna paused, her energy shifting as she said, "I need to talk to you about something."

"What's wrong?" he asked.

"I've been thinking about the question you asked me a few days ago, about who might want to screw with the film and if it might be personal against me."

"Yeah?"

"At first I dismissed it, but then something happened, and I had to wonder if maybe... I should say something."

"Is everything okay?" CJ asked.

"Yes, it's just not something I'd like everyone to know." She exhaled, as if the words were reluctant prisoners escaping her mouth. "A while back, I...had a thing with someone. A producer. And he was married," she added, her gaze dropping to her boots.

"Doesn't sound like you," CJ said, not a judgment, just a fact.

"It wasn't." Anna glanced away, heat rising in her cheeks. "And when I came to my senses, I ended it. Badly."

"Bad enough to mess with your work?" CJ asked.

"Maybe." Anna met his eyes again. "I got this text, out of nowhere, asking to meet, asking if I needed any help with the production. I shut it down, but...the timing is off. It's got me thinking—maybe he orchestrated all of this to get me to come back to him, like he was going to swoop in and save the day."

"Could be a coincidence," CJ offered, but they both knew better. Coincidences didn't run rampant in their world. "But I think I should tell Harold."

"I hate naming names in this business because it always has the potential of biting you in the ass later, but given how Erica had been inadvertently hurt during the last incident, I don't see how I can withhold my concerns if there's even a hint of bad behavior happening because of me. His name is Bob Wendell."

"Thanks for telling me," CJ said, the gears in his head already turning. Harold would definitely want to hear if there was someone willing to go to such lengths to get even over something personal.

"Okay, then." Anna squared her shoulders, the confession's weight visibly lifted. "That's all I've got for now. See you tomorrow."

CJ's production assistant popped up, and CJ climbed into the golf cart, ready to rinse off the trail dust and make a quick call to Harold to share what Anna had told him.

Wrapping early meant he could actually sneak in a nap before heading off to Erica's for the night, which was sorely needed.

Once back at his trailer, he wasted no time in calling Harold to share the information with the caveat that it was pure speculation and that it would be best to handle this discreetly. But Harold's tone told CJ that he had reason to believe there might be merit to the theory.

"Bob Wendell has a reputation for a wandering eye—that much isn't speculation, but it doesn't surprise me that he might try to orchestrate something to shift a situation to his advantage. I've caught him in the past doing shady shit and I chose to overlook it, but this is going too far."

"We don't have proof," CJ reminded Harold, but the wheels had already been set in motion. "Just make sure he's actually guilty before you potentially destroy a career."

Harold chuckled as if CJ's warning was cute. "You just worry about your end of things. I'll handle this situation. Thanks for letting me know."

CJ clicked off, wondering if he'd just made a big mistake or if he'd rectified one. Time would tell.

Later that night, CJ didn't have time to worry about Bob Wendell because Erica was agitated from the moment he stepped into the house.

"Is everything okay?" he asked in alarm when he caught Erica pacing. "What's going on?"

"I don't even know where to start," Erica said, stopping to stare at CJ in distress. "Glenna the Bad Witch showed up and started stirring all sorts of trouble—which is on brand for her, and normally no one pays attention, but now it's different. I think the resort's in real trouble and no one wants to admit it—and if that's true, then I think my job is in jeopardy."

"Hey." CJ's voice was a gentle interruption, warm and steady. He patted the seat beside him on the sofa, beckoning her to sit. "I don't think wearing a hole in your carpet is going to solve anything."

She complied, a frazzled sigh escaping her as she sank down next to him. He could feel the tension radiating off her, see the worry creasing her brow.

"Talk to me," he urged, his tone wrapping her in an embrace as his arm followed, drawing her in close.

"Bookings are down, cancellations are up, and I know it's because of all the bad publicity the resort has suffered as of late, which is unprecedented, honestly, but..." Erica started, her voice warbling. "Laura's doing all she can, but...if this keeps up, I might be out of a job. And with the baby on the way, I—" She broke off, biting her lip.

CJ absorbed her fears, choosing silence over empty reassurances. He could assure her that she had nothing to worry about, that he could easily take care of her and the baby, but that would do nothing but poke at a fiercely independent woman like Erica, so he just stroked her arm and listened.

"Feels like I'm staring down the barrel of a loaded gun," she whispered, leaning into his chest.

"Whatever happens, you're not alone." His words were simple, but they carried the weight of his conviction. CJ's heart ached with the urge to whisk her away from all this, to wrap her up in the safety of his world back in LA. Yet he held back, understanding that her independence was not his to take.

When he didn't offer to snap his fingers and solve everything, she actually seemed relieved, which seemed counterintuitive, but he was starting to understand Erica's complicated brain and knew she had to find a solution that worked for her.

"Thanks, CJ." Her breath hitched, and she seemed to draw strength from his presence. "Just having you here— it means everything."

He pressed a kiss to the top of her head, breathing in the scent of her shampoo. In that moment, he was her fortress against the chaos, even as his own walls threatened to crumble.

He didn't know how or when it'd happened, but he was desperately, hopelessly and possible ridiculously in love with Erica Pike.

So how the hell was he supposed to tell her that without sending her sprinting for the hills?

Chapter 26

Erica's heels clicked a steady rhythm on the polished tile as she navigated the familiar halls of Mariposa. The scent of fresh lilies, strategically placed to welcome and soothe, mingled with the undercurrent of anxiety that had settled over the resort since the assault. She pushed open the door to Laura's office with a tap of her knuckle, her practiced smile wilting at the sight of her boss.

Laura stood motionless, her gaze lost beyond the windowpane, where the relentless sun carved sharp shadows across the courtyard. "You okay?" Erica ventured, the words slicing through the hush that clung to the room like cobwebs.

"Thinking about axing Clive and Glenna from the wedding guest list." Laura's voice was flat, but the muscles in her jaw twitched.

"Seriously?" Erica's brows shot up. "What brought this on?"

"I've just been thinking… I think Glenna fed the story to the press about the assault, and if that's the case, I don't want her anywhere near what is supposed to be the happiest day of my life."

"Not that I don't support your decision, but why would she do that?"

"She wants to smear the resort's reputation when she knows it's imperative for us to shine."

"How would she even know about the assault to tell the press anything?" Erica asked, confused.

"If she had someone on the inside whispering into her ear, she'd have everything she needs."

"Do you really think anyone here would be willing to do that?" Erica asked, horrified.

"I don't want to, but it's the only thing that makes any sense."

"Okay, even if that were true—and I sincerely hope it's not—what's in it for Glenna and Clive to ruin the resort?" Erica asked.

"The family has chosen to keep a certain situation regarding the resort very private, keeping it strictly within a tight circle because we didn't want to alarm anyone. Plus, frankly, it's no one's business what goes on behind closed doors."

"What's happening?" Erica asked, afraid of the answer. "Is the resort bankrupt?"

"No, not at all," Laura assured Erica, creating a wave of relief that nearly weakened her knees. "The resort is doing very well. It's a land ownership issue that has my father threatening to get his grubby hands on the resort for the cash. He wants to liquidate all assets, but we as a family stood against his wishes, which is why it's so important that Sharpe Enterprises agrees to the merger."

Erica's heart hammered against her rib cage, a drumbeat of anxiety as she absorbed the gravity in Laura's gaze.

"We're banking on the merger. Without it…" Laura let the sentence drift, unfinished yet understood.

"Without it, Clive wins?" Erica ventured, recalling the man's hawkish eyes and the way his presence seemed to linger like a storm cloud over their every move. She'd never liked the man, which now seemed warranted.

Laura nodded. "Exactly. He's circling the resort, waiting for a slip. The land dispute has given him an opening, and the sharks—" Her hands cut through the air, mimicking the feeding frenzy of lawyers that had descended upon them.

"God, Laura." Erica's mind reeled. "I didn't realize things were this dire."

"Few do, and that was by design. Appearances are everything. We can't have people thinking the resort is in any trouble or we'll lose even more bookings, which we sorely need right now."

"Is my job...?" Erica couldn't finish the sentence, her throat constricting around the fear of the unknown.

"Everyone's is." The words were blunt as Laura's gaze met Erica's. "Even mine. But we're doing everything to keep this place in our control."

The room seemed to shrink, the walls closing in with the weight of their shared burden. And yet amid the encroaching darkness, Erica felt a flicker of something defiant kindle within her. She loved Mariposa and the Coltons; she'd do whatever possible to help.

"Then count me in the fight. I'm not about to watch Mariposa get squeezed to death by your greedy father and his bony-crony wife."

Laura cracked a reluctant smile at the dig. "So you think I should uninvite them to the wedding?"

"Why in the world would you keep Clive and Glenna on the wedding guest list after all this?"

"I guess to keep up appearances? Foster some sort of goodwill? Maybe appeal to my father's nearly nonexistent kernel of familial loyalty? I don't know."

"I think that kernel is damn near microscopic at this point."

"Yeah, you're probably right." Laura rubbed at her forehead, her shoulders dragging beneath the weight of everything happening. "God, what a mess."

Erica leaned against the edge of Laura's desk, her fingers tracing the grain of the wood as if seeking answers in its swirls and knots. The office was quiet, the tension between them palpable, like the charged air before a storm.

"I appreciate your loyalty, Erica," Laura said. "But if you need to leave, to be with CJ and start something new… I'd understand."

Startled, Erica straightened, her gaze snapping to Laura's. "Resign? Now?" Her words came out sharper than intended, a defensive edge to them. "That's not even on my radar, Laura."

"You're so loyal. I know you'd probably be willing to go down with the ship if need be, but I don't want that for you. You need to do what's right for you, not just what's right for the resort."

"Mariposa is more than just a job," Erica said finally, her voice steady. "It's home. And you…you're not just my boss." She let the words hang, a testament to the bond they'd forged.

"Thank you," Laura whispered, gratitude and respect woven through the simple phrase. "I feel the same way about you."

Erica nodded, a silent vow passing between them. Uncertainty might cloud her personal horizon, but here in the heart of Mariposa, her course was clear. Whatever the future held, she'd face it head-on, with the resort's soil beneath her feet and its fight coursing through her veins.

Now if only it was as easy to figure out her future with CJ.

CJ unfolded the checkered tablecloth with a flourish, masking his nerves with a practiced smile. The Crescent Moon Ranch sprawled before them, an expanse of tranquility far removed from the chaos of movie sets and flashing cameras.

Now that the production had wrapped, he was free to actually spend some quality time with Erica that didn't revolve around their hectic schedules. Today it was all about enjoying each other's company.

He watched Erica's face light up as she took in the rolling hills and the distant silhouette of horses grazing, her delight more soothing than the gentle Arizona breeze.

"Wow, CJ, this is...it's beautiful," she breathed out, the stress lines that had taken residence on her forehead seeming to smooth away with each passing second. "It's wild how you can live near someplace and yet still be a tourist. I can't believe I've never been here before now."

"Only the best for you," he replied, arranging the picnic with precision—a spread of her favorite fruits, artisanal cheeses and a jar of the marinated artichoke hearts she'd been craving endlessly since the pregnancy had started.

Erica laughed, a sound he'd come to cherish, as she popped a strawberry into her mouth. "You're spoiling me rotten, but I don't mind. Please feel free to continue. God, I needed this. How'd you know?"

"We've both been under a lot of stress. I needed this just as much as you," he admitted. "I've never in my life been under so much pressure than I have with this production. I'm glad it's wrapped, but also, I'm proud of the work. They say nothing worth having comes easy, so hopefully all this drama will translate to a film that makes it all worth it."

"I'm sure it'll be amazing. From what I could see, it's an amazing story."

"Thank you," he said with genuine pleasure at her assessment, settling across from her at the weathered picnic table. Their conversation meandered through comfortable territory until, bolstered by the serene setting, CJ broached the subject that had been gnawing at him.

"Erica, can you ever picture settling down in LA?" he asked, trying to keep his voice light.

Her expression shifted, the hint of a frown marring her features. "LA?" She shook her head, auburn hair catching the sunlight. "I… No, I can't. It's not the place I imagine raising our child. I mean, it's not exactly a place I picture as a place with solid values. When I think of LA, I think of shallow people and transient moral values, which is the last place I'd want to raise a family."

The words hit CJ like an unexpected punch, deflating his buoyant mood. "LA has some good people," he said, offended. "Every place has its good and bad points. I wouldn't say that one place is inherently better than another. It all depends on where you live. I, for one, live in a very nice and safe neighborhood with great neighbors."

Erica shrugged. "Well, you asked me and I told you. No, LA has never been on my radar as a desirable place to live, much less raise a family."

"But my career—it's there. I need to be seen, available. You know how this works. My career isn't like most people's and requires a certain flexibility."

"Sure, but Arizona is where I feel at home and where I have the most support," Erica countered. "The only person I would know in LA is you."

"Am I chopped liver?" he quipped, but there was something else behind his words that he couldn't quite hide. Most women would happily relocate if they were in Erica's position. But then, he hadn't fallen in love with those women. He wanted Erica—but he wanted Erica to follow him to LA.

"Of course not, but that's not how I operate. I need more," she said simply, stunning him with her brutal honesty.

But wasn't that what he appreciated most about Erica? The way she didn't pull punches, the way he always knew that she'd give it to him straight, no matter if he didn't like what she had to say?

Yeah, but right now, he'd love a little less of that blunt honesty. However, if that was how she wanted to play it... "Erica, let's be real, I can take care of us in a way that you can't. It doesn't make sense for you to stay here. Come to LA with me, and you'll never want for anything. I promise."

Her gaze narrowed. "Except autonomy. When did I give the impression that I wanted to be a kept woman, like some pretty bird in a golden cage? I am capable of taking care of myself and this baby, even if it's not to a Hollywood Hills standard—and frankly, CJ, it's offensive for you to even say something like that to me."

Heat flashed through CJ as regret tasted bitter in his

mouth, but his pride wouldn't let him apologize. A part of him felt he was right, even if he wasn't.

"You're being stubborn and short-sighted," he bit out. "C'mon, Erica, think it through. Don't let your mouth overload your ass. I'm offering you the world on a plate. If you want to get a job or something in LA, I won't stand in your way—I'm just saying you don't have to. Take up a hobby or something. That's what most of the wives do anyway."

Erica rose, her nostrils flaring. "CJ Knight, I am not a 'woman who lunches' or whatever you're trying to make me enjoy. I have a career I love, and I'm good at it. How dare you imply that I don't deserve the same consideration in a decision that should hold equal weight? I need a minute to calm down before I say something I truly regret—though, lord knows, you're choking on your whole damn foot!"

He watched her walk away, her figure growing smaller, feeling the rift between them widen with each step she took. The thought of spending a few more days wallowing in the aftermath made his skin itch. Decision made, he packed away the uneaten food, the silence around him now oppressive.

The drive back to Erica's place was excruciatingly silent, but the tension in the air was enough to choke a horse.

"I think I'll go back to LA," he announced, his voice devoid of the warmth he so desperately wanted to offer.

"Okay," she said simply, without turning to look at him.

By the time they reached her place, it was a done deal. The hurt between them was a chasm that couldn't be jumped without falling to their death a mangled mess.

Swallowing the lump in his throat, CJ packed up his bag and left without saying much more of anything else.

What else could he say? He wasn't entirely sure if he was truly in the wrong and she was being stubbornly prideful, or he was woefully out of line and ought to beg for forgiveness.

He should've said something about calling later, but he didn't because, frankly, he didn't know what could be said. Neither were willing to budge and both felt solidly they were in the right.

An impasse.

By the time he landed in LA and caught an Uber back to his place, he was tied in knots but numb at the same time.

He walked into his place and found Landon in the kitchen making a cheesy panini. "Hey, man, you're back! How was filming?"

"Eventful," CJ admitted, feeling a weariness that permeated his soul as he sank down onto the stool at the kitchen counter. "How were things here?"

"All good," Landon promised, hefting his gooey sandwich, offering, "Want me to make you one? I picked up some of the good gouda from that cute mom-and-pop in Santa Barbara we found that time we were hungover following that wild Golden Globes after party. You remember, that time you—"

"Yeah, I remember," CJ cut him off, the trip down debauchery lane not needed. "But no, thanks. I'm good. I'm mostly exhausted. I feel like I could sleep for days and still need a few more winks."

"Sleep's important, man," Landon agreed, crunching into his sandwich with a groan of appreciation. "Mmm, that's criminal. Damn, it's going to kill my stomach later, but for now, I'm in heaven."

CJ smiled, rubbing at his gritty eyes. "Anything else going on?"

"Oh yeah," Landon said, recalling as he chewed. "Have you heard about Bob Wendell?"

CJ perked up with wary interest. "What about him?"

"The guy's been playing puppet master with people's lives. It's real sinister movie-plot type stuff. I mean, honestly, if it were on paper, I'd say it was a little over the top, but this shit's real. He's probably going to jail. It's wild what people think they can get away with in the digital age. Receipts are everywhere, man."

"Seriously?" CJ said.

"Yep. He's toast," Landon said, taking a huge bite. "Turns out he's been strong-arming women for…favors, if you catch my drift. And if they didn't play ball? Career sabotage."

"Damn." CJ shook his head, the news stirring a bitter sense of justice within him. "That's messed up."

"Understatement of the year, buddy." Landon finished his sandwich and wiped his mouth before tossing his balled-up napkin into the trash like he was an NBA player. "Nothing but net, baby."

CJ realized Harold had really pulled no punches, chasing down a lead that had turned out to be the jackpot. He mostly felt vindicated for Anna. She'd been carrying that secret shame for too long, and now she could let it go.

He released a pent-up breath, relieved on that score, at the very least. Too bad his situation with Erica wasn't so easily solved.

As if reading his mind, Landon asked, "So, what's the deal with Erica and the kid?"

Hell, if I know. He could only shrug. "Things are kind of…up in the air right now."

"Look, CJ," Landon said, his tone unusually serious. "Far be it from me to dispense life advice, but don't be a jackass, all right? Chase your bliss. Because this place?" He gestured to the clustered cityscape beneath his sprawling estate. "It's nothing but a recipe for heartbreak."

"Easy for you to say," CJ muttered, but the truth of Landon's words stung. Still, he shot back, "When have you ever taken anything seriously?"

Landon's gaze turned somber for the briefest second. "Not soon enough, man." He flashed a lopsided grin as he shouldered his duffel bag. "Anyway, got a new gig lined up. I'll keep you posted."

As the sound of Landon's Uber faded away, CJ stood alone, the silence echoing loudly in the empty house. He tried to picture a kid running amok this place but couldn't manage it. His house was gorgeous and everything he'd thought he'd wanted when he'd purchased.

Now it felt hollow, like a movie facade. He didn't have anything in this house that felt distinctly representative of him as a person. Sure, it was decorated with style and class, but nothing stood out as his. By comparison, Erica's place was ten times smaller but was packed with warmth and personality. Photos lined the walls, knickknacks representing adventures and holding memories were sprinkled throughout her house, and a cozy night spent in her little house felt more inviting than a lifetime spent in this cold place.

Was this what he wanted to bring a child into?

CJ slumped against the door frame, hating how morose he felt. The air felt thicker somehow, charged with a truth too raw for the glitzy veneer of LA. Landon's words clung to him, a tattoo on his conscience.

"Chase your bliss," he muttered under his breath, the syllables tasting like a dare.

He shook his head, trying to dislodge the knot in his stomach. Landon, the eternal drifter, had lobbed a grenade of insight that left CJ's defenses in shambles. A guy who couldn't hold down a job to save his soul, yet there he was, doling out life lessons that rang with an uncomfortable clarity.

"Damn it, Landon," he said to the empty room, feeling the fissures in his well-constructed facade.

Had he screwed things up with Erica? Was she right? Was it better to raise a family outside of LA? Of course he'd seen the effects of privilege and wealth in this town— useless nepotism was a constant reality—the drug use, the moral decay of youth gone wild without any guardrails. But he'd raise his kid differently, he wanted to protest.

Except he didn't know the first thing about raising a kid, much less raising a kid with the kid of guidance it would need to avoid the pitfalls common to movie-star kids.

He hated that term, along with *A-list* and *celebrity*, but it was the reality of his life.

CJ's phone buzzed, a jarring intrusion. He glanced at the screen—another meeting, another chance to be seen. It should've spurred him into action. Instead a weary sigh slipped from him, the allure of the spotlight dimming.

With a final glance at the city below, he grabbed his keys, decision hardening like cement in his veins.

"Time to find some damn bliss," he grunted, determination etching itself across his features. He flicked off the lights, stepping out into the night, a man on a mission to rediscover what mattered most.

Chapter 27

CJ watched the moonlight drape like a sheer curtain across Erica's bare shoulders, her skin shimmering with an ethereal glow.

She lay beside him, her hand delicately poised on her collarbone, the new wedding ring catching slivers of silvery light. How had he gotten so lucky? His heartbeat echoed *forever* with each pulse as he committed to memory the way her chest rose and fell in gentle rhythm.

"Beautiful," he murmured, not solely for the modest band adorning her finger but for the entirety of the moment—their moment.

"Thank you," she said softly, her eyes lifting to meet his, brimming with shared dreams and silent promises. "For this, for everything."

He reached out, brushing a stray lock of hair from her forehead. The familiar rush of being impossibly blessed to have her swelled within him in the private moment.

Erica shared a smile in the quiet of their bedroom before a small frown pulled on her brow. "Whatever happened with that production assistant that got busted for sabotaging your set?"

"Ahh, in the excitement of making you my bride, I forgot to tell you. Have you ever heard of a producer named Bob Wendell?"

"Vaguely? What about him?"

"As it turns out, he was blackmailing women in the business. It was vile—career advancements traded for... for favors." His jaw clenched at the thought, disgust souring his tongue.

"Blackmailing? How did you—"

"Anna Wilson," CJ answered, still amazed at how things unfolded. "Apparently she had a fling with him, but when she ended things, he snapped. Hired someone to ruin her film, figuring she'd be desperate enough to go back to him. But it all unraveled when I stepped in."

Erica sat up, blankets pooling around her waist, her eyes wide with shock. "You stopped him?"

"More like inadvertently exposed him. The assistant he used flipped on him, handed over texts that led right back to Wendell. And then...the floodgates opened. Other women came forward, stories worse than the last."

Erica reached for his hand, squeezing it tight. "God, CJ. That's horrific, but... I'm so proud of what you did," she said.

"Thanks, babe." CJ smiled, appreciating her support. "It feels good to be on the right side of a story. Oh, and you know our missing wrangler? Turns out it was simply a case of a family emergency. The guy had to leave town, and he was out of cell range wherever he was at, so he couldn't let the production manager know what was happening."

"Are there places on the planet that don't have cell service?" Erica asked.

"Apparently."

"Well, I'm glad it wasn't anything related to Allison," she said quietly, as if even mentioning the poor girl's name had the power to draw bad energy their way. "Okay, no sad talk allowed tonight. Let's talk about brighter things."

He chuckled, the mood in the room lifting. "Like baby names? What do you think about Arizona?"

"Arizona?" Erica laughed, the sound dancing in the air. "Absolutely not," she teased, though her smile hinted at the possibility that she might consider it.

"Ah, well, you make me work for every victory," he said, grinning. "And that's just one of the many reasons I love you."

"Good," she replied, snuggling closer. "Because with me, life will never be boring."

"Wouldn't have it any other way," CJ whispered, pulling her into his arms as they settled back into the embrace of the night.

CJ watched the play of moonlight on Erica's face, her features softened by shadows. Her fingers were still entwined with his, a lifeline in the quiet aftermath of their conversation.

"Harold Greene," she murmured, breaking the silence. "Never thought I'd say this, but I've got to hand it to him. He did the right thing in the end."

"Agreed." CJ nodded, the image of the usually stern-faced executive softening in his mind. "There's talk about another project he wants me on board with. Early days, though."

"Another project?" Erica's brow quirked up, curiosity alight in her eyes. "That could be something."

"Could be," CJ echoed, cautious hope threading through his response.

A pause settled, their breathing the only sound until CJ broke it with a question that had been gnawing at him. "Any news on the person behind the assault at the resort?"

Her sigh was a soft gust as she shared, "Trail's gone cold. I'd hoped they could at least solve that mystery, just so everyone could feel less jumpy at every shadow. It would've been nice to have some good news to cling to. The Sharpe merger's looking shaky."

"Damn," CJ muttered, thinking of the sprawling resort that had become more than just a place to them. Mariposa would always have a soft place in his heart because of Erica.

"But you know me," Erica continued with a chuckle. "I'm not going anywhere. I'll stand with the Coltons, come hell or high water."

"Then so will I," CJ declared. "Whatever it takes, Erica. We're in this together."

"Always," Erica whispered, her eyes meeting his.

In the way she challenged him, made him strive for every little win, CJ found a thrill he'd never known. In this room, with her by his side, he could see the stretch of years ahead—unpredictable, demanding but utterly irresistible. And as he pulled her closer, feeling the warmth of her skin against his, CJ knew without a doubt that with Erica, the word *boredom* would forever remain uncharted territory.

"Whatever the future holds," he murmured into the space between them, "I know it's going to be one hell of an adventure with you."

"Wouldn't have it any other way," Erica whispered back.

And CJ finally understood what he'd been missing all this time—the thing that money couldn't buy but his heart had recognized immediately—the love of a woman worth building a life with.

* * * * *